RISING TIDE

ALSO BY JENNIFER PALGRAVE

The One That Got Away

RISING TIDE

JENNIFER
PALGRAVE

Published by Town Belt Press, Wellington, New Zealand, 2021: townbeltpress@xtra.co.nz

Printed by Your Books, Wellington, New Zealand

Cover designed by James McDonald

JAMESMCDONALDBOOKS.COM

Cover art © Judi Lapsley Miller

www.artbyjlm.com

ISBN: 978-0-473-56050-8

Catalogue record available from the National Library of New Zealand.

❀ Created with Vellum

"It's *there*, in the background. Always. Increasingly urgent. Its ominous hum is the soundtrack to every other story we tell."

— Ingrid Horrocks on the climate crisis

1

Lauren Fraser stirred and stretched out a sleepy arm, fumbling for the snooze button. Only seven o'clock, earlier than she liked. Unfair, wasn't she semi-retired? But it was a busy day ahead. Packing for Melbourne, finishing a piece of editing and taking Monty for a walk. She sighed, stretched and threw back the duvet.

Revived by the shower, she peered at herself in the bathroom mirror. Her reflection stared back: a well-cut cap of soft grey hair, dark eyebrows over blue eyes. Her nose prompted the usual recurring argument. Too prominent or Roman and distinguished? She moved on, trying an experimental smile–was that a new wrinkle? Someone had told her they were laugh lines, and at least her forehead wasn't lined from frowning. Not too bad, considering her age, she concluded, then chided herself for conceit.

How would she compare with the Melbourne group? It was the second year of the ageing study. In 2017, she'd scored a free trip to Cambridge, where the whole cohort of sixty-something women who were students back in the '70s had been brought together, questioned, poked and prodded. At least they hadn't measured wrinkles, but who knew what they'd be up to this year. The second year and the research team was already spending less lavishly. This time the Antipodean alumnae were to be segregated in Melbourne at St Catherine's Hall while the current student residents were on a break. No visit to Julia and the grandchildren in Brighton, no catching up with Rachel and her other English friends.

Lauren rubbed a cream onto her face, spreading it hopefully over the laugh lines. Anti-wrinkle? The manufacturers should be sued. She looked at the time–quarter to eight already, she needed to get breakfast on the table.

She was writing 'to do' lists in her head as she spread marmalade on her toast and listened to the news. The usual miscellany of all the ills of the world, human stupidity or natural disaster. Sometimes both at once. In an even tone a reporter was talking about thousands missing after a tropical cyclone of unusual intensity swept across an African country. Climate change, Lauren thought. It was becoming more obvious all the time. She felt guilty taking a plane to Australia. International air travel poured carbon into the atmosphere. That was a good reason not to be flying to England, she supposed. She'd have to make up for it when she returned. She'd just joined a new group, the Wellington Climate Protection Society, and it would keep her on the ball.

She smiled as she remembered the public meeting that had inspired her to join. The main speaker, Nat Spiller, had opened with a stunt–abseiling down on a rope from above the stage. It made everyone sit up, laugh nervously. He'd used it to challenge them, demand that they do outrageous things before it was too late. Not that Lauren saw herself scaling buildings or sitting in the middle of crossroads or–her train of thought was interrupted by a news item close to home.

She took a bite of toast, as she listened. 'The survivor of yesterday's shipwrecked yacht, the *Lucinda,*' intoned the newsreader, 'has now been discharged from hospital. Police are asking members of the public who might have seen any activity on the South Coast road yesterday evening to come forward.' Lauren wondered why on earth they would be looking for anyone. Did they think Cornish wreckers were luring boats onto the rocks?

The news continued, another Wellington item. 'A virtual reality model has been developed of rising sea levels and their impact on Wellington City. Members of the public will see what Wellington would look like under a variety of scenarios, up to six metres of sea level rise.'

Lauren felt smug. Fun to be ahead of the news! She and her friend Pam had heard about the model through the Climate Protection Society and already signed up for the experience. 'I guess I'll be OK up here in Roseneath but the beach might have disappeared,' Lauren had said to Pam.

'We don't all live in lovely apartments on top of a hill,' said Pam, 'and anyway, you might have to wade to town.'

Lauren's apartment, one of a block of six with a harbour view, had been a good buy. Pam's burrow, as Lauren thought of Pam's ground-floor apartment, on flat land in Te Aro, was much more likely to sink beneath the waves. Would Pam even notice? Lauren wondered. She was so seldom home. Pam spent her retirement at the community gardens on Mt Vic where she fed herself and numerous friends and acquaintances from her richly crowded plot of vegetables. When she wasn't gardening, she was working on environmental issues, volunteering now after a career in the public service.

Lauren pulled herself back to the present, switched off the radio, put her breakfast dishes in the dishwasher and made for her desk. That editorial work next. Why did some children's authors think they had to cram every story full of facts? She sighed, thinking about the piece she was working on. Talk about information dumps....

By eleven she was ready for a break. She put on a jacket and outdoor shoes, felt in her pocket for a dog treat, left her apartment and knocked on her neighbour's front door. 'Coming!' Lauren could hear Phyl padding down the hallway, and much closer, paws scratching on the door. When Phyl opened it, she steadied herself against the door jamb, as Monty pushed past and leapt up at Lauren, tail wagging. 'No, Monty!' they both said in unison.

Monty was an adorable mutt, a mixture of Staffy and who knew what else. Lauren said, 'I promise I'll give him a good run. I'll take him down to Owhiro Bay and we can walk towards Red Rocks. That's a favourite for both of us.'

'It's very kind of you, Lauren. I just didn't get him out much at all over the weekend.'

Lauren clipped on Monty's lead and as they walked up the path to the road, he strained forward. Lauren twitched the lead to slow him down. He was getting a bit boisterous for Phyl. She was a tall woman, still sturdy and upright in her early eighties, with her bearing befitting an ex-cop. She was frailer than she used to be, though she'd be loath to admit it.

Monty safely stowed in the back seat of her car, Lauren drove off. The route took her across town and up the hill to Brooklyn, to join the slow procession of trucks heading for the landfill off Happy Valley road. The trucks turned off, freeing Lauren to pick up speed, until she reached the Owhiro Bay settlement. She signalled to turn right, along the coast, and gasped. On the rocky shore was a yacht. It lay on its side. Waves were battering it and it bumped up and down helplessly, captured by the rocks. It was a shocking sight, like a great wounded white bird.

A Greek chorus of bystanders gathered on the shore, as if in mourning. The sight of the foundered yacht tugged at Lauren. Where the road widened she pulled to the side and stopped. Must be the yacht mentioned on the news. 'Shall I leave you here, Monty? No, you'd better come.' She reached for his leash in the glovebox and clipped it on his collar. 'No, it's not your proper walk yet,' she admonished him as he crouched eagerly, preparing to bound out of the car.

Keeping the dog on a tight leash, Lauren picked her way over the pebbly beach and joined the cluster of people. A woman was holding forth, obviously enjoying the limelight. She was shortish, slightly overweight, a fringe of straight brown hair almost down to her eyes. She looked cheerfully rounded, like an old-fashioned russet apple. 'I live just opposite.' She gestured to a tumbledown house across the road.

'I was just getting tea when an orange light flaring from the sea made me look up. I went out to the footpath and I could make out the yacht, close inshore and near the rocks. I ran down to the beach for a closer look. There was a guy, it looked like he was stretching down over the side, trying to grab at something, perhaps free something. It must have distracted him, he was drifting onto the rocks. It was frightening.

'I heard a sickening crunch–that's when he hit the Sirens. Then another crunch, the boat was held fast.'

She paused and one of the onlookers said knowledgeably, 'The Sirens, eh. They're vicious–there's lots misjudged them over the years.'

Lauren was curious. The Sirens were well away from the shore. She asked the woman, 'But how did the boat get right in here?'

They all looked at the yacht again, now lying helplessly close to the shore.

'I ran into the house to phone 111 and while I was telling them they'd better get someone out here quickly, I saw through the window a big wave taking the boat off the rock that held it. It was nearly surfing, side on to the waves and then it crunched on to those rocks closer in. The guy was pitched off. I could just glimpse the orange of his lifejacket as he was tumbled around.'

Lauren shuddered. It sounded awful.

'So what did you do?' said the man who'd commented on the Sirens.

'I went back to the beach. There were a few other people around by then. One guy was wading in and another was on his cell phone. I told him I'd already called emergency services. The sailor wasn't far from the beach. He was close enough in to get his footing. A guy helped him onto the beach and I got a good look at him. Quite an old guy. He must have swallowed a lot of water, he was choking and spluttering. Stumbling, too, the guy who'd gone in was holding him up but as soon as he got a little way up the beach he just fell over right in front of us.'

'So was he in a bad way? He ended up in hospital, didn't he?' This time it was a woman who'd just arrived. She had left a pram on the path as she picked her way down to the beach: Lauren supposed there was a sleeping baby inside it.

The russet woman said proudly, 'Well, he'd just plopped himself on the sand. I looked him over, he was breathing, didn't seem to be bleeding or anything. I asked him if he was all right, and he mumbled something, I had to lean over, ask him again, and...'–she paused for dramatic effect–'...that was when he said there was someone out there, he thought they might be drowned.'

An excited murmur ran through the small crowd. Lauren was horrified. She found herself hanging on the woman's words, like all the others.

'He passed out then. I couldn't get anything else out of him. And then a police car arrived and an ambulance. They got him away quick smart. '

The guy who seemed familiar with the coast said, 'Even if he wasn't hurt he might have had hypothermia. Cook Strait never warms up much–it's still pretty cold in November.'

The woman agreed. 'And he was in the water for a few minutes. He might have knocked his head, too.' She began to peter out, sounding breathless. 'As well as being half drowned.'

'Did you hear anything about the other person, the drowning? Or was that the end of it?' someone asked.

'No, it wasn't.' The woman picked up the story again, enjoying her audience. 'I told the police he'd mumbled something to me about a body out there. They talked to everyone else there, too, but I was the only one who'd heard what he said. Soon there was a helicopter flying with its searchlights over the water. Police cars going up and down the road. Then there was a diver going in, I reckon it must have been the police dive squad. And that police launch came into the bay after a while.'

'Probably the Lady Elizabeth,' the man said helpfully.

'Whatever,' said the woman. 'And there was an inflatable out from the shore, too. Then after I'd gone home again the police came and knocked on my door. They wanted to check my story. I told them there was no mistaking what I'd heard. "Someone out there. Might be drowned." That's exactly what he said.' She looked triumphant. 'Must have been another crew member on the boat, fell overboard perhaps.'

'So you didn't see them bringing anyone in?' The questioner was new to the scene, another dogwalker. Monty barked at the new arrival, a large Labrador, and Lauren had to keep him in check. The Labrador ignored him with a lofty expression.

'Well, I could hardly stay up all night looking at them.' The woman sounded offended.

'There hasn't been any further announcement on the radio,' someone else said. 'Just about the wreck and that there was a search. I was listening to the news just before I came out.'

Lauren stood for a moment more. The conversation seemed to be going nowhere. She stared again at the yacht unbelievingly, then gave a nod to the hero of the hour and made her way back to the car, Monty surprisingly obedient by her side

'Good dog,' she said absentmindedly as he leapt into the car and she slipped his lead off. She felt distracted, edgy. Before she could close the door on him, Monty licked her hand.

'You sweetheart, you know I'm upset, don't you.' She ruffled his fur, then shut the door.

She drove off again and from the car park at the end of the road she trudged along the gravelly sand towards the seal hangout at Red Rocks, as Monty bounded back and forth.

Lauren gazed out at the sea–it was grey today and somehow sinister–had they found the missing person, or were the waves tossing around a body just out there? She shuddered and tried to concentrate on exercising Monty. He covered twice the distance Lauren did, as he retrieved and returned sticks she threw. Half-way along the beach, she stopped–she didn't want Monty anywhere near the seals. He'd had a vigorous run and she needed to get home for a late lunch.

Arriving home, Lauren stopped to check the letter-box. Nothing today–of course, it was a Monday, not a mail delivery day. Damn the post office. She caught herself–when did she last post a card or a letter? She was part of the problem. All email and Facebook these days.

As she mused, Monty was pulling at the leash. She bent down and let him off, knowing he would head straight down the path for home. By the time she reached the top of the stairs, Phyl was opening the door, responding to Monty's excited scrabbling. 'Hello Monty, came home all by yourself today?' Then, 'Oh, hello Lauren, I know you're busy today, but come in for a quick cuppa later–it would be good to have a chat before you go away.'

Lauren took herself next door to Phyl's when it was time for an afternoon break. She settled in the living room, enjoying the harbour view, while Phyl rattled around in the kitchen. When she emerged, she handed Lauren a frilly cup and saucer and offered a plate of Anzac biscuits. Lauren resigned herself to another of Phyl's brittle offerings.

As Phyl sat down opposite her, Lauren said, 'Monty and I had an unexpected adventure this morning.' Phyl raised her eyes, looking a little stern. 'Yes?' Lauren was amused–sometimes Phyl looked so much like the cop she used to be, she could just imagine the older woman pulling a pencil and notebook out of her pocket.

'I spotted a wreck down at Owhiro Bay. A yacht hit the rocks there yesterday evening. It was breaking up. There was such a crowd on the foreshore, we stopped to see what was going on. Apparently the yachtie managed to make his way to shore before they took him off to hospital.' She was surprised at herself, her voice had a tremor in it. 'The boat looked awful, Phyl, and they think someone else was still out there.'

'I heard something on the radio. His crew, perhaps? It seems a bit odd. The weather was OK last night, he must have really lost his way to end up on the rocks.'

'He was an old guy, according to a woman on the beach. She said that search and rescue were out for hours–a helicopter and the police launch. Nobody there seemed to know if a body had been found.'

'We'll know soon enough, I dare say.' Phyl sipped her tea and looked pensive. 'The *Lady Liz*, eh–or her successor. That brings back memories–I remember the *Wahine* disaster, it was so rough, the harbourmaster wouldn't let the police boat go out.'

'So what were you doing that day, Phyl? The 50th anniversary a few months back, wasn't it? You took part in some commemorations?'

'I was on the scene with the force at Eastbourne, helping people ashore...' –she grimaced– '...and retrieving bodies.' She examined her finger nails, short and stubby but well cared for. 'That was the first time I'd ever had to deal with drownings. There were bodies washing up onto the shore long after everyone who survived had been rescued–and some of them were in terrible shape. It's not something I'll ever forget.'

Lauren gave a convulsive shudder. 'I can imagine. I was a teenager then, you know I grew up in Seatoun. My father helped people on the beach–he went off and stayed half the night. Mum baked batches of scones and took them down with thermoses of tea. Dad looked shattered the next morning.' She mused, 'So much anguish. The survivors, the rescuers, the bereaved. I don't suppose that there was any counselling offered to the police back then? Or did you just talk about stuff with your colleagues.'

Phyl gave her an offended look. 'No to both your questions. I guess I'm old school, but I do believe you just have to learn to deal with anything the job throws at you.'

Lauren thought Phyl was wrong but couldn't help admiring her staunchness. No use arguing with such an ingrained perspective. 'God forbid that anything like the *Wahine* should happen again. It was bad enough seeing one broken yacht and thinking of one poor soul maybe drowned out there. Odd, too, given the weather wasn't too bad.'

Phyl shook her head. 'You can never rely on the sea being safe. But we'll never get a storm like that again, I reckon it was a oncer.'

'They're supposed to become worse with climate change.'

Phyl looked sceptical. 'I don't necessarily believe all that stuff about the weather–but if there are changes afoot, we're in God's hands.'

'It wouldn't hurt to give God a hand to slow down climate change.'

Phyl laughed and Lauren was relieved she hadn't taken offence. It was a risk taking a dig at someone's beliefs.

2

Lauren heaved a huge sigh as she settled into her seat on the plane to Melbourne. Her neighbour, who'd had to get out to let her into the window seat, grinned at her and raised his eyebrows. Lauren twisted her mouth in what she hoped was a deprecating smile and then ignored him. She also ignored the blandishments of the inflight entertainment system. She needed some thinking time.

But perhaps it wasn't thinking as much as letting her thoughts go into free flow. She was still upset about that boat wreck. Behind her eyelids she saw images of the stricken yacht, trapped amongst the dark rocks, the foam surging through. Then her mind threw up an image of a body floating helplessly in the water.

She sighed again and shifted in the seat. And Phyl! That was a surprise, she knew Phyl was devout, but that shouldn't make her a climate sceptic. Surely people were past that, unless they were conspiracy theorists or oil moguls.

Another big sigh and she leant against the seat, tilted it back and shut her eyes. Climate change! The science was one thing. But Lauren knew feelings had to be engaged to drive home what was happening to the planet. A documentary that showed a polar bear swimming, swimming, swimming towards an ice floe no longer there. People on a Pacific island 'paradise' holding out empty plastic water containers to the camera. Some music floated into her mind, a new piece she'd heard, referencing climate change. It sounded reedy, scratchy, disturbed. Visceral, that was the word.

Surely everyone would be committed to preventing climate change if they understood emotionally what was happening. She thought of the charismatic Nat Spiller again, speaking at the public meeting her friend Pam had taken her to. He was sober as he set out the science, talking about what New Zealand scientists in the Antarctic were discovering. Then he was fiery as he talked about actions the audience could take. Pam thought he was great–but then he was her niece Ellie's partner, and Ellie was Pam's favourite niece. Lauren distrusted charismatic men. They always seemed to want women to make the tea. But after all, that meeting had driven her to the climate protection group, that her friend Michael had been urging her to join. The government needed pressure put on them. They weren't acting fast enough, maybe the coalition was making things difficult.

The plane struck some turbulence, and her stomach lurched. Oh yes, more turbulence during plane flights was to be expected in the future. That would probably be enough to stop her flying, her body protested. The turbulence died down again, she put the seat upright, and excused herself to the guy on the aisle, squeezing past awkwardly. Why would anyone willingly go on international flights anyway! She joined a queue for the plane toilet, pretty sure that like her, many were hanging about just because it was good to stretch and stand up.

She was still mulling over climate change as she walked along the aisle, apologised to the guy and settled back in her seat. She didn't think people would be wowed by the Wellington Climate Protection Society, such a sedate, uninspiring name. It was in tune, though, with the way the group was proposing to work. All the time-honoured tactics for pressure groups: attending council meetings, writing letters, making submissions, organising meetings with movers and shakers. Old fashioned stuff, not much of a presence on Facebook and none on Twitter or Instagram. Or whatever new communication system the internet threw up. It would be more fun to belong to something like Extinction Rebellion, the new activist group she'd heard about. They were into civil disobedience, direct action. But what the Wellington Climate Protection Society did was necessary. And she had the right background for that sort of work.

A pity about Harold Stevens, the guy who had called the first meeting, shortly after the public meeting Nat Spiller had organised. He looked to be in his late thirties, not a natural leader and so old womanish. She checked herself. She knew lots of spirited, spunky, imaginative old women. No, Harold was just himself. Used to work at the Ministry of Transport, now a consultant. Not an attractive man. He had a slight stoop. Average height, but that stoop made him look smaller, and the way he peered through his wire-rimmed glasses somehow cut him off from the world. His hair was carefully cut and his clothes were clean and tidy, but he had an old-fashioned look: a neat green jersey, a Viyella shirt with carefully ironed collar and cuffs (how long had he had that?), brown trousers with a sharp crease and well-polished brown leather brogues. He had seemed uncomfortable in front of those assembled at the meeting, and looked past them rather than at them as he explained how the group would work.

People had certainly got restless as he droned on about how important it was to keep within the law. And Lauren could hardly believe it when he proposed that the next meeting would be a formal AGM with the election of officers. But the attendees had gone along with it. Lauren supposed that, like her, they were prepared to put up with him because the need to take action was so urgent.

Now Lauren wriggled, reclined the seat again, her thoughts taking a different direction. It seemed hypocritical to be worrying about climate change while on a plane. Deirdre. An image popped into her mind. So far she'd been trying not to think about Deirdre, because if she started she might not think about anything else. They hadn't been in touch very often since Deirdre had been sent to Canberra for a top cop secondment, just a few desultory emails. No phone calls. Lauren had resigned herself to thinking that their friendship, which had looked as if it might become something more, would not survive the separation. So she was surprised when Deirdre had responded with enthusiasm to Lauren's news that she would be visiting Melbourne in November. 'I've been planning a weekend in the big smoke for some time,' she'd said in her last email.

That was followed by a phone call where they arranged to meet up after Lauren's meeting finished. Lauren sank into a reverie. Deirdre. Her strong and slender build, those sparkling brown eyes belying her range of stern expressions. She had looked amazing in those leather pants the last time they went out together! It had been one of their few social occasions. Lauren had most often seen Deirdre either in uniform or in the nondescript garb of the professional woman.

She drifted, recalling their first meeting, the instant attraction. What was it? Was there any pattern in her relationships? Kristen had been completely different in looks, blonde and lively, whereas Deirdre imparted a cool authority that Lauren found maddeningly compelling, even when Deirdre had been telling her off for interference with police work last year.

She switched tracks and thought, as so many times before, of her first love, so long ago, so tragic, a young woman so different from both Deirdre and Kristen. Political, intense, sturdy. Don't go down that track, she told herself, opening her eyes and looking around. I'm just not the type to have a type, she said firmly to herself. That made her chuckle and her seat mate glanced at her again. He looked as if he were going to say something but was stopped in his tracks by the intercom announcing their imminent descent. Time had flashed by. Lauren readied herself to disembark.

She made her way to the new automated passport control. She lined up her passport correctly, planted her own feet on the feet painted on the floor, adopted a serious expression and with a click and a whirr she was through.

The huge luggage hall echoed with a babble of voices. She pushed her way through the crowds, found the right carousel and before long her lime green suitcase with its rainbow ribbon floated gracefully in front of her. Then it was through Customs, by putting herself in what she thought of as the non-smugglers queue, and she was liberated into the arrivals hall. She bought a Skybus ticket from the machine and stepped into the warm Australian late spring sunshine. November, a lovely time to visit one of her favourite cities.

She made her way to the back of the Skybus, to get the best view, pleased she didn't have to concentrate on driving. Melbourne's skyline grew ever taller, new matchbox-thin skyscraper apartments startling her as they entered the central city.

She was looking about appreciatively when her phone rang, making her jump. Who on earth? She fumbled for it, and saw the name. 'Hello Pam, what's up?'

Instead of Pam's usual matter of fact tone, there was a desperate edge to her voice as she replied, 'Have you got a minute, Lauren?'

Lauren said again, 'What's up? I'm on the Skybus, just going into Melbourne.'

'Oh, of course,' said Pam, 'I'd completely forgotten.'

'Forgotten?' Lauren couldn't believe Pam had forgotten. They'd been talking about Lauren's trip just the day before. For the third time she said, 'What's up?'

This time Pam replied, 'Oh Lauren, Nat's been drowned.'

Lauren searched mentally for a context. Nat? Then she clicked. She was shocked. 'Nat Spiller? Ellie's partner?'

'Yes.' Pam's voice shook.

'That's awful, Pam....' Then she remembered. 'Was it Nat the police were searching for when that yacht was wrecked at Owhiro Bay?'

'Yes, nobody knows how it happened–he was found in his wetsuit. He didn't have his snorkelling gear on, but he was a strong swimmer. You know–he was so athletic.'

'But why was he in his wetsuit? Wasn't he on the yacht?'

'No, the yachtie had spotted him half-drowned. He was trying to haul Nat in and that's when his boat went on the rocks.' Pam sounded close to tears. 'But Lauren, I'm really sorry I've bothered you, I wouldn't have if I'd remembered you were away. But could we talk about the whole thing when you get back. Ellie's distraught.'

An image crystallised in Lauren's mind. Ellie, as she'd seen her at a book launch. Ellie brushing back her unruly curly hair with one hand, wine glass in the other, laughing and leaning close to her aunt.

Pam was still talking. 'It's more complicated than it sounds–I need someone clear-headed.' She cleared her throat; her voice was cracking again.

The bus was heading down the ramp into the terminal area. 'That's really bad news, Pam. He was an inspiration to us all. You look after yourself–make sure you talk to other people–and I'll see you when I get back.'

She put her phone back into her handbag, and stared out the window, now hardly noticing her surroundings as the bus rattled through the depot. Nat Spiller: brilliant, visionary, creative. She'd enjoyed listening to him so recently. If anyone could get across the notion of climate change viscerally, it had been him. What a terrible loss, and awful for Ellie. The couple were still quite young, probably in their mid thirties. Nat should have had years of accomplishment ahead of him.

She worried too about Pam, so generous to her friends, but reticent and inclined to withdraw into her burrow. It would have been hard for Pam to ask for her support. It wouldn't have happened if Pam had remembered she was away. More complicated than it seemed? What could that mean? Lauren sighed–she would just have to put it out of her mind until she got home.

3

Lauren decided she didn't have the energy to cope with Melbourne's tram service, so she lined up with other travellers and got a taxi to the college. The taxi dropped her off at a handsome traditional brick and sandstone building on Royal Parade. She called in at the office and was given directions to her room. It was the usual student affair, a single bed, a chair, a desk, a wardrobe, a mirror and hand basin–but a delightful outlook onto an inner courtyard, graced by mature elms. The shared bathroom was down the corridor. Lauren was pleased she'd brought a dressing gown and slippers. Midnight encounters should not be too awkward.

She threw her suitcase on the bed, hastily collected her handbag and room keys, and pinned on the name badge the office had given her. She was just in time for the first session. She studied the map and found her way to a common room where the group had already gathered.

Glancing round the room quickly, Lauren saw no-one she knew. Most of her friends at Cambridge were Brits who had continued their lives in Britain after university. As had Lauren, who stayed on for several years, marrying her university boyfriend, starting a family and a promising career in publishing before returning to New

Zealand in the 1980s. None of the Antipodeans looked familiar, even though everyone here would have been at last year's meeting.

Lauren apologised for her late entry. The group were already seated in a semi-circle, all name-tagged. The convenor looked ready to go with a PowerPoint display set up on a screen in front of them. Her assistant handed Lauren a folder of papers. She glanced round the room again. There was definitely no one she recognised from last year's meeting. It occurred to her that her friend Charlotte might have been here, now that she'd taken up with Brett again. Brett had said he was planning to buy a property in the New South Wales highlands.

Brett...memories flooded her and she found it hard to concentrate on the words of welcome from the research team. Brett, the sponsor of the study, her old acquaintance from Cambridge days, the super-rich philanthropist–and the amoral profiteer who was responsible for her hair-raising adventures of the previous year. She shuffled through the papers she'd been given and flinched when the researcher, winding up her introduction, thanked the study sponsors. The name Brett Wilson, spoken aloud, pierced her consciousness, she drew in her breath sharply and to her embarrassment started a fit of coughing. Everyone in the small group turned to look at her as she groped in her handbag for tissues. The assistant brought her a glass of water. 'Are you OK?'

Lauren nodded and sipped. She was regaining control of herself. The bastard! He got away scot-free! But two deaths on my conscience. No, she berated herself, stop thinking like that. Get out of my life, Brett, I've dealt with it, put it behind me. I'll never poke my nose into anything like that again. Shut up and concentrate, she told her wandering mind.

THE MORNING SESSION hadn't begun until 10.30 allowing participants time to arrive from their various starting points, if they hadn't got in the night before. With her early morning start, Lauren felt she already had a working day behind her when they broke for lunch. But she was keen to chat to her fellow alumnae. There were two women from her year, she just hadn't recognised them forty years later.

The three sat down to lunch together and began swapping news as well as stories of student days. One of them, Jean, a Scot, had come to the lucky country with her husband in the eighties, forging an arts career in Sydney. She had recently retired from a senior position at the state art gallery. The other, Rosie, who Lauren now remembered as rather a scamp, was someone who'd hung out on the fringes of her circle, boy mad and always off with some new young man, working her way up the social list. She had left suddenly towards the end of her final year, called back by her parents. There was a story there, Lauren remembered, about a hasty marriage. Rosie said she hadn't had time for a career, with her family and her charities. Jean smiled at Rosie. 'The gallery's certainly benefited from the donations you and your husband have made.'

Their reminiscences were tailing off when a woman across the table interrupted them with a command not to be cliquey. Her name tag announced her as Miriam Smith, two years behind Lauren at Cambridge. She was a short, powerfully built woman with a commanding voice and an infectious laugh, wouldn't suffer fools gladly, Lauren supposed. And she registered on Lauren's gaydar.

Lauren said, 'We had to catch up with news of our year–you young things weren't of such interest, you know.'

Miriam laughed. 'That's right, you older students could scarcely give us the time of day. Anyway, most of you were arts types, and I was doing a science degree.'

'What discipline?' Lauren enquired politely.

'Marine biology, and in recent years I've been engaged in climate science. I'm partly retired now but I can't give it up, there's too much urgent work to be done. I'm off to Antarctica again this summer, it might be my last trip.'

Over the course of the next three days Lauren enjoyed getting to know the women in the group. They joked about the meals which seemed scarcely to have improved from their own college days. Except for a more international flavour to the gluey sticky messes.

After the first day's session of tests, questionnaires and tasks–the most alarming of which was an MRI scan over at the hospital, which Lauren found claustrophobic–the group wandered across campus to a pub which was popular with university staff. Sitting in the garden bar in the fading spring sunshine they swapped stories of their lives.

Lauren found herself warming to Miriam, who had come to Australia on her own, straight after finishing her Cambridge science degree. She was one of the first wave of women to climb the academic ladder in the sciences and she had clearly developed a thick skin. She told stories about her male colleagues, especially the Aussies who played practical jokes, mostly not very funny. Funnel-web spiders in the ladies' loo ('We were lucky to have a loo,' Miriam said), creepy-crawlies on the lab bench and so on. But Miriam loved her new country and her new life. She did not speak about relationships but Lauren had a sense that she had had her share of domestic happiness.

Miriam, although she described herself as 'retired, sort of' seemed wedded to her career. Now an emeritus professor at Monash, she had become involved in Australia's Antarctic programme. She told Lauren that she worked closely with New Zealand geologists on core sampling.

As they walked back to the hostel, Miriam fell into step with Lauren. 'There'll be a couple of New Zealanders in a group of my friends going out to dinner on Thursday night,' she said. Lauren scarcely had time to envy Miriam being able to avoid the hostel meals before Miriam smiled warmly at her. She carried on. 'Would you like to come out with us? I think you'd enjoy the group. Not just because there are Kiwis to make you feel at home.'

ON THURSDAY, Miriam took Lauren home with her before the dinner. The house was a typical Australian brick bungalow in a quiet street in Brunswick. They pulled into the driveway and Miriam ushered Lauren into the dark hallway and through to the kitchen at the back. The house had clearly been renovated, the modern kitchen opening up into a sunny enclosed porch running the width of the house and overlooking the back garden.

Miriam indicated a comfortable well-used sofa on the porch for Lauren to sit on while she busied herself getting drinks and snacks. She brought out two generous gin and tonics, finished with ice and slices of lemon. Lauren took an exploratory sip. 'That's the best thing I've tasted since I got here,' said Lauren. 'Lucky you, living on the spot. Staying in the college is well and good, but I'd just as soon leave behind student rooms and college food.'

Miriam laughed as she put a platter of cheese and crackers on a side table and sat herself down on the couch next to Lauren.

They clinked glasses. 'Here's to...' Their toasts overlapped. 'I was going to say, here's to the good old days,' said Lauren.

'L'cheim, a toast to a long life,' Miriam said. 'Were you happier then or now, do you think?'

'Cambridge was an eye-opener for an inexperienced young Kiwi, but I guess I had the resilience of youth and I settled in quickly. Drama club, parties, walks in the countryside, inevitably ending in pubs–and I enjoyed my studies. It was a golden time, but I'm more comfortable in my skin now. How about you?'

Miriam looked thoughtful. 'I adored my studies, I knew science was my bent and when I discovered biology that was it. I was a city kid, not one of those children whose outdoorsy fathers take them fossicking at the seaside. The family wasn't well off, my parents escaped Germany in 1939, lucky to have connections in the East End. Schmidt became Smith, you know the story. I felt the brunt of the English class system at Cambridge, never at ease in social situations and as for boyfriends... soon enough I found I liked girls better.' She gave a broad chuckle. 'Not that there was anything going on at Cambridge, just a few unrequited pashes. I acted like one of the boys, that's how I got through. What's your story?'

They hadn't talked about being lesbian before now–but Miriam's gaydar had clearly been working too. She fixed Lauren with a penetrating stare. Lauren felt pinned like a specimen in a glass case. She almost felt an urge to wriggle. Better take the bull by the horns.

'I didn't come out till my thirties.'

Miriam raised an eyebrow. Lauren felt impelled to explain. 'I had a steady boyfriend by my final year. He was English–not one of the privileged ones. We married and stayed in England where our children were born. Then I decided to go back to a good job in Government publishing, because Mum and Dad were getting on. He managed to get an academic job. I didn't realise it, but my marriage was about to go on the rocks. Two children, everyone settling into life in New Zealand and then I hurled a spanner into the works. First love, really.'

Miriam's attention was fully engaged. 'Yes, you'd walk a hundred miles over tacks for that person who...'–she paused, looking embarrassed–'...lights up your world.' Her tone shifted. 'I should tell you that my life partner died two years ago. We met soon after I arrived in Australia nearly forty years ago.'

Lauren was about to take a bite of cracker and cheese and stopped, frozen. 'I'm so sorry,' she said. 'You must be bereft.'

'It's been hard,' Miriam acknowledged. 'It's my work that's kept me going. Jane was keen that I retire and we do some travelling, not just on scientific expeditions. I hadn't got my head around it, when suddenly she became ill and only two months later she was gone. '

Lauren was moved. She felt really drawn to Miriam and was touched by her struggle to express what was clearly a burden she carried with her all the time. 'Was Jane a scientist too?'

'No, she was an academic, a historian. I still have all her books, can't bear to part with them.' She looked around the slightly dishevelled sunporch. 'She was so house proud, too. I find it difficult to keep up to her standards, I'm afraid.'

Lauren shrugged. 'Housekeeping's not for everyone! Tell me more about Jane. What was her field of history? Was she Australian?'

They passed the next half hour with Miriam proudly recounting stories about Jane. She took Lauren into their library. It was a lovely room, with bookshelves ranged around three walls, two armchairs and two standard lamps on either side of the sash windows on the fourth wall. Lauren checked at the sight of those two chairs. So awful to lose your life companion, she thought.

Miriam was pulling out some of Jane's books. She gestured Lauren into one of the chairs and handed her one. 'This one's my favourite. She delved into the nineteenth century history of women and crime–the courts, criminals, police–and it was a rip-roaring read as well as sound scholarship.'

Lauren leafed through it, looking at some of the plates and the chapter headings, reading a paragraph here and there. 'It looks fabulous, Miriam, I'll try to get a copy from the library when I get home.' She paused. 'I've been rather close to historic crime myself, recently. My friend Ro Wisbech is a historian, and she's just had a book published about women in the fourth Labour Government in New Zealand. While she was researching it, she stumbled across the attempted murder of our Prime Minister at that time, and the two of us ended up trying to find the people responsible.'

Miriam sank down into the other chair. 'Really?' she said. She leant forward as if not to miss an iota of Lauren's story. Lauren proceeded to give a concise version of her and Ro's recent adventure.

'And you worked out all that without police help?' Miriam sounded impressed.

Lauren wondered if she was blushing. 'There was a senior cop, a woman who helped us, at least when we weren't getting in her way. After everything had settled down, she and I went out together a few times and I thought something might come of it. No such luck, she got seconded to Canberra–just like my ex-girlfriend who got promoted to Sydney. Deirdre's visiting me in Melbourne when we've finished being guinea pigs–it'll be lovely to see her, but bittersweet, too.'

Miriam looked astonished. 'Goodness, I didn't think the dating scene was flourishing in our age group. Bad luck, anyhow!'

'Yes.' Lauren made a face. 'I don't know what the pull of Australia is, but you're getting lots of Kiwi lesbians.' They laughed.

Miriam glanced at her clock and said, 'Oops, it's time we were setting out.'

In the car, Lauren said, 'Any time you're in Wellington, you're welcome to stay. It would be lovely to keep in touch.'

'As a matter of fact,' Miriam paused and then smiled winningly, 'I am coming through pretty soon–just before going to Christchurch and on to the ice this season. I've promised Esther, the post-doc I'm co-supervising that I'd take a look at the marine lab where she's based.'

4

As they set out towards Lygon Street, Miriam explained that the area was Melbourne's Little Italy. From previous visits Lauren was familiar with the enchanting line of restaurants. She recalled lunching alfresco there. Tables, cheerful with their red cloths and cane chairs spilt out on the footpath and green umbrellas under the leafy plane trees sheltered the customers from the warm sun. She'd savoured a steaming latte and the best pizza ever.

This time it was evening, slightly before seven. Miriam had reserved a table and as they walked in, an older man with a big girth and a big smile to match bustled from the cavernous depths to greet her like an old friend. They were seated right at the front by airy open windows giving onto the busy footpath. The restaurant was filling up fast, both inside and out. They definitely had the best seats.

Lauren was looking forward to meeting the group. 'They're the sort who see you through the good times and the bad,' Miriam said. 'Karen, who was Jane's oldest friend, used to make me get up in the mornings after I lost Jane. She'd phone and if she wasn't satisfied with how I sounded, she'd come over with coffee and croissants. Then there's Barbara and Dave, he's the only bloke–but a good one.'

Lauren was amused at Miriam's half apology for having a bloke at the dinner. Miriam continued, 'And I've asked young Esther as well. She's the post-doc I told you about. She's very excited about coming down to the ice this summer, a first for her.'

Miriam was still painting mini-portraits of her friends when the first group arrived, the others hard on their heels. There was a bustle of introductions, followed by a hubbub of advice about the menu, before the waitress could take their orders for food and wine. Lauren let Miriam order for her. An adventurous eater, she found that was the best way to experience an unfamiliar restaurant. Then the group settled down to serious chat. Esther was on one side of Lauren. She turned out to be a young woman with dark hair, spectacles and a trace of acne, looking appropriately nerdy and awkward. On Lauren's other side was a well-dressed woman whose portrait Miriam hadn't got to. She appeared to be in her late forties, although Lauren was finding it increasingly difficult to judge the ages of anyone a few years younger than herself.

The woman turned towards Lauren and Esther, saying, 'Hi, I'm Alison. Miriam must have sat us Kiwis next to each other on purpose. No doubt she thinks we'll all know each other already.' She gave the impression of being easily in charge of any situation thrown at her.

Lauren laughed and said, 'Good to meet you, Alison. And Esther, Miriam's spoken about you. I understand you're going down to the Antarctic with her this summer?'

'I am,' Esther replied, raising her eyes to meet Lauren's. 'I'm not an old hand like Miriam.' She turned to Alison, looking shy. 'You may not remember me, Alison, but I did do a class with you a couple of years back.' Alison nodded graciously and Esther went on, 'The trip, it's such an opportunity....' She trailed off, mumbled something unintelligible about her work and cast her eyes down at the table again, as if she'd already said too much.

Alison spoke reassuringly, 'It does seem overwhelming to contemplate, but people adapt amazingly quickly. It only seems like yesterday that it was my first time. I gnawed my fingernails to the bone in the weeks leading up to it, and then Antarctica was love at first sight and I forgot all my fears.'

She turned to Lauren. 'I'm not on the same team as Miriam, but we both work with core sampling. I manage the New Zealand summer programme,' she said with a rueful expression. 'But I try to minimise the administrative stuff so I can get on with the science.'

Lauren nodded. 'I do understand the pull. I used to manage a team and I enjoyed it, but I was always keen to get back to my desk to do what I thought of as the real work. I was in publishing, and I'm your arty type, not science. That said, I have enormous admiration for our scientists and their dedication to helping the planet survive. And...'–she hesitated, unsure of whether she might unleash a torrent of technicalities–'I'm not sure that I understand core sampling. I know it's to do with climate change, but how does it work?'

Alison smiled approvingly and winked at Esther, who blushed slightly. She began to expound in a practiced manner. 'Our geologists drill down many hundreds of metres to extract cores of ice from different levels. We bring the frozen cores back to New Zealand to examine them for levels of greenhouse gases–that tells us how temperatures in the Antarctic have changed over hundreds of thousands of years.'

Lauren nodded and Alison went on, warming to her subject.

'Back in the Pliocene era, several million years ago, there was a warming period rather like what we see today. Miriam's team–she's a marine biologist, as you know–is examining core samples from that era for minuscule traces of life. It all helps us understand how temperatures and sea levels around the planet rise and fall over time. It's ongoing work, it's urgent and I think we'll both keep going as long as we're fit enough and they let us.'

'Thank you, Alison, that was really clear. The other person I've heard explain the science well was Nat Spiller, the climate change activist.' She paused, then said, 'You won't have heard the awful news, I guess. He drowned last weekend.'

'Really? I can hardly believe that.' Alison sounded shocked.

'He'll be such a loss.'

'He was such a good intermediary between the science community and the general public. I didn't approve of all his tactics, but he made sure Wellington didn't ignore the climate change issue.' She leant across Lauren to Esther and said, 'Did you know him, Esther?'

Esther shook her head, murmured, 'I knew who he was, though. That's upsetting.'

Their pasta dishes were arriving and there were general murmurs of appreciation as the steaming plates were set in front of them. Lauren was pleased that hers was gnocchi. She didn't fancy attempting an intelligent conversation while trying to wind spaghetti onto her fork and keep it from dripping down her chin. She brought the conversation back to a less gloomy topic.

'I guess you do need to be super-fit to work down there?'

'Well, if you're there to go onto the ice and actually work hard, it certainly helps. But that doesn't apply to everyone who goes to the ice–the politicians who fly in for a photo op, or the media people, artists and writers there for short visits–they need to be healthy but their experiences won't be too rugged.'

'No slogging through ice storms, I guess.' Alison laughed and Lauren continued, 'Are the arts programmes worthwhile? I did see a contemporary dance troupe whose choreographer had visited the ice. It was mesmerising.'

'It's important to have people spread the word about how special the Antarctic is–and how crucial our scientific work is. We scientists haven't always been so good at getting our work widely known, though we're trying a lot harder now.' Her face clouded over. 'Especially since the climate predictions are so dire. People think of Antarctica as beautiful, wild and remote. And it is, but life as we know it depends on it staying that way.'

She gulped and looked down at her plate. Was she trying to suppress a sob? Lauren didn't know how to respond. A 'there, there' wouldn't be right–the thought of the Antarctic's ecosystem being breached was horrifying. She took a deep breath and put her hand lightly on Alison's arm.

'I do so admire what you're doing. And it's not just up to you lot, everyone has to get on board. I'm getting actively involved in climate politics because that's where I feel I can make a difference. And our work completely relies on what you climate scientists tell us.'

'Of course.' Alison was recovering herself. She reached for the carafe and poured herself another glass and put another splash in Lauren's and Esther's glasses. 'But it would go more smoothly if we didn't have the odd colleague who's unhelpful.' As she replaced the carafe on the table, she leant across the table and interrupted Miriam, who was deep in conversation with Dave about something to do with molluscs, if Lauren had heard them right. Alison said, 'Did you hear that, Miriam? I was talking about rogue scientists. You know who I mean and the bastard is down again this season.'

For Lauren's benefit, Miriam explained. 'There's one of your Kiwi scientists who's off-side with the rest of us. Not exactly a climate change denier–they wouldn't even get onto the programme–but a young guy who's trying to make his mark in the academic world. He seems to think he can best do that by seeking controversy. Calls himself a climate sceptic. Just what we need at the moment, his work is eagerly picked up by all the climate deniers.'

'Yes,' said Alison, turning to Lauren. 'We're all furious at him. Of course there's always room for disagreement in science, that's what it's all about, but he takes every shred of evidence against global warming and pushes it as hard as he can. And do you know, Miriam?' She leant across to get Miriam's attention again, 'It seems that he's being paid by some property developer in Wellington to come up with facts and figures favourable to them. I heard that on the rumour mill. Apparently it involves predictive mapping that will minimise future flood impacts around the city.'

'Sounds like he's sailing close to the wind in career terms,' Miriam replied.

'Well, it's not that simple, academic freedom, you know.'

'No, but he's not going to get invited onto panels like you and Dave. When's your report coming out?'

Miriam explained that Alison and Dave were working on a very important intergovernmental report with scientists from many countries. Dave stroked his beard, removing a strand of spaghetti, and said, 'It's only a few weeks now, it's being signed off.' He paused, 'It's a bit hush-hush, of course, but...' Alison threw up her hands and glared at him. Dave looked apologetic. 'Well, I'm not letting the cat out of the bag if I tell you the report's going to make it clear that we're really in the shit but we can do something about it if governments just take it seriously enough.'

'That'll be the day,' retorted Miriam. 'Look at ours. Bunch of clowns, some of them know what's going on but they're busy pandering to their right-wing supporters or else they're climate change deniers.'

It was beginning to sound like a conversational ground the others had been over many times, so Lauren decided to throw in something new. 'Have you heard about the virtual reality demonstration Wellington City Council put together about climate change? They've done it so that ordinary people can get a handle on what rising sea levels will mean. An environmentalist friend and I are already booked in to see it.'

'Great that the Council's brave enough to do that,' said Alison. 'Most councils seem to want to stick their head in the sand. Afraid they'll have to pay out if they could have foretold which properties would be endangered.'

Dave interjected, 'I guess it's our fate to have our work turned into video games!'

Lauren was amused but protested all the same. 'Well, if it takes video games, then let's encourage them. You scientists can point the way but everyone else needs to understand, so as to make the changes we need.'

As Miriam drove her back to the hostel at the end of the evening, they chatted comfortably. Lauren reflected that it could have been an evening out with her own circle in Wellington. Conversation flowed easily, serious topics of the day were discussed, teasing and laughter forming an overlay to the firm friendships of long acquaintance. The gathering had been universally despairing of getting any laws to stop carbon emissions.

'I always feel so proud of our Prime Minister when I'm in Australia, you're all so envious. You know, before she was in power, Jacinda said climate change was her generation's nuclear-free moment. But Labour's first term is being hampered by being in a coalition.'

'You're still doing better than us,' Miriam replied. 'Some of us thought that Malcolm Turnbull might not be too bad despite being on the wrong side. But he was held hostage by climate change deniers. Now he's gone, we're in an even worse pickle.' Clearly upset, she almost missed a turn, correcting rather quickly, and swore under her breath. She said soberly, 'I fear for my country.'

Lauren felt there was no comforting response. Now Miriam was slowing down as they approached the hostel entrance. 'Thank you so much, Miriam, it was a lovely evening–good food and great company–and it was fun to meet the Kiwis. Esther must think she's struck it lucky to have you as a supervisor. And I'm sure Alison's a great colleague. We'll hope that, what was it? –"climate sceptic" doesn't give you all any grief.'

'Yes, it's good to have Alison down there, we'll watch the climate sceptic!' As she spoke, the car came to a halt outside the college. 'See you in the morning. And'–she looked mischievous–'in case I don't see you on your own. I hope you have a wonderful reunion with your policewoman tomorrow night.'

5

They were to meet at the Oyster Bar at David Jones in Elizabeth Street. Lauren worried that she might not spot Deirdre. It had been a few months, the bar was crowded, and Deirdre wouldn't be in uniform, not that she'd worn a uniform on their dates. Stop being ridiculous, you must be nervous, Lauren told herself.

The stools at the bar were all taken and the tables seemed to be occupied too. The crowded room had a jostling, cheerful Friday night air, people finishing work and starting their weekend with a treat ... or a date. Lauren was uncharacteristically early. After the final session with the group, she had caught a tram into the city for some shopping. She window-shopped for a while and then got serious. It was her time-honoured tradition to go clothes shopping in Melbourne–absurd, since Wellington had very good shops, but then she didn't always have completely free time at home. So she'd been to Myers, nosed up and down the fashionable laneways and lastly, David Jones. By five o'clock she was thoroughly fed up but had acquired a pair of jeans that fitted her slim figure closely, a summery top that she wouldn't wear in Wellington until January probably, and some trendy shoes that were both sporty and elegant.

A couple stood up, freeing two seats at the bar. Lauren dived for them, plumping her shopping bags on the spare one. She ordered a glass of mineral water. Then a hand on her shoulder. 'Champagne, surely?'

Later that evening, they found themselves having dinner in a small French restaurant in one of the laneways, a cheerful place with what looked like regular customers, checked tablecloths, baskets of bread, red wine in carafes. After champagne and half a dozen oysters, it could have been a comedown, but the buzz of the place kept the lift from the champagne going. Lauren no longer felt nervous and Deirdre seemed very relaxed. Lauren reflected that Deirdre looked smart in anything, even the casual clothes she was wearing. Her jeans fitted beautifully, emphasizing her long legs, and her Italian leather jacket was soft and well cut. The black jacket set off her brown eyes, which sparkled–not at all the jaded Friday night look that Lauren remembered from her own years of being chained to an office desk.

Over steak and frites with a green salad, they caught up with each other's news. 'How are Michael and Kiano doing?' Deirdre wanted to know. Deirdre had met Lauren's friend Michael Peston the year before when he identified a suspect in Lauren's investigation.

'I'll be seeing Michael regularly, because we've both joined a climate protection group. He and Kiano are doing well, apart from being obsessed with Mandela.'

'Mandela?' Deirdre looked puzzled, then laughed. 'Oh, their dog–I remember, he was just a pup, that time we went to their party.'

Lauren remembered the party well. It was afterwards that Deirdre had come home with Lauren who was full of nervous expectation–would tonight be the night? But Deirdre had broken the news that she'd just been seconded to Canberra for several months. An exchange programme with the Australians for senior police. She'd acknowledged her attraction to Lauren but made it clear that things between them could not develop. Not at this time anyhow. Lauren had been disappointed but not devastated. Perhaps a little relieved. She was not at all sure that she wanted to set sail on the bumpy waters of a new relationship. Nevertheless, there was that zing.

And it was still here. Their eyes met, they brushed each other's hands as they refreshed their glasses. 'Dessert?' asked Deirdre.

Lauren was inclined towards austerity when it came to desserts, and was conscious she'd indulged in a tiramisu the night before. 'I don't need one.'

'What's need got to do with it? We're out on the town. I'm having the crème brûlée.'

If there was one thing Lauren enjoyed, it was cracking the lid of a custardy crème brûlée, and this place would surely deliver the best, if the meal so far was anything to judge by. 'I can resist anything except temptation,' she said.

'Oh, very good.' Deirdre did not appear to recognise the Oscar Wilde quote and Lauren decided to let her think her dining companion was witty and original.

Digging her spoon into the crisp golden crust and dipping into the creamy mess underneath, Lauren was bereft of conversation. It was too delicious and she gave herself over to the sensations. So apparently did Deirdre. There was a satisfied sigh.

'Done?' asked Lauren.

'Not a smidgeon of space left.' Deirdre patted her lean tummy.

There was a chill in the air, but the evening called for a spring walk. At first, the pair wove their way among many pedestrians on a street noisy with trams, buses and cars jostling along at a slow pace. 'Let's keep walking,' said Deirdre. 'Canberra's just a small town, not the sort of place you can enjoy strolling around in the evening. I'm a city girl at heart.'

'Where are you staying?' Lauren asked. 'Which way shall we walk?'

'I'm on the outskirts, just down Royal Parade and across the Park.'

'Same direction as me, though I must be a couple of stops further along the tram route, the far side of the university.'

Time passed quickly. They were enjoying each other's company. The traffic noise died away as they took a well-lit path through the park. 'There it is.' Deirdre indicated a neon sign. They paused outside, a moment's awkwardness. 'Would you like to come up for a drink?'

'Why not?' said Lauren, brushing aside a cautious feeling that nearly made her decline the offer.

The room was small but pleasant. Deirdre surveyed the contents of the mini-bar. 'Wine? Whisky? Gin? What do you fancy?'

Lauren was still feeling the effects of the champagne and the rough red. 'A very small whisky. Plenty of water with it, thanks, otherwise I'll be decidedly tipsy.'

Deirdre unscrewed the cap of a little bottle of Johnnie Walker and carefully divided the contents into two tumblers. She went to the bathroom to add a finger of water to each and then searched in the icebox. There was an ice tray but the contents were only half frozen. 'Damn cheap hotel! But here's to you, Lauren.' They clinked glasses.

There was only one chair so Lauren sat on the bed. Deirdre looked as if she'd planned to sit there, but changed tack and moved towards the chair. It was wobbly and looked uncomfortable. Lauren laughed and patted the bed beside her. Deirdre joined her and before Lauren knew what was happening, they were kissing. Delicious hungry deep kisses, but each balancing their whiskeys, awkward too. Lauren broke free to put her glass down on the carpet and suddenly remembered. 'Oops, what time is it? The hostel main door closes at eleven and I don't have any other way of getting in.'

Deirdre turned and put her glass on the bedside table, then consulted her watch. 'Twenty to eleven.'

'Oh.' Lauren was momentarily stunned. Could she get there if she ran? Wasn't there a phone number to call on the information sheet. Did she have it with her?

Deirdre looked at her directly. 'My professional opinion,' she paused–Lauren thought she was going to offer to pick a lock or something–'You'll just have to stay here with me.'

A heartbeat. 'I couldn't think of anything better.' And they were in each other's arms again.

~

LAUREN TRIED to slip unobtrusively past the college office but was greeted cheerfully by the receptionist. 'Jean McKenzie was looking for you, she wanted to say goodbye but didn't see you at breakfast.'

'Skipped breakfast, decided on an early morning walk.' Lauren lied smoothly and made her way towards the stairs. Damn! Jean was coming down. 'I heard that, Lauren. Skipping breakfast: that must be the secret to your slim figure.' She went on, 'We're all checking out this morning and I wanted to say goodbye. So did the others. What a shame you weren't there.'

She chatted on and Lauren felt mortified, in fact she felt nineteen again. Climbing the wall of her Cambridge college late at night, her boyfriend giving her a leg up. Crashing down on the other side, going over on her ankle and her yelp bringing out the porter. That had led to a dressing down. You'd think a woman now in her sixties could do discreetly what she liked. Lauren escaped to the privacy of her room. She had quite decided on her walk back to the college that while last night had been glorious, it was not something that should be repeated. But a shock of memories kept coming back to her. Deirdre's lovely body, herself awakening to touch and warmth after such an interval, the sheer delight of intimacy.

Damn the police force, sending Deirdre to Canberra! After her experience of a long-distance relationship when her last girlfriend was transferred from Wellington to Auckland and then to Sydney, she certainly didn't want to try that again. She sighed. Meanwhile she would be seeing Deirdre again before she left Melbourne; Deirdre had said she could take her to the airport.

LAUREN WAITED at the college entrance for Deirdre to pick her up. Deirdre was driving a rental up to Ballarat to stay with a cousin overnight. They'd agreed on a coffee before she dropped Lauren at Tullamarine for the flight home.

Lauren had said her goodbyes to the other women in the project. Promises to meet up next year wherever the investigators decided to bring them together. The four days with the alumnae group had been good, and getting to know Miriam was a standout. She looked forward to her visit.

A small featureless car pulled up and a smiling Deirdre got out, greeting Lauren with a peck on the cheek. Lauren put her suitcase in the boot, grasping it assertively to make sure that Deirdre didn't try any gallant gestures.

They drove towards the old road north at Richmond. Lauren enjoyed this part of Melbourne. With its assortment of discount shops, street art and funky cafes, the inner city suburb had the vibe of Wellington's Cuba Street or Auckland's K' Road. Deirdre scored a park in a side street and the pair wandered down the main road till they found a café that appealed to them. It was full of nooks and crannies. They chose a quiet booth towards the back, away from the banging of the baristas and the chatter of customers.

A moment of awkwardness and then they both started to speak at once.

'I was going to say…'

'I don't think…'

Deirdre winced and Lauren gave a half smile. She reached across the table and put her hands over Deirdre's. 'I don't want to think of what happened as insignificant, but I don't hold with the lesbian way of doing things. In bed one night, moving truck the next day.'

Deirdre looked relieved. 'I must confess, I was wondering what I'd got myself into, even though we did have a marvellous time.' They looked at one another, and then away, each of them with a small smile.

'Let's just put it in the too hard basket for the time being.'

Deirdre nodded, 'Sounds like the best thing.' She grinned wickedly at Lauren. 'I am growing quite fond of you, though.'

'*Quite* fond? *Quite* fond? You…' She matched Deirdre's grin. 'I hope that's an understatement. You wouldn't let me get too big-headed, that's for sure!'

They both laughed, the awkwardness dissolved and they agreed to keep in touch every so often. 'Do you use FaceTime?' Lauren asked. 'I'm preferring that to Skype for calls to the grandchildren. It comes through like an ordinary phone call rather than having to make an appointment to meet on the computer.'

'FaceTime?' Deirdre wrinkled her nose. 'I'm afraid we're more incompatible than I first thought.'

Lauren was surprised. 'I would have thought you'd be up with the latest.'

'No, it's the great divide, the Macs versus the rest. You've got an iPhone, I see,' she said, peering across the table. 'And I've a Samsung. But you can download WhatsApp, it's the same sort of thing, works across all devices.' She grabbed a serviette and wrote it down. 'Check it out.'

Lauren agreed and they began to speak of other things. Lauren's thoughts were turning back to her ordinary life in Wellington. She told Deirdre about the new climate action group. That reminded her of the shocking phone call she'd had from Pam. 'I heard bad news when I first arrived here–apparently one of Wellington's main climate change activists has been drowned.'

'Who was that?'

'Nat Spiller. Have you heard of him?'

'Oh yes,' said Deirdre. 'Were you involved in his activities?' Deirdre's face was impassive.

'Oh no, I hardly knew him–he was the partner of my friend Pam's niece and I didn't know him personally, but I admired him immensely. He was a real climate change hero, smart and imaginative. He organised brilliant protests, street theatre–you know, he wasn't afraid of the authorities. Quite a different approach from my group.'

She paused. Deirdre was listening intently. Lauren had a sudden thought. 'Of course, you're one of the authorities. I suppose you're not that keen on law-breakers.'

Deirdre laughed. 'I've got a poster of Nelson Mandela in my flat,' she retorted. She paused, before speaking again. 'How did it happen, do you know?'

Lauren told her the story, all about seeing the wrecked yacht, how the yachtie had said that someone was still in the water, and then the shocking news from Pam that Nat's body had been recovered.

'Was he a strong swimmer?' Deirdre asked.

'Pam says so. She said he was wearing his wetsuit when he was found.'

Deirdre was silent. 'What?' said Lauren.

'Nothing, it's just my work here.' She paused. 'I can't talk about it, but I'm placed with a group that deals with threats to national security. That includes protest activities.'

Lauren started to say something indignant but Deirdre interrupted, 'I know what you're thinking. But the police do have to be involved and it's tricky, balancing freedoms and behaviour that crosses the line.'

Lauren pursed her lips. 'Okay, but what's that got to do with Nat Spiller? He was just going for a swim.'

'Oz is a more divisive society than EnZed, I'm discovering. There've been a few instances of activists coming to harm.'

'What?' Lauren was astonished. 'What are you suggesting?'

Deirdre looked as if she wished she had never raised the topic. 'Nothing, really. No doubt the police will be looking into it since it's a sudden death.'

Lauren's stomach churned. Could someone have had it in for Nat because of his activism? Surely not, that kind of thing didn't happen in New Zealand. She mentally corrected herself. Of course, there had been the Rainbow Warrior sinking. But there didn't seem to be anything more to say. She looked at her watch. 'Look at the time, we'd better go.'

They walked companionably to the car. Half an hour later they said their goodbyes on the kerb at the airport's two minute drop-off. This time Lauren didn't object to Deirdre handling her bags. It gave Deirdre the perfect excuse to get out of the car and give her a hug.

6

There was a soft knock at the door. Lauren had taken tea and toast back to bed, a rare indulgence. Who on earth could it be, she wondered as she grumpily pulled on her dressing-gown and slippers and padded up the hall.

'Pam!' Lauren was horrified, Pam looked beyond tired, her face was haggard. 'Come in, come in.' She took her by the arm and steered her down the hall.

'I know you only got back last night and I didn't mean to just show up. But I haven't been sleeping so I went for an early morning walk. Somehow it took me across Mt Vic and then I remembered you'd be back, so...' She waved her hands as if in explanation.

Lauren was embarrassed at herself for having felt grumpy. It wasn't at all like Pam to intrude. She was normally as reserved as a pipi hiding in its shell in the sand, detectable only by its air bubbles. Lauren hugged her, ushered her towards a comfy chair and offered her a drink.

'Just a glass of water, thanks. Sorry,' Pam said again, a tear rolling down her cheek.

Lauren returned from the kitchen with water and tissues. 'What's going on?' she asked gently.

'Ellie's so upset,' Pam sniffed. 'She's confiding in me because she can't talk to her mother. Lauren, Ellie keeps saying Nat's death wasn't an accident. She keeps raging and crying and saying he never would have drowned and that someone must have murdered him.

'I need to talk to you about all this, Lauren. You dealt with something like this last year, and I respect your judgment.' Lauren's heart sank. Pam continued. 'There's no one else I can confide in.' Lauren's heart sank further.

'Pam, I'm no expert on crime. Murder! It sounds extraordinary!' Lauren could hardly believe her ears. 'Has Ellie got anything to go on? People drown all the time, even the most experienced swimmers and divers. Don't the police think it's accidental?'

Pam shrugged, visibly pulling herself together. 'It's hard to get anything out of her, she's so upset. I was with her when the police came around to tell her about the autopsy and let her know when the body would be released. They listened to Ellie sympathetically but I could tell they just think she's hysterical with grief. In the end the senior cop said as much. He didn't put it that way, of course, but he did ask her if the doctor had prescribed her any pills to help with sleeping.'

Lauren paused, taking this all in. 'And had her doctor? Who is it, anyhow?'

'A woman from the Terrace practice. I took Ellie down, although it was hard to persuade her. She gave Ellie sleeping pills but Ellie said she's not taking them because she wants to keep her focus until the police start taking her seriously.'

'Well, she won't keep focused if she isn't getting any sleep. Perhaps you could encourage her to take them.'

Pam put her head in her hands. 'I've tried but she's just being impossible.'

'Do you think she could be right?' Lauren was thinking fast, wrestling between disbelief and her knowledge that what tearful women say is often discounted.

Pam shrugged, hands outstretched helplessly. 'I just don't know. Of course she's grief-stricken, but she's usually very sensible. I can't act as if I don't believe her, she trusts me. But if I did believe her... well, I wouldn't know what to do next.'

'Did she suggest anyone who might have a grudge towards Nat?'

'Not really, she muttered something about climate change politics, but she's been pretty incoherent.' Pam bit her lip. 'But maybe sensible enough not to go round making wild accusations.'

'That's something.' Lauren frowned and thought for a moment. 'The autopsy. Was there any room for doubt about what happened? Did the police give her a written report?'

Pam looked surprised. 'I don't think so, they just said it showed he had a large gash on the back of his head, consistent with being dashed against a rock, and that the injury didn't kill him, rather, he drowned. They believed that he must have been knocked off his feet by a wave while he was out there. He must have been floating unconscious for a while because the guy from the yacht thought he was still alive.'

'So they've interviewed him? They must have been doing some sort of investigation.'

'Maybe, but I think it was a journalist. Caught up with the guy as soon as he was discharged and got a story out of it. You wouldn't have seen it, it was in the *Dominion Post* while you were away in Melbourne. Well, I know you usually read the news online, but perhaps...'

Pam was wittering, Lauren thought. She needed to have something concrete to focus on. 'Perhaps you could get hold of the autopsy report.'

Pam perked up. 'I knew you'd have some ideas, Lauren, thank you!' She blew her nose and looked thoughtful. 'Could you get it please, Lauren–you've had contacts in the police.'

Lauren almost smiled–her most recent contact was hardly professional. She said, 'I could ask Phyl next door what the procedure is. If the police summarised it accurately to Ellie, it might not help, but you never know. There'd be details and there might be room for doubt about how Nat got the blow to his head. Or if there isn't any room for doubt, it might help persuade Ellie that she's barking up the wrong tree.'

Pam looked more herself, her cheeks less blotchy. 'That would be really helpful, Lauren. And you'll come to the funeral, won't you? It's at three o'clock on Tuesday at Old St Paul's.'

Lauren agreed. She was no stranger to supporting friends at funerals when their parents died. This was a little different. She couldn't help thinking that if Nat had been murdered, the funeral gathering would be a good place to get to know what was happening on the activist edge of climate change politics. She told herself to stop it, it all sounded too unlikely.

Pam left and Lauren shut the door, walking slowly back into her living room. She went over to the window. She loved her view, but she wasn't seeing it as she gazed into the distance. Murder, hard to believe, horrifying if it were true. Could Nat have been attacked because of his climate change work? Would that have been an attack on the whole environmental movement?

7

Lloyd Spiller was trying to use work as a distraction from his misery. Spiller Developments owned a multi-storey building in downtown Wellington. Most of it was leased but Lloyd's empire took up two whole floors at the top of the building. Lloyd liked to walk up the steps from the street level, take the lift to the second to top floor and tread firmly up the final set of twenty stairs. Although he was a big man, tall and heavy set, his sixty-odd years sat lightly on him. His hair might have been turning grey and his skin weathered, but he prided himself that he was just as fit as his sons, and as sharp as ever. He knew he was respected in the business community and he couldn't imagine retiring. He expected fair dealings from business partners and loyalty and hard work from his staff– but he didn't expect them to work any harder than he did.

He would arrive from the lift at the reception desk at precisely eight o'clock, and nod to the blonde young woman. He never remembered the receptionist's name, they were interchangeable. Upstairs, he would proceed down the corridor past the open plan offices to his big corner office with its view over the city and out onto the water. Big mahogany veneer desk; coffee table and tub chairs in one corner. He would call 'Good morning' to his secretary in her small office next door, then hang his coat on the rack next to the hard hat and orange vest. They reminded him of his beginnings and still occasionally came in useful. Then he would sit straight down at his desk and begin working through the pile of documents already prepared for his decisions. Print-outs of emails, legal files and so forth. His secretary would bring him a strong tea in a big earthenware mug.

The Wednesday following Nat's death was no different. The Spillers had heard from Ellie on Sunday evening that Nat hadn't returned home from snorkelling. They had a sleepless night that night, and early the next day their world was shattered by another call from Ellie. The police had found a body and were taking Ellie to the morgue to identify it. Lloyd couldn't stay at home. He'd gone too and yes, it was Nat. The rest of the day was a blur of distress, and he'd forced himself to stay home all of Tuesday. He'd called home his grown-up children, reckoning that they would be there to keep their mother company. Now he desperately needed his normal routine. He went into work at the usual time. What else was he to do?

But it was different, the blonde at reception had tried to talk to him. 'Oh, Mr Spiller.' He paused. 'Yes?'

'I'm so sorry,' she stumbled over the words. 'About your son,' she said. 'About Nat. He was a lovely man.'

He looked at her properly. Perhaps she wasn't as interchangeable as he'd thought. 'Thank you.' It was said gruffly.

He walked on up the stairs and along the corridor, walked into his office, called a good morning to his secretary and sat down at his desk. But where was the work? There should have been a couple of days' worth. His secretary came in. Mary Braithwaite had been with him for twenty years. She had his mug of builder's tea in her hand but no papers. 'Oh Lloyd,' she said. She never called him Lloyd. 'I'm so, so upset, that lovely boy, how could that have happened?'

Lloyd was incredulous. You tried to keep afloat with your normal routine and those around you wouldn't let it happen. Did she want him to scream in anguish, cry out to his dead son for forgiveness?

'Thank you, Mary.' For what? For making him wonder how Nat could have been so careless. For ruining the carefully built fortification of his own routine? He said gruffly, 'Could you bring me that report on the parcel of land in the Wairarapa we're considering?' He paused. 'And the file on the Lyall Bay project. I've asked Justin to come and talk with me about progress later in the week.'

She shrank back into her usual persona. 'Certainly Mr Spiller. And a letter has come in from Council about your proposal to swap the Lyall Bay land for a piece on higher ground. Shall I bring that in too?'

'Oh good. Yes, please.' He would usually have turned to busy himself with the pile of paperwork. The shiny surface of the desk defeated him. As she left the room he put his head in his hands and slumped over the desk. Oh Nat. Such talent. Such a waste. And no children to delight their grandfather.

By the time his secretary brought the papers he was sitting up again. He opened the Lyall Bay file. She'd put the letter from the council on top.

'...pleased to inform you....prepared to exchange your land in Lyall Bay, being Lot.... Council intends to use lower land as park-land....our engineers have surveyed....firm prediction based on the most recent scientific information that sea may cover it by mid-century.'

'Huh, so much for us dinosaurs,' Lloyd thought. Lloyd had reluctantly come to believe in rising sea levels. He hadn't become head of the firm without being able to move with the times. But the boy was going to hate it. His pet project. Lloyd wished he hadn't given it to him. Justin seemed to want to show his brother Nat that he knew better about rising sea levels. Didn't he have some tame climate change scientist in his pocket? That guy Derek Drysdall. He'd been hanging around Justin and Lloyd didn't trust him. A smartarse. Lloyd gave a kind of strangled cough, something between a choke and a sob. Justin didn't have to try and outdo Nat any more.

~

By Friday, Lloyd was still keeping up his routine. He was sitting at his desk, idly turning over papers in front of him when his secretary popped her head in. 'Your son's here, Mr Spiller. Are you ready for him?'

Lloyd nodded. 'Show him in.' He pushed his chair back from the desk and walked round to greet Justin.

'My boy,' he said gruffly and enveloped Justin in a bear hug.

It was an unaccustomed display of affection and Justin stiffened awkwardly. Lloyd released him and gestured to the chairs by the window.

'All we can do, son, is keep going. Nat would have expected us to do that.'

Justin muttered something inarticulate as he slumped into a chair. Several years younger than his brother, he lacked Nat's vitality. An unkind trick of genetics made him look like a blurred copy. Nat had had dark hair, bright blue eyes, a Roman nose and a generous mouth given to smiling. Justin's hair was mousy, his eyes light blue and his complexion had a pallor about it beneath his tan. He was quieter, his demeanour less definite. There was a blankness about him. Nat's friends–if they thought of him at all–unkindly blamed the blankness on a lack of brain power. Now, waiting for his father to sit down, he looked not at him but at the floor.

Lloyd had gone back to his desk and was sorting through some papers. He brought a sheaf over and put them on the table and settled heavily into a chair opposite Justin. 'Thank you for staying with us this week, son. It's meant a lot to your mother. Was she up when you left?' He looked uncharacteristically anxious. 'Those pills the doctor gave her really knocked her out. She was still asleep when I came to work.'

Justin looked uncomfortable. 'She's awake now but not up. Auntie Judith brought her a cup of tea and Mum asked to see me before I went out. She was on at me again not to go diving anymore. I'm not going to stop diving, Dad.'

Now he raised his head to look directly at his father. Lloyd was shocked. The boy was looking awful, as if he hasn't slept for days–reddened eyes with bags under them, mouth turned down, and no glimmer of a smile.

Lloyd blamed himself. He hadn't noticed how hard the boy was taking it. And he supposed that the swimming and diving was helping him cope. He said more gently than he might have, 'I know, son, but you mustn't upset your mother just now. This has been a terrible shock for all of us and you know how it's affected her.' He shuddered inwardly. He remembered the horror of Ellie's phone call, how his wife had wept and screamed at him in a way that demanded he hold himself together. He continued, 'I understand you need to get out into the sea'–Lloyd was proud that both of his sons were so good in the water. He checked himself, just one son now–'but perhaps take it easy for a while. And you probably need to settle down to work again, that'll help you cope. You haven't been in the office the last few days.'

Justin muttered something his father couldn't hear, so Lloyd went on briskly. 'Justin,' he said, 'I need to let you know the latest in the Lyall Bay development.'

The younger man sat up. 'Lyall Bay? I thought you'd be wanting me to tell you how the planning appeal is going.' There was a querulous edge to his voice. His father always seemed to be wrong-footing him. 'I think we're going to win. Derek Drysdall has lodged his submission and...' –his voice turned from shrill to quiet–'Nat didn't put in a counter-submission.'

'I tell you, son, it's dead in the water,' said Lloyd. His stomach lurched at the ill-considered phrase, but he went on grimly, 'We've spent enough time and money fighting for it. I'm not saying you haven't done well but the council isn't going to move on it. And now they've offered us a really good deal–a swap for some public land higher up–they'll turn the Lyall Bay section into parkland, until it's covered with sea water.'

Justin looked horrified. He shifted in the seat and stared at Lloyd. 'How come? I hadn't asked them to consider that. What am I going to say to Derek? I already owe him a few thou for the work he did on the submission and he's expecting more for appearances if there are hearings on the submission.'

'Don't be so pathetic,' snapped his father. 'Pay what you owe and tell him there's nothing more coming. I organized to offer a transfer as a backup, and it's paid off. It's not cheap to get out of a plan but we've got a good deal out of the council and that will more than make up for what we've spent on Lyall Bay. In fact it would be good if you told him to shut up about his ideas on sea-levels, because we want the council to think they've done the right thing, buying us out.'

Justin did not usually stand up to his father. But now he literally stood up, as if he could not contain himself. 'You could have told me you were talking to Council. It makes me look stupid! I could have done that, if I hadn't been sure Derek would carry the day. What a waste.... Now we'll have to withdraw the application.' His voice trailed off. Then he carried on. 'Derek's done a lot of work for us. And he and I thought we might go in together on that half-built house next door to our site in Lyall Bay. You know, where the owners went broke and the builders walked off. The place is going for a song and it wouldn't take too much work to get the project to completion. It's only a small house, but the views would be sensational. And it's got resource consent, it was planned before all this climate bullshit turned the council into nannies.'

'As I recall the lie of the land,' said his father. 'it's also on a bit of a slope.' Justin didn't reply and Lloyd continued, 'What you do with your own money is your concern, Justin, but it will not be a Spiller Developments project.' He looked at his son's face and relented. Now wasn't the time to be trying to stiffen him up. Justin was suffering with his brother's death. 'Well, you can make a business case and I might let you have a mortgage–the banks certainly wouldn't–but I want you fully engaged on the Newtown project. The other would be in your own time.'

Justin muttered, 'Thanks, Dad.'

There was a pause. Then with an effort, Lloyd said, 'I'll talk to you later about the replacement for the Lyall Bay development. I know you must be wanting to get back to your own place, but your mother would appreciate it if you stayed with us till after the funeral, and we can all go together.'

8

Lloyd had insisted on having Old St Paul's for Nat's funeral. He'd left the service details to Ellie but told her not to skimp, he'd foot the bill for Nat's send-off. Ellie would have preferred a natural burial for Nat at Makara, with his body unembalmed, feeding a tree above, but the state of his body after the long hours in the water didn't allow it. She'd organised a coffin and he was going to be cremated. So here they were. The wooden arches of the beautiful old church, once the Anglican Cathedral for Wellington, soared above the pews where Nat's friends and family were waiting for the service to begin. The wood, the brass fittings and the stained glass windows combined to drench the whole building in colour and light.

Lauren followed Pam, directed by the usher to the front pew of the rows allocated to the Petersen family. A distressed-looking older woman who must have been Ellie's mother sat on the aisle end of the pew, clutching her daughter's arm and murmuring to her. Pam edged past her sister-in-law and Ellie and sat down stiffly on Ellie's left, with Lauren next to her.

Lauren turned around to scan the packed church. She caught sight of Harold Stevens, the chair of the Environmental Protection

Society. He looked miserable and was drab in a dark suit. But mostly the mourners were a colourful lot. The front rows on each side were, like Harold, a sober reminder of traditional funeral attire–black suits, black shoes. The front pews on the opposite side must be the Spillers, with the woman on the aisle presumably Nat's mother, crowned by a very elegant black hat–altogether a bunch of kaka at the front of an array of kakariki–Nat's and Ellie's myriad friends, every environmentalist in Wellington, she thought, looked to be dressed haphazardly from op shops. The women had brightly coloured hair and wore a cheerful miscellany of clothes: leggings, petticoats, skirts, dresses, t-shirts, blouses, often layered in a way that looked odd. Get over it, Lauren told herself, it's the modern trend. The men weren't as flashy as kakariki, they were more like the kiwis they were intent on saving, brown and hairy, with their long hair, beards, woolly jerseys, cords. What she thought of these days as her funeral gear, her black trousers with a narrow self-stripe in the fabric, fine-knit top and a maroon fitted jacket, seemed positively conservative. Even if the jacket was stylishly fastened with a long zip, and she was wearing her dark red shoes.

She shook herself mentally, not the time to be thinking about fashion. She couldn't help wondering who Ellie thought might have killed Nat. Were they present? She turned her attention to the families occupying the front pews. Ellie's was small and close; Pam of course, Ellie's mother and then another elderly woman, perhaps a maternal aunt, in the row behind, who was leaning forward to whisper in Ellie's ear. The sprawling Spiller clan took up three rows. The craggy, handsome man next to the woman in the black hat, looking every bit the elder statesman, must be Nat's father. The next row held a family, a woman about Nat's age, pale with a furrowed brow, alternately leaning forward to talk to the black hat, and glancing at the children on one side of her and a man on the other, presumably a husband. The other Spiller mourners were no doubt aunts, uncles and cousins.

Then the coffin was carried in. Pam pointed to the pallbearers with a whisper: 'Nat's brother, Justin, front left, Ellie's brother, front right, the rest cousins of Nat's, I imagine.' The coffin was placed at the front and the pallbearers dispersed. Nat's brother stood uncertainly, until he was grasped by his father and pulled into the front pew. Ellie's brother sat by his mother, causing the rest of them to shuffle along. The church hushed and the celebrant began speaking. It was a secular service. Nat had not been religious in the conventional sense but Ellie had obviously tried to take his family's feelings into consideration. The church itself, though deconsecrated, still felt like a hallowed place. The music that interspersed the tributes and talk of Nat's life included Psalm 23, as well as Leonard Cohen's 'Hallelujah', sung by a musical friend of Nat.

Lauren imagined that most of the mourners related to Cohen's 'Hallelujah' better than 'The Lord's my shepherd'. The funeral demonstrated that most people didn't sing at church any more. She listened carefully to the tributes. The head of the environmentally aware architecture firm, Nat's former employer, talked glowingly about his work, two of his friends spoke admiringly about his more flamboyant protest actions, and Ellie's brother remembered how much his family had enjoyed having Nat as part of it. There was a bemused feeling in the church. How could someone so vibrant, so alive, not be here? Laughter, at some of the anecdotes, and the occasional muffled sob. Ellie was by turns laughing and weeping. Lauren could see that Nat's mother was sobbing. His father was putting on a brave face, but twisting a large white handkerchief in his hand. When it was the Spiller clan's turn to speak, a man who introduced himself as Nat's Uncle Mark faced the mourners. Pam whispered to Lauren, 'He's in the firm too. Lloyd's younger brother and the CEO in waiting.'

'Many of you know that Nat was,' he hesitated, 'at odds with his family. We loved him, though, we all loved him, his charm, his enthusiasm. We didn't agree with his stance, but,' and he repeated himself, 'that didn't stop us from loving him. We didn't see much of him, it was too tiring. You all knew him, he couldn't let you get away with anything, he'd be correcting you and arguing with you.' There was a ripple of recognition and amusement through the assembly. 'But this is such a sad day for us. Nat's family know that he was trying to do the right thing for Wellington, for New Zealand, and indeed his planet.

'Lloyd has asked me to announce that Spiller Construction will be making an annual award in his name. The Nat Spiller environmental award will be worth $100,000 and will be given annually to assist an innovative environmental science project.' It was unexpected, people looked at one another, one or two people clapped and then remembered where they were. That was the end of the speeches. The celebrant read out a Celtic blessing and the pallbearers took up their positions again. They walked out with the coffin, behind them the Spillers and Ellie with her supporters.

People stood, stretched, nodded to friends, formed little groups. Pam and Ellie were swept up by friends of the Petersen family, so Lauren edged in on the environmentalists. Old friends of Nat were exchanging memories; belly laughs and guffaws occasionally cut across the bleak mood. The other topics of conversation were the puzzle of his death and the Spiller turnaround. 'How on earth could he have been caught out like that?' 'Must have been a freak wave.' 'Or perhaps he got cramp?' 'It's a treacherous bit of coast–look what it did to that yacht that tried to rescue him.' 'Still can't understand it.'

'And the proposed award: Can you believe it? $100,000.'

'What about that crazy development they were pushing? You know, the owners would have been swimming in their living room in another twenty years.'

'Is the award blood money? Sorry they alienated Nat, trying to make up for it....'

As they talked, the mourners were making for the side room where refreshments were set out. The proposed memorial was on everyone's mind. Between bites of sausage roll or egg sandwiches, as people balanced their tea and coffee, the chat was first about what the likely terms of the prize would be and second, what this said about Spiller Construction.

'Not all developers are the enemy of the environment,' said Jack, a close friend of Nat's, 'but Nat certainly thought his family firm was. What a turnaround! Do you think as well as donating a prize they might start building environmentally friendly subdivisions? Imagine if they took them off the grid, and made power dependent on wind and sun!'

The idea was taken up and soon a little group of Nat's architectural colleagues was virtually designing a green subdivision. Voices rose and sounded cheerful as more suggestions were made, and then someone would remind the others about Nat and they would be sober again.

Ellie interrupted the conversation. Visibly pulling herself together, she said, 'You're all invited back to my place. Nat would have liked you to come and have a drink.' Lauren would have slipped away, but Pam wanted her support. Lauren agreed, realizing it would give her more of a feel for Nat's world. Ellie's brother offered them places in his car, and drove them the short distance to Ellie and Nat's apartment further up the hill in Thorndon.

When Lauren got out of the car she was surprised at Nat and Ellie's choice of flat. It was in an old apartment block, and as they all went in from the entrance, Ellie's brother leading the way, they went down a set of stairs rather than up. Surely not a gloomy basement flat?

It wasn't. The building took advantage of the slope of the land and their flat opened out onto a deck and the back lawn for the whole block. It included a small but carefully tended vegetable garden that had to belong to Nat and Ellie. It looked like enough for two.

It was an odd trigger for sadness, but Lauren was sorry that now Ellie would harvest the produce just for herself. Which of them, she wondered, was the gardener. Perhaps Ellie, given her aunt's enthusiasm for gardening. Probably both of them, Nat would have been into self-sufficiency.

Someone was speaking to her. 'Sorry? Oh, thank you, a gin and tonic if I may.'

Ellie and a friend were handing around drinks to everyone. Ellie's mother and aunt were already ensconced into the two comfy armchairs, both managing cups and saucers. Everyone else seemed to have a glass. Some of Nat's environmental buddies were standing at the kitchen end of the long open room that served as kitchen, dining and sitting room and there was another small group over by the couple's extensive book collection.

A pool of sadness hung over the wake, continually interrupted as life reasserted itself. Everyone had a story about Nat–the time he used crampons to shin up the trunk of a huge threatened totara; when he darted out of a respectful crowd, to hand deliver a petition to a Governor-General; the night he'd spent in police cells practising a persuasive speech for the District Court–all that and a lot of talk about the new award. 'Fancy old Spiller coming round.' 'Terrible that it took Nat's death to do it.' And the company sobered again.

Then more Nat stories: how he'd organised sit-ins, led marches, presented petitions and once even got onto an oil rig and climbed to the top, refusing to come down even when the weather turned sour. 'There wasn't an aspect of the environment he wasn't dedicated to. He'd even been to the Antarctic on a Greenpeace expedition.'

'Yeah, that would require some fortitude. The Southern Ocean and its 50-foot waves!'

'But it was Wellington's south coast that he loved,' someone else said. 'He really grieved when the data came out about sea level rise and what would happen to it.'

'Perhaps it'll still be lovely, the shoreline will just be in a different place,' said Ellie's brother. That didn't go down well. He was fixed with several pairs of disapproving eyes and several raised eyebrows. He continued defensively, 'I heard he was writing a submission against the proposed Spiller development in Lyall Bay. I really admired him for that. A hard thing to stand against your own family. Do you think they'll can that development now?'

Lauren was all ears. Now that was a hint of trouble, and of course close relatives are top of the list when it comes to murder. But she didn't dare ask any questions in case it spotlighted Ellie's suspicions, and Ellie was keeping control of herself.

'Given their proposed environmental award they might,' someone else said. 'Not likely, though,' replied another. 'Nat told me that the family had gone to the expense of hiring a tame "expert".' He waggled his fingers to indicate quotation marks. 'The guy was arguing that the Council's all wrong about how soon and how big the sea level rise would be.'

An astonished voice. 'A climate change denier? Now?'

'This fellow's a scientist who actually works on climate change. He's even on the Antarctic summer programme.' By now Lauren was eavesdropping unashamedly. They must be talking about the guy Miriam and Alison had complained about when she was in Melbourne.

The same voice, still astonished. 'That's extraordinary. I thought there was a consensus. Doesn't everyone know climate change is already happening? And all we can do now is stop it from getting worse?'

'That's true.' Jack was an oceanographer and spoke authoritatively. 'But there's not a consensus about how much sea rise and how soon and where. It's not like pouring water into a bath. The levels don't go up evenly. Ice sheets melting at one pole can make the seas rise near the other pole. Some warming events can even lower sea levels in particular places.

'But I know the fellow who's in the Spiller group's pocket. His name's Drysdall, Derek Drysdall. He's a real outlier. Hardly anyone else thinks sea rise is going to be that minimal around here.'

'Ah,' said somebody else. 'A lukewarmer!'

Jack ignored the crack and continued. 'He's one of the scientists from Vic who go down to the Antarctic most summers. A meteorologist. I spotted him at the funeral, he was talking to Nat's brother. Nat had told me how tight Derek is with Justin.'

There was a slight pause in the conversation. Everyone was processing what this might mean. 'They must be paying him a lot, to put his reputation on the line!' one said. Finally, someone else said, 'I don't think what one scientist says will have much effect on the Council. They will have taken their cue from sources like NIWA and the UN reports and won't be swayed.'

Heads nodded.

Ellie was holding herself together. Lauren watched her, white-faced, shoulders held stiffly, pushing her way from group to group, offering drinks and snacks, listening woodenly, trying to smile as she went from one to another.

Then someone stepped back as she was coming forward with a couple of refills. They collided and a glass of red wine splashed all over Ellie's shirt. 'I'm terribly sorry. I'll get a cloth,' said the guy who'd stepped back.

Ellie burst into tears. The incident had broken the dam. 'Don't worry, it's not the shirt.' The guy looked perplexed. 'It's Nat, Nat should be here,' she wailed and her voice rose. 'Why can't you all see? Nat didn't have an accident. He wouldn't have. Someone must have killed him.' She choked. She stood in the middle of the room, tears running down her face and wine dripping from her shirt onto the floor. There was a frozen silence. Pam stepped forward, took her niece gently by the arm. 'Come on Ellie, let's go to the bathroom and clean you up.'

9

Lauren was waking up slowly and not very happily. She lay in bed analysing how she felt. Her mouth was dry and her head wasn't throbbing but certainly twinging. Just like a hangover. Then she remembered the funeral, the wake, that ghastly scene with Ellie. Its aftermath, as Nat's friends tried not to show their disbelief. She groaned. Pam had phoned her afterwards and extracted a promise from Lauren to go with her to see Ellie today. Pam wanted reinforcements and she wanted Lauren to be able to hear for herself what Ellie was saying and try to get some sense out of her. Damn, Lauren thought, she would have to put off coffee with her friend Ro. She had been neglecting her lately.

By the time she'd collected Pam from outside her flat, Lauren had pulled herself together. Nothing like a couple of paracetamol, a hot shower and a freshly ironed shirt. She hoped she appeared both sympathetic and efficient.

Ellie answered their knock, looking tired and pale. She hadn't slept well, but was still keen to talk to them. Lauren hoped Pam hadn't built her up too much, she did feel there wasn't anything useful she could contribute. Just be a witness, she told herself.

She looked around, reflecting that, like herself, the room had a morning after feel to it, with too many chairs jostling for space against the walls and a few half-empty glasses on bookshelves that hadn't been cleared away. Ellie sat them at the table, made coffee and sat down herself, looking expectantly at Lauren. 'What do you need to know?'

Lauren winced inwardly. Pam must have told Ellie about the Lange investigation. There was no way in hell that Lauren was going to be seen as some sort of private investigator, but it was clear that she was expected to run the conversation. She tried to be gentle. 'Why do you think Nat's death wasn't an accident, Ellie? Surely the police would have been onto it if there was anything odd about it?'

Ellie took a deep breath and dabbed her eyes with a handkerchief. 'I just know he wouldn't have been so careless. He's been snorkelling off the south coast for years, and he's always'–she corrected herself–'he was always meticulous about safety. He knows–knew–how dangerous the sea could be and he respected it.' She stopped. 'When the coroner released Nat's body,' her voice shook, 'the police came around and told me what was in the report. They said his death was consistent with an accidental injury followed by drowning. That doesn't mean it *was* an accident, does it?' She looked bleakly at Lauren, who dropped her gaze. 'You've been in the public service so you know how weaselly officials can be.'

Lauren didn't want Ellie to feel she was taking the same attitude as the police. Nor did she want to seem too readily convinced. Her job was to be neutral, yet any signs of doubt would probably have Ellie incoherent in floods of tears. 'Your Nat was so admired, Ellie, he did such great environmental work. Can you think of anyone who would have wanted him dead?'

Ellie sounded bitter. 'There were always people wanting to quibble about what Nat did. Nat knew that to force change he often had to take drastic action and ask others to help. Sometimes actions outside the law. He said that sometimes you have to do outrageous things to make people notice that the planet's dying.'

Pam interrupted, 'But Ellie, people who disagree with you don't usually harm you. Quibbling is one thing, killing's another.'

'Aunt Pam,' Ellie seldom used 'aunt' to Pam, it was a sign of frustration. 'There were people who hated Nat, they were jealous, I think, because he had vision and they just plodded.' Tears were running down her cheek.

'Who in particular just plodded?' Lauren asked the question quietly.

'That Harold Stevens, for one,' said Ellie.

'Harold Stevens?' repeated Lauren. Her voice rose in astonishment. 'The one who's started the Wellington Climate Protection Society?'

'Yes,' said Ellie. 'He and Nat had a big row. Harold thought you had to obey the law all the time. When he found out Nat was going to climb up the Beehive and plaster a banner across it, he had the gall to tip off the cops. They turned up really early in the morning when Nat and a mate were getting their ropes and things out of their car boot in a side street near Parliament. They took them off to the police station for questioning and so they never got to pull it off. Harold was so smug the next time he saw Nat and actually admitted it, as if it was something to be proud of. He was just a pompous ass. He told Nat that the environmental movement shouldn't get a bad name and wouldn't benefit from stupid pranks.'

Ellie went on, sounding reflective. 'Nat said Harold was always a plodder. They'd known each other at school. His family were fundamentalist Christians, some weird sect. He was always so buttoned up.'

This was giving Lauren new insight into Harold, but Ellie's idea of him as a potential suspect seemed completely wild. 'How come Harold's so into saving the environment? He worked for the Ministry of Transport as a draughtsman and he said he's now a consultant. Where did the environmental stuff come from?'

'He was a loner, always been a keen birdwatcher. Nat said it was because he wasn't supposed to think about human birds.' Pam winced.

Ellie gave a wan smile and went on, 'Maybe he wasn't even interested in girls. Nat did respect his knowledge though. Harold was upset about what humans were doing to the planet. Bird habitats, especially. But then he got obsessed with climate change and our shorelines. Something about his grandparents' house falling into the sea up north somewhere. And of course the Hutt Valley, where he lives, is very low-lying.' She gestured vaguely and said, 'You'll have to ask Nat for more detail. Oh,' she wailed as she realized what she'd said. Pam moved to give her a hug and Lauren said, 'Would you rather we talked about this some other time, Ellie?'

'No, I want you to find out who killed Nat.'

Lauren took a deep breath. This isn't what she had in mind at all. What on earth had Pam been saying to Ellie. She was cross, but suppressed her anger. 'So what happened after the row?'

'I don't think they saw each other again. Apparently Harold said he was going to start his own lawful organisation to fight climate change and I know Nat was surprised when he actually did. I think he might have stirred up Harold by sending him a mocking email. He said something to that effect but I don't really know, except that Nat thought he wasn't capable of running an effective organisation.'

'Mmm,' said Lauren, remembering the inaugural meeting. What Ellie said about his background made sense of the way he'd seemed at that. Buttoned up, prissy. Hardly a murderer, surely!

'So you think Harold was cross enough....'

'I know it may sound weird.' Ellie was defiant.

Lauren sighed inwardly, sat silent for a moment. Then, 'You said people were jealous of Nat. Were you aware of anyone else as angry as Harold?'

Ellie considered. 'No, the other person who'd had a big falling out with him was Derek Drysdall. And that was quite different.'

Derek Drysdall–that name again. 'How was it different?'

'Derek was another one who was at the same school as Nat, but younger. He was a friend of Justin's. Nat said Derek was bright but always competitive. They're all part of the snorkelling and diving crowd. Derek's now a climate scientist. And Nat thought he twisted data. He was furious with him.'

'Sounds unethical,' said Lauren, 'but why was Nat particularly furious about it?'

Ellie looked surprised at the question. 'Oh, of course, you probably don't know. The Spillers are starting a development at Lyall Bay. Nat couldn't believe they'd sell spots there. Residents will be paddling around in gumboots in another decade or so. But they got Derek to write a submission in their favour–he'd apparently boasted that he could produce data that would minimise the risk. Nat went to see him about it and came home fuming. He told me he was going to write a submission that cast doubts on Derek's scientific credentials. But that required a lot of careful investigation and he didn't have time!'

She buried her face in her hands. Lauren and Pam looked at each other. Enough? said Pam's eyebrows. Lauren nodded and opened her mouth to thank Ellie and say their goodbyes, when they were startled by a doorbell chiming.

Ellie looked up. 'Can you get it, please, Pam?'

Pam was astonished to see Justin Spiller standing awkwardly at the outside door. 'Oh, was Ellie expecting you?'

'No, but my father wanted to check on some stuff. Can I come in?' as Pam continued to block the doorway.

She moved aside. 'Oh sorry, come down.'

As they entered the room Ellie and Lauren looked astonished, too.

'Justin, this is my aunt's friend Lauren Fraser. Lauren, Justin Spiller.' Lauren and Justin nodded to each other. Lauren said, 'We didn't meet at your brother's funeral, but I saw you there. I'm sorry for your loss.' He barely nodded and addressed himself to Ellie.

'Dad asked me to come over and see if there's anything you want help with. And he'd like you to come for lunch on Sunday.'

'Oh.' Ellie seemed to shrink and looked at Pam. 'Pam, you could come too? Is that OK?' The second question was to Justin, who looked surprised.

'I guess so.' Pam was also surprised but managed to say thank you.

There was an awkward pause. Justin seemed to have nothing more to say. Ellie was the same. Then she said, 'Lauren's here because she's going to help us find out how Nat died. She's got a reputation for sleuthing.'

Lauren was annoyed but she kept her eyes on Justin, who looked startled. 'What? Nat drowned, you s–'. He broke off. Lauren wondered if he was going to say stupid or silly. Instead, he looked at Lauren with some interest. She could feel him assessing her. A woman, grey hair, older, what could she do? 'Good luck with that,' he said. 'I'll see you on Sunday, Ellie.' He nodded and left.

'Doesn't sound as if he thinks there's anything suspicious about the death,' said Lauren.

'Oh, they wouldn't want anything messy to emerge.' Ellie sounded bitter. 'It might be bad for business. They're all weird. Nat and I hardly saw anything of them. You know Nat's father wanted him to go into the business. He thought Nat's environmental passion was just a phase. He didn't get it. And Nat said his father couldn't understand when Nat criticised anything in his developments. That Lyall Bay one was the last straw for Nat. But his father still wanted him to join the firm. He hadn't quite given up hope.'

'I suppose his brother was being groomed in his place, was he?'

'Sort of,' Ellie sounded doubtful. 'But I think Nat's father wasn't sure if Justin was up to it. Nat's uncle Mark will probably take over.' She paused. 'Unlike their mother, honestly, talk about spoilt youngest. She thought Justin could do anything. Yes, he's a good builder, and yes, he swims like a fish and is admired in the snorkelling/diving community, but CEO of a construction and development company? I don't think so.'

'He worked with his father, though?' Lauren thought she should find out as much as Ellie could tell her about the family, now that she'd begun talking about them. Lauren would need to know Nat's background if Ellie turned out to be right about his death. But what was she thinking? It seemed that the idea of her running an investigation was solidifying against her will. Even in her own mind!

'Yes. Nat said their father had put Justin in charge of the Lyall Bay project–a bit of a test. Nat thought it was too much of a test, because the development had to go through the Environment Court and success seemed unlikely. Nat was quite protective of Justin.' She started sniffing again. 'They used to snorkel together and Nat was always giving Justin advice–but I don't think they had been recently. Nat was too angry about Justin's commitment to Lyall Bay. He thought Justin had been captured by Derek with his silly reassurances.' She blew her nose vigorously. Tears were still trickling down her face.

'Hey, Ellie,' said her aunt quietly. 'We'll stop pestering you now. Your mum's coming over soon, isn't she?'

Ellie nodded, looked at Lauren. 'You'll find out more, won't you?'

'I'll do my best,' said Lauren, mentally kicking herself. She and Pam stood up and said their goodbyes. Ellie stood up too, and Pam gave her a warm hug before the younger woman opened the door and stood watching them climb the stairs. As they reached the top, Lauren glanced round at Ellie's woebegone face. She said to Pam as they made for the car, 'I hope you realise any involvement is completely against my better judgment. But,' and she thought of Ellie's face again, 'I will look into it...with your help,' she said sternly to Pam. 'We have to either find evidence to put in front of the police so that they take her seriously, or if we can't find anything, make her realise it was an accident.'

'Thank you so much, Lauren.' Pam sounded effusive but Lauren cut her short.

'Let's get on with it then. I'll drop you home and get in touch later, when I've thought all this through.'

LAUREN WAS FIDGETY THAT EVENING. She'd been wrestling with herself, caught between annoyance at being dragged into an investigation, and anger that Nat might have been murdered. They couldn't afford to lose someone like Nat. Could it really have been because of climate politics? Not if it were Harold, that would have been jealousy. If it were Derek, to stop him being exposed as a shonky scientist. She decided that she'd had enough of it all at the moment.

She'd give the matter some serious attention after a good night's sleep.

She was trying to read a book, but her thoughts kept drifting away. It had held her attention until now but suddenly the plot seemed absurd and the characters wooden. She got up, plumped up the cushions on the sofa, went into the kitchen and turned on the jug. She stood there, frowning and tapping her fingers on the bench top. The jug came to the boil and she poured the hot water onto a teabag and continued to stand staring at it. Then she shook herself, said aloud, 'Right, I will,' and marched back to the chair she'd been sitting in. She picked up her phone and stood, found a phone number in her contacts and pressed the call button. As the phone connected, she remembered that she should have used WhatsApp. She shrugged, waited and a smile broke out.

'Hello, I hope you've finished work. It must be about six thirty your time?'

There was a pause, as Deirdre answered. 'Yes, quite right. I'm driving home but I've got the phone on speaker.'

'Just as well I didn't use WhatsApp then,' said Lauren.

She could tell from Deirdre's voice that she too was smiling, as Deirdre said, 'Yes, you'd have had a great view of my thigh.'

Lauren went on, 'Deirdre, I know we agreed not to talk too often but I really need to get your advice about something that's going on here.'

'I'm always pleased to talk to you, Lauren.' Deirdre's tone of voice was soft. Lauren relaxed back into her chair. 'You'll never believe it, Deirdre ...' She hesitated, wondering how to phrase news sure to be unwelcome. '...I seem to find myself caught up in another murder investigation.'

Deirdre coughed, or perhaps it was a snort. 'Lauren, what on earth do you mean. I won't believe what? And what murder?'

Lauren took a deep breath and tried to explain coherently: 'You remember we talked about Nat, Pam's niece's partner, who drowned. The environmental activist.'

'Yes, yes,' replied Deirdre. There was an impatient edge to her voice.

'You suggested that it might not be that straightforward.'

'Did I?'

'Yes, you did. Well, Ellie thinks it wasn't an accident, it was murder. And Pam got me around to talk to her about it. And....'

'Oh Lauren.' If Deirdre hadn't been driving, Lauren thought she would have put her head in her hands. 'Never mind what I said. You can't keep poking your nose into police matters. Remember what happened last time. You were in trouble, your friend Ro was in trouble. You put yourselves at risk *and* you trampled over a police investigation.'

Lauren felt snippy. 'Well, we solved a crime that the police hadn't got anywhere with, didn't we! Even if you did shut it down in terms of historical record.'

Deirdre acknowledged that, but said again that Lauren should leave any enquiries to the police.

'Yes, but they won't take Ellie's suspicions seriously.' Lauren almost shouted.

'They're the ones who have the most information. What could you possibly add?'

'Well, I thought of asking Phyl to run me through the autopsy procedure. I want to get hold of the report. It might not be as clear cut as the police said.'

'Good luck with that,' Deirdre said. 'You won't be able to, you're not a family member and even if you were, the police might be holding onto it since it sounds as if they considered opening up a homicide investigation.' She paused and added, 'Even though they clearly decided not to. There'll probably be an inquest and the report might not be available before then. An inquest will take months.'

'Thanks for helping.' Lauren said bitterly. Surely this whole business wasn't going to run her relationship with Deirdre off the rails. Such as it was.

Deirdre's voice lightened up. 'Look, I'm just giving you the standard police view. I can't stop you poking your nose into it. You're a force to be reckoned with, Lauren, when you've got the bit between your teeth. So keep in touch. Oops, there's a bit of traffic here, I'm going to have to concentrate. Bye.'

Lauren made a face. Oh well, at least Deirdre was trying to keep things on an even keel, even if she did disapprove. Bedtime! she thought and tried again to push it all out of her mind.

10

The next day, Lauren decided on a brisk walk to get the brain working and help to mull things over. She grabbed a jacket and knocked on Phyl's door. 'Would Monty like to come for a short walk with me?'

Phyl laughed. 'Is the Pope Catholic?' Indeed, Monty was already there, tail wagging frantically, big brown eyes looking at Lauren. As she bent down to put on the lead Phyl handed her, Phyl said, 'How would you like to come to lunch when you get back? A friend in the Wairarapa was over yesterday and brought me some field mushrooms they'd picked themselves. I need someone to help me eat them.'

Lauren was already being pulled away. 'Thank you very much, Phyl. I love mushrooms–as long as they're not death caps,' she called over her shoulder as Monty led her down the steps and up the path to her car.

The walk over, and Monty returned to his owner, Lauren looked in briefly at her apartment, tossed her jacket on its hook in the hall, and then headed back to Phyl's. A lunch invitation from Phyl was unusual. She'd enjoy someone else's cooking and it was the perfect opportunity to interrogate Phyl.

She laid out the story to Phyl after they had happily demolished the mushrooms. They were still sitting at the table over cups of coffee. 'So you see, Phyl, I'm not at all sure Nat was murdered, but I'd really like to help out Pam. I wish she hadn't given Ellie the impression I can walk on water, but if I can get the full autopsy report, I might be able to reassure Ellie and make things easier for Pam. Although I suppose it might show–'

Phyl had been listening quietly but now she interrupted. 'Lauren, you won't be able to get the autopsy report. For one thing, you're not family and for another, it might not be available if there's still the chance of a homicide investigation.'

'Damn,' said Lauren, 'just what Deirdre said.'

'Well of course she did,' said Phyl, 'I trained her up well a million years ago. So did you see her when you were in Australia?'

Lauren hoped she wasn't blushing. 'Briefly,' she said. 'She's well and she's enjoying her time there–her secondment has already been extended. I'm not sure when she'll be back.'

Phyl picked up the coffee pot and looked enquiring. Lauren held out her cup. As Phyl poured her a second cup, she said, 'And I suppose if you talked to her about this business, she told you to leave it alone?'

'Might have,' Lauren screwed up her face as she acknowledged it.

'Good advice,' said Phyl. 'I agree with her.'

As Lauren thanked Phyl for lunch and made her way to her own front door, she couldn't help feeling like a child who has been reprimanded. Her stubborn streak asserted itself. What had she expected, cops always stick together–it was a good idea, getting hold of the autopsy report and she was going to find a way! She'd promised Pam that she would investigate and she would.

Auntie Google came up with Coronial Services as the place for online information about autopsies in New Zealand. Lauren clicked onto the website. The information was clear and concise, a model of plain English. Lauren's thoughts drifted back to her career in government publishing. Plain English, that was the mantra back then, and she had been involved in projects seeking to overcome the fusty, arcane and unintelligible writing that seemed to drip off public servants' pens. Concentrate, she told herself, stop reminiscing.

'What happens during a post-mortem' was the page she looked at first. Lauren knew nothing about post-mortems. She had never been next of kin, or even very close–touch wood–to anyone who had died unexpectedly. What she knew she had picked up from grisly scenes on TV cop shows. Green and white tiled mortuaries. The pathologist picking up a buzz saw. First-time cops going pale and fainting or vomiting. The most horrific injuries described in a deadpan voice.

The coronial webpages were nothing like that. They explained the procedures in an almost friendly manner. Nat's body, recovered from the water, would have been taken to the morgue at Wellington's regional hospital. The coroner would have been notified. Ellie must have given permission for a post-mortem when she went to identify the body, but she had probably been too shocked to take much in.

A 'full post-mortem', or autopsy, the website helpfully explained, involves taking samples of bodily fluids and genetic material and in addition, cutting the body, 'similar to a surgery'. Lauren shuddered.

The police told Ellie they thought Nat had incurred his head injury through being dashed against the rocks. But how did they know someone hadn't pushed him against a rock, or even hit him with a rock? And would the pathology report, as they called it, throw any light on this?

The website confirmed what both Deirdre and Phyl had told her. It seemed as if Ellie would not have much chance of having a copy sent to her. But since she had been in shock when the police told her what the pathologist had concluded, perhaps the police would agree to go over it again with someone she trusted. It seemed unfair that Ellie could not access the evidence that the police used to decide whether or not a death was due to accident or homicide. Where was the justice in that?

~

Lauren felt lucky. She found a parking spot just opposite the central police station. She was halfway through the swing door when she realised she hadn't put coins in the meter. Probably the worst place in town to forget. Not that parking wardens had anything to do with the police, they were filling the council's coffers.

The second time through the door, she went up to the counter and asked for Constable Braeburn, the name on the card Pam had got from Ellie. She was asked to wait and was relieved when a young man in uniform poked his head into the reception area only a few minutes later. 'Come this way,' he said and led her to what she supposed was an interview room. Bare, scruffy grey carpet, a table with spindly chrome legs and a scratched laminated surface.

Braeburn slapped the file box he was carrying on the table and invited her to take a chair, as he sat down opposite. 'Ms Petersen said you'd like to talk to the police on her behalf.'

Lauren nodded and was about to speak when Braeburn asked her to produce identification. 'Just to be sure you are who you say you are,' he said, almost apologetically.

Lauren scrabbled in her handbag for her driver's licence, which he examined carefully, looking up at her to check her similarity with the photo. Satisfied, he nodded to her to begin.

'I'm investigating Nat Spiller's death on behalf of Ellie Peterson, his partner.'

'Oh, you're a private investigator. Do you have a licence?' the young man asked.

Lauren felt wrong-footed. Warmth rose to her cheeks and she hoped she wasn't blushing. 'No, I'm not a private investigator. I don't believe a licence is required to ask questions on behalf of a friend. I'm not being paid for my time,' she said snippily.

Braeburn shuffled a little. His air of authority seemed to keep slipping. Lauren wondered how long he'd been in the force. She decided to steer the conversation directly to the matter at hand. 'Ellie was told by the police that the pathologist's report confirmed the police view that Nat's death was an accident. As you may know, she is finding that hard to believe. I understand that the police didn't actually show her the report or offer her a copy. Her aunt suggested that I follow up, because she wasn't sure it would be helpful for Ellie to see the report, given that it might contain upsetting detail.'

'Quite right, too,' said Braeburn. 'We don't make a habit of showing the reports to relatives, not that they are ours to show. Technically, that's for the DHB–they're part of the deceased's medical records which are confidential to the person they're about.'

Lauren decided it wouldn't be at all helpful to ask how the police got them then. As if anticipating, the officer went on to say, 'The coroner has authority over the records since such reports are commissioned by the coroner in the case of deaths occurring in unusual circumstances. If there's any chance that a death may have resulted from a criminal act, the coroner then shows the report to the police.'

He sounded as if he'd swallowed a textbook. Lauren bet he was only a year or two out of police college. 'So you have the report with you?' she asked, nodding at the file box. 'Can I see it?'

Braeburn looked flustered. 'I don't have the authority to show it to you.'

Lauren drew herself up, exasperated. He caught the look she gave him and went on hastily. 'But I've been told that I can describe its contents.'

He reached for the file box, slid it awkwardly across the table and delved into its contents, rustling the papers. 'Here it is.' He pulled out a couple of sheets of paper, arranging them in front of him.

Lauren craned her head forward and Braeburn looked at her severely enough to make her sit back again. She tried to read the document upside down but soon realised it was better to concentrate on what he was saying. He'd begun to read, when Lauren interrupted him. 'OK if I take notes?'

Braeburn shrugged. 'Shouldn't be a problem. Now, I'm not going to read the whole thing, I'll summarise it.' His tongue poked out the corner of his mouth as he visibly concentrated.

'A 35-year-old man brought to the mortuary after being taken from the sea on the south coast.... I conducted a full examination after obtaining consent from the next of kin...healthy male, etc...skin pale and mottled from immersion in seawater, probably for some hours...visible head wound on the back of the skull, with severe bruising and lacerations sufficient to cause significant bleeding....Internal examination....

He paused and looked up at her. 'Now, are you sure you want to hear this?' He had an uncomfortable expression on his face.

'Carry on, I've a strong stomach.' Lauren wasn't sure that was true, but she wasn't going to be bested by a young policeman.

'Stomach contents,' Braeburn continued. 'Signs of a meal several hours before....Blood tests, no signs of alcohol, illegal drugs or medications. Heart healthy, no signs of disease. Lungs filled with seawater indicating drowning as the cause of death.

'A cut was made to expose the brain....' Now Lauren did begin to feel squeamish. 'A subdural haematoma was present, evidenced by pooling of blood between the dura mater and the...' He stumbled over the unfamiliar words, as Lauren tried to focus on the meaning of the Latin terms, to combat her rising gorge. 'Arachnoid mater sufficient to cause dizziness, lack of muscle control, possibly loss of consciousness within several minutes of traumatic force being applied.'

Braeburn ran his finger down to the bottom of the last page. 'Conclusions...death by drowning, precipitated by a concussion arising from blunt force trauma.' He looked up from his notes.

Lauren pulled herself together. 'Blunt force trauma? Doesn't that mean being hit on the head?'

'The police investigated very thoroughly and concluded that the trauma was most likely sustained from the deceased losing his footing and being thrown against the rocks by a wave.'

'But you can't prove that?'

'We interviewed witnesses...'

'But there were no witnesses, surely?' Lauren interrupted.

Braeburn continued stolidly, '...and experts as well as family members, and there was no evidence of suspicious behaviour. The police decided not to open a homicide investigation.' He slapped the papers back into the file box, stood up and said, 'There you are, then. Thank you for coming in.'

It was maddening, Lauren thought as she walked back to her car. She'd been pinning her hopes on the autopsy report clarifying the cause of Nat's death. Instead, it left open the possibility that he had been attacked. She tapped on Phyl's door when she got home and told her about the frustrating interview. It took some time, as Monty kept distracting them. He whined and jumped up, obviously expecting a walk. Lauren concluded, 'Surely they can't dismiss what Ellie says just because they can't find evidence of an attack. Isn't it their job to consider all the possibilities?'

Phyl leaned against the doorjamb, looking irritated. 'Lauren, they did some investigating and they will have weighed the balance of probabilities. You can't open a homicide inquiry any time someone dies accidentally. Most accidental deaths are just that, accidents. You can't have a murder investigation whenever someone falls off a ladder and hits their head.' She looked as if she was going to say something more, but a buzzer went off in the kitchen. 'Sorry, I have to go, something's in the oven.' She hauled Monty inside, protesting, and shut the door.

Being thwarted made Lauren more determined. Cops all seemed to take the same line, whether it was Deirdre or Phyl or the Wellington police. Washed their hands of it, all too much trouble to think outside the square. She decided not to contact Pam or Ellie right away, she wanted more time to think and something positive to show for her efforts.

If she were going to look into it any further, talking to the yachtie, who had actually seen Nat drowning, was the next obvious line of inquiry. She wasted no time, opening up her laptop as soon as she got inside. How to locate the man? She had heard the news on the radio but hadn't done her usual trawl through the online news sites while she was in Melbourne. She looked back on *Stuff* and found the item easily. It had been big news. The wrecked boat, the sailor coming ashore and the search for the drowned man. There was a photo.

Lauren shuddered. *Lucinda* lying on the rocks at Owhiro Bay, just as she recalled it.

There were a score of stories about Nat after his death was made public, but Lauren ignored these. Ah, here it was, a story about the yachtie. He was identified as Steve Painter, and the journalist had caught up with him soon after his discharge from hospital. Another photo, an ordinary-looking older guy with an unfriendly expression, standing in an open door. The article said he lived at Evans Bay and it sounded as if he lived on his own, though that wasn't clear.

The journalist didn't seem to have got much out of him. It sounded as if the guy...now what was that expression? Door-stepped. Perhaps the journalist and photographer had turned up without warning and were sent on their way. The journalist had also spoken to the President of the Boating Club, who said that Steve was an honoured longtime member and that the Club would do all they could to help him. Poor old guy, Lauren thought, he's lost his boat. Perhaps that meant losing his world.

If Steve Painter still had a landline he might be in the White Pages. She reached for the phone book she kept on the small table where her landline lived. Bingo! That was easy, not many Painters in Wellington and only one in Evans Bay. S.E. Painter. A street number in the 400s on Evans Bay Parade. She went to Google Maps and checked it out. Yes, as she thought, one of the row of older houses opposite the marina.

When she phoned, the guy said he could see her the next Wednesday morning. He sounded bemused and none too friendly. Not surprising, as her explanation for wanting to see him probably sounded odd. However, he agreed.

11

Ro Wisbech parked her battered old Toyota Echo at an awkward angle in Maida Vale Rd. It had been hard to get herself going this morning but she hadn't seen Lauren for ages, not since her Melbourne trip. And then Lauren had stood her up for a coffee date, claiming something more important and clamming up when Ro asked her what it was.

If she was honest with herself, Ro was still cross with Lauren. Their adventure last year had been incredible but it had killed Ro's scoop. All that historical evidence they'd uncovered now sealed up in archives just because the police thought they might get a prosecution going. Ro jumped out of the car and slammed the door. She began striding down the path, her thoughts in a whirl, then pulled herself to a halt. 'Stop it,' she told herself. 'Lauren is my best friend outside of the academic world. She's really sharp and she's the person I turn to if I'm in a pickle. And I'm in one right now. So get over yourself!' She screwed up her face and took a couple of deep breaths. By the time she reached Lauren's door she had a smile at the ready.

'Hi, Lauren, you okay with Red Rocks?' Being Wellington, a strong gusty wind was blowing that morning. It was a northerly, so

Ro had decided on the south coast and that they might as well go right round to Red Rocks and look at the seals.

'As long as you haul some of this stuff,' Lauren replied. She'd packed a large picnic lunch for them both. 'I'm not up to carrying a 20kg pack any longer. It's one-day tramps and day packs.'

'No problem,' Ro replied. She shuffled around in the boot to pack Lauren's heavier items in her own backpack, then squashed her tall, rangy figure into the driver's seat, flicking her unruly red hair away from her face. They drove across the city and then along to the end of Happy Valley Road, turning as they reached Owhiro Bay.

'That's where the broken yacht was,' Lauren said as they passed the rocky outcrop where the boat had foundered. 'I saw it the morning after the wreck when I was taking Monty for a walk.' There was no sign of the wreck now.

'What wreck was that?' said Ro.

'You know, the yacht that hit the rocks when the skipper was trying to save Nat Spiller from drowning. You must have heard. It was all over the news. The papers, radio, TV....'

'Nat Spiller! He's dead? That's shocking.' She bit her lip, almost embarrassed. 'I haven't been keeping up with the news,' she explained.

'That's not like you,' Lauren responded.

Ro decided to be honest with her friend. 'I guess I've been feeling down. When I get like that I read late into the night–trash, mainly–and lie in in the morning. If it wasn't for the cats jumping up and whining for their breakfast I'd probably stay in bed till noon.'

She gripped the steering wheel harder. By this time they were driving along the beachfront road, past the odd mix of decrepit and swept up houses that hugged the shore. 'Don't you need to get to the office?' Lauren asked.

'Lectures have finished for the year. I've got marking to do, so I spend the afternoons on that. I only go in if there's a meeting I can't avoid, or a supervision session. But I've only got one PhD student at the moment and she's self-sufficient. Haven't seen her for a month.'

'Nice work if you can get it.' The joke was automatic, but Ro could hardly believe that Lauren had said it. She glanced at Lauren, who was biting her lip. 'Sorry, Ro. I just hadn't realized you were in such a state. I guess it's hard to motivate yourself when you're down. Would it be better for you if you did have to turn up every day?'

'Maybe so. Maybe it would just make it worse.' Ro felt a prick of guilt at her earlier crossness with Lauren. It was a huge relief at having spoken out. She wouldn't have felt able to confide in her colleagues, she reflected. Academic friends were her mainstay in terms of socialising, but in the end they were competitors, too. It didn't pay to show weakness.

Lauren placed her hand on Ro's arm. 'A good long walk, that'll help you get sorted.'

The little car bumped into the car park at the end of the road. They shouldered their packs and began trudging along the gravelly track, sometimes together and sometimes single file. The track ran beneath steep hillsides, rocky with the odd bush clinging on, and eaten away by the workings of an old quarry. The sea was grey and choppy, separated from the track by a shingly, pebbly beach.

How many millennia before the pebbles turn to sand? Ro wondered. The stark environment matched her mood, but in an odd way, was also a corrective. She turned and said to Lauren, gesturing at the landscape. 'Humans and their troubles are not so significant, are they?'

Raising her arms out wide to the sea, Lauren declaimed. 'How slow untroubled by any grouch of mine or yours, Father Ocean tumbles in the bay.' Ro gave her a quizzical look. 'James K. Baxter,' Lauren responded. 'He wrote it about the Wellington coast.'

'That's apt.' Ro gazed at the ocean, then aimed a kick at a mound of pebbles, sending them flying. 'Sexist prick that he was.'

Lauren raised her eyebrows. 'You're right. But a great poet. Anyhow, let's not debate that now.' As they walked on she brought Ro back with a direct question. 'Why do you think you're feeling low?'

'I know *why*,' retorted Ro, 'but I can't do anything about it. It's postpartum depression only I didn't have a baby, I had a book.'

Lauren laughed. 'Go on.'

'Lots of kudos when it was launched, you'll remember, and my friends read it, but it's all died down now. I guess women in the fourth Labour Government was always going to have a niche audience.' She stopped walking and looked fiercely at Lauren. 'It would have been different if I'd been able to talk about poison plots against the Prime Minister.'

Lauren said, 'Oh, come on Ro.' This was a well-rehearsed argument between them. She sounded impatient. 'You need a new project. Stop harking back to what might have been.'

Ro bit her lip, trying not to flare up. 'Are you telling me to buck up?'

Lauren looked suitably chastised. 'I'm sorry. That was tactless.'

'Hmph.' Ro acknowledged the apology but her wide generous mouth, given to smiling, was now a thin line. She walked on in silence.

Lauren said in an appeasing tone, 'I've been meaning to tell you about this really neat woman I met in Melbourne. Miriam Smith. Her partner died a couple of years ago. She was a historian, Jane someone. Wrote a book about women in crime.'

Ro made the connection. 'That'll be Jane Standish. Really good value. Shocking that she died so young. I met her at a couple of conferences.' She paused, trying to remember a Miriam Smith, but drew a blank. 'Is Miriam an historian too?'

'No, she's a climate scientist,' Lauren replied, looking relieved that their conversation was on track again. 'Past retirement age, but she still goes down to the ice every season. She invited me out to dinner one evening with her friends and they included a couple of Kiwis who are going down this summer. There's a lot of women involved in the programme these days. It's great.' They stood still for a moment, catching their breath. They'd picked up speed along the gravel track, which was rising towards the rocks. Out to sea a flock of seagulls wheeled and soared, dived and rose. Lauren continued, 'Somebody said the birdlife in the Antarctic was amazing, mainly penguins but some hardy sea birds as well. It would be lovely to see it, but after Erebus no more scenic flights from here.'

Lauren shrugged her shoulders underneath her pack and made to move on again. Ro was struck by a sudden thought. She stood perfectly still, needing time to let it consolidate, so she waved Lauren on. After a minute or so she ran to catch up.

'That's it! Lauren, you're a wonder.' Lauren looked startled at the sudden change in Ro's tone of voice. 'The Antarctic. I've read something recently about the way it's usually portrayed: all men, all heroes, man against the elements. It's nonsense these days, and earlier, too. Women have been involved in Antarctic discovery for decades now.'

'And?'

Ro gathered her thoughts. Her mind was racing. 'I could do that! Write a history of women in the Antarctic. Come right up to the present. I could use documents, oral histories, other sources.' Ro began walking fast, then stopped suddenly, turning back to Lauren who was now struggling to keep up. 'This is the time of year they advertise those places for artists and writers in the Antarctic summer programme. Or it might have been earlier.' She frowned.

'Sounds like a great idea,' Lauren puffed. 'What's more, you're sounding more like yourself every minute.'

Ro grinned, jumped up and down, waving her arms, her red hair flying behind her.

'That's exactly what I mean,' Lauren laughed. 'And I'm just remembering, the group in Melbourne were talking about those fellowships. They sound wonderful. Miriam is coming through Wellington, did I say? I'll make sure you meet her. She won't be at Scott Base, but apparently there's a lot of mixing with the American base. That's where she'll be. I don't understand exactly why, but it's to do with the project she's working on.'

The track seemed to have got slightly easier, with more vegetation on the slopes to their right and the gravel packed down. Now rather than trudging they were walking. At least Lauren was. Ro felt really excited, she was virtually skipping. They talked on but Ro felt distracted, mulling over what she could say in an application. Would it be seen as a serious project or a bid for a free trip?

Now they reached a great hump in the track. It suddenly rose up, not for a long distance but high enough that the view to the other side was blocked. 'Ah, we're nearly here,' said Lauren. They made the short climb and looked down. The same rocky foreshore.

But were they all rocks? The rank smell and the occasional movement said otherwise. A large group of seals, beautifully camouflaged, lay about, swam, came back to the beach. Ro wrinkled her nose. 'Let's not eat our lunch too close,' she said. 'Do you think a group of seals should be called a stink of seals?'

'It's all the adolescent males,' Lauren said. 'They're driven out while the mothers are busy with the babies. The family group might have a different name. Is it a pod of seals? Though I think they all smell.' She in turn wrinkled her nose. The pleasure of watching the seals outweighed the smell assailing them. The two women gazed at them for some time, enchanted at the way they were getting on with their lives unperturbed by the humans.

Then Lauren unpacked a picnic rug from her backpack, and they spread it out at some distance from the seals. They had eaten the food–a veritable feast, Ro thought admiringly, licking egg and bacon pie crumbs off her lips–and were sipping coffee from Lauren's thermos when they were startled by the roar of an engine. The unexpected noise, alarmingly close, made them both jump. 'What on earth?' said Ro. But as she spoke they saw the source, a huge black four-wheel drive came hurtling over the hump they'd walked across, swooshed past them fast, spraying gravel and carried on.

'What a monster,' said Lauren. 'And what stupid driving. Going so fast when they couldn't see the other side.'

'Pity it's not a Sunday,' said Ro, 'wish they'd ban cars every day of the week. We'd have the track to ourselves then.'

Disturbed now, they swallowed their coffee, packed away the lunch things and said goodbye to the seals. As they walked back Ro felt much more cheerful. Now that the new idea was packed safely away in a corner of her mind, she could pay attention to Lauren.

'So have you been flat out with work since you got home from Melbourne? I'm surprised I haven't seen you.'

'Not overwhelmed,' said Lauren, 'Just a comfortable amount. I was completely up to date before I left. It's not work that's been keeping me busy, it's Pam and her niece Ellie, you know, Nat Spiller's partner.'

'How so?'

'I haven't talked about this to anyone.' Lauren sounded diffident.

'Come on, Lauren, I've unloaded on you–why don't you do the same?'

Lauren laughed. 'I guess it would be good to tell someone I can trust not to blab.' As they walked she explained what had been going on and how Ellie thought Nat had been murdered. 'She seems to think that because I helped you with that cold case last year, I should be able to find out who killed Nat,' she said. 'I do think Pam put her up to it. But how would I know whether she's right? He might just have drowned, that's what the police reckon. So I'm reserving judgment until I've talked to the guy who tried to rescue him. I'm seeing him on Wednesday.'

Ro had listened attentively, saying almost nothing. Now she spoke. 'Poor Ellie, if she's right and no one's believing her. Lauren, you know I'd be happy to help if there's anything I can do.'

Lauren looked surprised and pleased. Ro was feeling buoyant and expansive. By now they had reached the car and stowed their backpacks in the boot. Ro folded her lanky frame up into the driver's seat, while Lauren got into the passenger side, saying 'Thanks, Ro, I'll remember that.'

12

Some of Ellie's and Pam's stress had rubbed off on Lauren. Ellie's suspicions hadn't been allayed when Lauren phoned to tell her about the meeting with Braeburn–any more than Lauren's had. Lauren told her she would be talking with the yachtie soon and would report back on any developments. She felt oppressed by the weight of Ellie's grief.

But by Monday morning, two or three social events had taken her out of herself–she'd enjoyed a concert and been picked up by the walk with Ro. She was ready for anything again. When she checked her work and appointments for the week ahead, she saw that the proposed visit to the city council's virtual reality experience was the next morning. Something to look forward to, was her first thought, but then she frowned slightly. Would Pam be up to it? She'd borne the brunt of Ellie's distress for two weeks now and was still spending a lot of time with her. However, it would do Pam good to do something completely different. And Lauren was keen to hear how the lunch with the Spiller clan had gone and what Pam had made of them all. Perhaps after they'd finished at the Council, she'd see if Pam could stay and have lunch with her in a café and get the story.

So on Tuesday morning she texted her friend, 'Don't forget, it's virtual reality with Dwight at the city council, 11am today. See you in the foyer.'

A beautiful November morning, so Lauren walked to the city alongside the gently lapping waves of Oriental Bay. A couple of hardy souls were trying out the water, but it was scarcely warm enough yet for swimming. Wellingtonians usually waited for January, midsummer. Lauren's thoughts drifted to the forthcoming visit. What will rising seas do to this beautiful beach, Wellington's most popular stroll? She pulled her jacket tightly to her chest as the wind picked up a few notches and the waves began to dance.

Pam looked pale, despite her sun-hardened complexion. She was pacing round the foyer as Lauren walked in. They hugged briefly and then asked at the reception desk for Dwight Albermarle. 'Take the elevator to the eighth floor.'

Dwight was there to greet them. The building seemed oddly quiet, given that the floor was shared with the mayor's office. 'They've all gone,' Dwight said. 'I'm the last one here and I'm packing up my stuff. We're off to the Terrace.' The Council buildings were being earthquake strengthened. The 2016 big shake that destroyed the Kaikoura coast had rattled Wellington–and Lauren too–in a terrifying manner. A number of public buildings were declared unsafe and some even demolished. It gave the central city an eerie feel.

Dwight did not look like the average bureaucrat, tall and craggy, with a shock of curly hair. He'd commandeered a big meeting room as a playroom for him and his equipment.

They stood awkwardly as he juggled with wires, a couple of laptops and waved around a headset and what looked like X-box controls. 'Who wants to go first?'

Pam and Lauren looked at each other. 'You go,' Pam said rather nervously. Lauren stepped forward and tried not to flinch as Dwight awkwardly placed the headset, juggling it to get the goggles into position. All fitted, she was in complete darkness, immediately disoriented. She wiggled her toes to help retain her sense of standing upright. Dwight placed a control in each of her hands. 'Ready?' he asked.

Lauren nodded, an awkward movement with the weight of the headset. 'Sure.' She tried to sound confident.

A new world burst in on her, she froze and let out an involuntary scream. She was standing on the rooftop of Te Papa, the National Museum, looking down at small figures, many storeys below. She felt her arm being gripped and Pam's voice reassuring, said, 'I'll hold you, you started to sway. 'I'm on top of Te Papa,' said Lauren. 'If I take a step forward, I'll fall off.'

Dwight laughed. 'It takes people different ways. Look towards the horizon, that'll help your balance.'

Lauren raised her eyes and Wellington's harbour was before her. The sensation was definitely three dimensional although it looked a little cartoonish.

'Now use the hand controls. Press that button on your right.'

The hand controls allowed Lauren to adjust the level of sea rise. She could see lines and numerals set against the view. It appeared to be set to one metre, and as she pushed the button it ramped up to six. She turned towards the city and, following Dwight's instructions, leapt forwards off the building. She let out another involuntary squeal and Pam tightened her grip.

'I've landed on top of another building and I can see up Lambton Quay. It's sloshing with water. Oh, over there, the waterfront buildings–the wharf's disappeared. So has the park. I can just see the tip of the Len Lye sculpture waving. Gosh!' All thoughts of how this might affect people were far from her mind. It was like being in a thrilling disaster movie. She plucked up her courage again and began to leap from one building to the next, striding over the city like a giant. But whenever she looked down, vertigo threatened to overcome her. After another few minutes, she decided she'd had enough. 'Here you are, Pam' she said, wrenching off the head set.

Pam stepped back, laughing. 'I'm not sure now.'

'Go on,' said Lauren. 'Like Dwight said, just keep your eyes on the horizon.'

Pam squawked that she was in the middle of the harbour. Then she played around with the controls for a few moments and announced, 'Right, I'm off to the south coast.'

Lauren watched a screen that showed, in 2D of course, what Pam could see. With a bit of practice Pam soon got the hang of the controls and was striding over the Brooklyn hills and across to Cook Strait. Not normally an expressive person, Pam jiggled on the spot and let out cries of delight. 'I'm heading towards the airport now, along the coast road. We won't be driving around there in future, that's for sure. Oh look! The airport's not under water.'

Dwight interjected, 'No, it's built well up–the only thing is you'll have to take a boat to get there.'

'Now for Oriental Bay. Well the beach is gone but the road's still there–that's not so bad.'

Dwight countered, 'With the sea level up a meter or two it will pour into the stormwater drains and the old networks just won't cope. Just because things look all right on the surface doesn't mean they will be.'

Pam took off her headset. 'Wow, that was amazing. Just about as good as a helicopter ride.'

Lauren, now that she was feeling less green, agreed. Dwight, who was an enthusiastic guide, continued the patter he must have given dozens of times. Then, conscious of taking up his time, they thanked him and left.

On the way down in the lift, Pam placed her hand on Lauren's arm and said in a voice full of emotion, 'It's just starting to sink in. I'm glad I don't have children.'

Lauren thought of Adam and Tamsin, her bright-eyed grandchildren in England; Brighton where they lived was on the coast too. How could she not be glad for their presence in her life, but yet....

As they walked briskly along Oriental Parade, Lauren was trying not to imagine the future of the road hiding blocked sewers and broken infrastructure under its surface. The virtual reality experience had seemed fun–just as she'd joked with the scientists in Melbourne about turning their work into video games. But now the implications were hitting her. She said, 'How can our little policy group do anything in the face of such a looming catastrophe?'

Pam was silent for a moment, searching for words. 'How can we not? We must try to understand the science and then push the powers that be to use it to make good policy–whether it's for mitigation or adaptation.'

Lauren sighed. 'We had high hopes for the new government–but the coalition has put the brakes on farsighted action for the whole country. I guess we have to cultivate our own garden.'

Pam looked mystified.

'Voltaire,' said Lauren. 'I'm not talking about the community garden, it's metaphorical. In other words, everyone has to look after their own patch.'

'Oh,' said Pam. Now they had reached the café and were absorbed in ordering paninis and flat whites.

Lunch restored their equilibrium and Lauren asked about Ellie.

'The Spillers are a weird family–that Sunday lunch Ellie inveigled me into going to was awful. They ignored her when Nat was alive but now they're all over her. Nat's mother wanted her to come and stay with them "for as long as you like, Ellie". So they could weep together, presumably. It was creepy. Now Ellie just wants to get back to work.'

Lauren said, 'That's a good idea, it'll stop her from brooding all day.'

Pam sipped her coffee absentmindedly and continued. 'Nat's father, Lloyd, was creepy too, but in a different way. He was obviously very upset but he was still trying to act the paterfamilias. He asked Ellie about her financial commitments, almost as if he were interviewing a potential employee. He said he wanted to make sure that Nat hadn't left her with any debts and that she could manage on just her own income. Ellie told me later that he made her feel like some Victorian widow who, if she wasn't careful, might be pulled into the family home and made to spend the rest of her days spinning wool in a corner.'

Lauren tried to picture Ellie as meek and mild in a crinoline but the image just wouldn't come. She laughed wryly. 'Go on.'

'Ellie made it very clear to Lloyd that she was financially independent. She and Nat had separate bank accounts and she was already starting up work again and there was plenty of work around. Spiller looked really miffed.

'Then the real drama started up. I was just a fly on the wall. I think they'd forgotten I was there, so I sat quietly through it.'

Lauren was by now completely engaged. She pushed her coffee cup out of the way and leant forward, hands clasped on the table. 'So–the real drama?'

'Mrs Spiller cut right across Lloyd and said to Ellie, "You've been looking quite pale. You're not in the family way, are you dear?" At that Ellie burst into tears. Lloyd leaned towards her, looking her up and down for all the world like a man inspecting a horse for sale. When Ellie regained some control, she blurted out that she wanted a child but Nat refused. He didn't want to bring a child into a world being wrecked by climate change. Lloyd Spiller pushed his chair back, stood up, and walked out of the room.'

'But why? Wasn't that a bit of an overreaction?'

'Ellie told me later she knew what it was all about. Apparently when Nat and she had discussed having a child, he had told her that his father was putting pressure on him. The father had a studbook mentality about the family. He thought Nat was best placed to pass on the Lloyd Spiller name and the Lloyd Spiller qualities. Nat was disgusted.'

'Huh,' said Lauren. She felt indignant on Ellie's behalf, annoyed at both Nat and his father for pulling their father-son dynamics into the issue of having a child. Maybe his decision was to spite his father as much as it was about climate change. But she put the thought aside as Pam continued.

'Catherine, the daughter, has a couple of children but she took her husband's name, so her offspring don't do it for the Spiller dynasty. Justin, of course, is the youngest and he might well become a father, but Lloyd sees him as a weak link in the chain, a poor copy of his brother.' She paused and thought for a moment. 'Actually, Justin pricked up his ears at that part of the conversation. I noticed, because he'd just been slouching around and not contributing to anything. Then he looked quite uneasy when his father stalked off.'

Lauren waved away a waiter who came to ask if they wanted more coffee. 'Was that all?'

'No,' said Pam. A tremor of excitement or nerves, crossed her face. 'Nat's mother went off to the kitchen and we could hear cross words being exchanged. Then she called Catherine in to help with bringing out the meal. We all sat down at the table. I made sure to hide in the furthest corner, next to Justin, unfortunately. I really don't like that young man, I just can't fathom him. He's nearly thirty but he seems like a teenager.

'Anyhow, the meal passed awkwardly. I thought Ellie was composed, but she started looking upset again when we were having our dessert. Lloyd's attitude must have been rankling, but she suddenly burst out with it.'

'With what?' Lauren thought Pam was starting to wander. Up to this point she'd been a great raconteur. 'I thought we'd already had the family drama. Bloody strange dynamics. Less Victorian novel and more 'The Sopranos'...without the gang connections, I daresay.'

Pam looked completely mystified and Lauren remembered she didn't have television. 'Never mind, so what happened at dessert?'

'Well, Mrs Spiller–Lorraine's her name, but I just can't bring myself to call her that–Mrs Spiller said something to Justin about how this all never would have happened if the boys hadn't been so keen on snorkelling and diving, and they didn't get that from her side of the family–rugby was their sport, apparently her father trialled for the All Blacks'– Lauren hmphed–'and she hoped Justin would now see sense. She was just wittering on, really, but Ellie lost it at that point and yelled, "Nat was brilliant in the water. You all don't seem to realise that he would never have taken risks. He wouldn't have drowned. Hasn't it occurred to you that the police have got it all wrong. He was murdered!"'

'At that Lloyd banged his fist on the table. "Nonsense!" he said firmly. "We won't have any of that sort of talk. It doesn't help anyone. And Lorraine, stop nagging Justin." Ellie took no notice of him. She looked directly at him and told him–'

Pam broke off with an apologetic smile. 'You won't want to hear this, Lauren, but I'm afraid she told him that she had someone looking into whether it was murder. Lloyd was livid and demanded to know who. She was reluctant, but he kept pressing her and she caved in and gave him your name. He said that he'd get your details and then he'd be speaking to you about it.'

Lauren's heart sank. She sighed. Everything was happening too fast and she felt in over her head. 'I'm not Miss Marple, you know. I'm only trying to help you support Ellie through all this. I'm still hoping I don't find anything to suggest Nat was murdered.' She thought again. 'But I'm surprised Justin hadn't told him about the investigation. Remember how cross he looked when Ellie told him you were looking into it.'

'He probably judged correctly that his father would have been furious. Family name and all that. I don't think he'd say boo to his father. When all this was going on he just kept quiet and stared at his plate.'

'Oh, well, I expect I'll be receiving a summons. Damn it, we'd better have some of that cherry tart to strengthen us.' She called the passing waiter.

13

They were walking back along Oriental Bay, when they ran into Michael Peston exercising his dog. Mandela, a chocolate brown Labrador, was nine months old and well grown. He looked at Lauren with his soulful eyes, and greeted her with a small woof of recognition before Michael noticed her. 'I didn't think you'd be cruising Oriental Bay these days,' said Lauren mischievously. 'I thought Evan's Bay would be your beat.'

Michael missed the quip, looked startled for a moment. 'It's a southerly, much more pleasant over here than down from our house, and the city council has finally allowed dogs on buses. Mandela and I hopped on a number fourteen at Kilbirnie and here we are. Mandela's first bus ride. He behaved himself too, apart from sniffing the driver's leg.'

Gay men, thought Lauren, they treat their dogs just like children. First bus ride, another developmental step. She tried to wink at Pam, but as usual it looked more like a facial tic. She smiled sweetly to cover the failure. 'We've just been to see the council's virtual reality show on rising sea levels–the one that was advertised at the Climate Protection inaugural meeting. Come and perch on one of these benches and look at the sea, while we tell you all about it.' Lauren thought they needed a break after the heavy talk about the Spiller family Sunday lunch.

The three of them sat on one of the benches looking out to the harbour, with Mandela sitting patiently by them. Pam and Lauren's descriptions tumbled over each other as they described their experiences to Michael. Pam flew over to the south coast, and the airport was still above water, but you couldn't get to it, the road was gone–Lauren was on the floor and wobbling about, never seen her look so scared–Pam grabbed my arm so I wouldn't fall off the building–Lauren, there *was* no building–well, I was on the roof of Te Papa–and you were standing above the monastery at Oriental Bay.

They finally stopped reliving it and Lauren said to Michael, 'You and Mandela will be wading along this part of Oriental Bay in a few decades.'

'Lucky us, to have that long. Yes, it does sound alarming. Wonder what the property owners think about such a vivid portrayal of the inevitable? They like to stick their heads in the sand–all too literally!'

'It was really scary; you make adjustments to get different amounts of sea level rise and it shows the city at high tide mark. One metre rise, bits of Oriental Parade, Evans Bay Parade, the main drag north through the city all under water. Two meters, and Lambton Quay is gone. Will I be willing to paddle to David Jones to buy that thousand dollar pair of red sneakers that I fancy?'

'Perhaps they'll need to change its name to Davy Jones's Locker.' Then he looked serious. 'Are you two coming to the Climate Protection meeting tonight? It'll be important–now we've had the inaugural meeting, you know Harold wants to have the first AGM and elect office holders. Poor Harold! Some of us have decided it will be the opportunity to replace him as chair. He's really not the right person to be fronting an effective organisation. In fact,' –he looked abashed– 'I've been asked to stand.'

'I'm planning to come,' Lauren replied. 'And it would be good to have a more with-it chair. Do you want to, though, Michael? Haven't you done with politics?' She knew Michael had had a difficult time as a gay MP years ago, before he became involved in development projects in Africa.

'This is different, it's not party political, it's lobbying. Your virtual reality experience might have seemed a bit of fun, but it won't be much fun if it all happens.' He paused and looked thoughtful. 'And it'll be disastrous for the developing countries where I've been working. There's probably time to stop the worst effects.'

Lauren turned to Pam. 'Will you be able to come, Pam?' Pam had been spending most evenings over at Ellie's. Her niece seemed reluctant to be by herself in the apartment.

'Yes, I am. Her brother Tim said he'd keep Ellie company this evening.'

Michael said, 'I was really sorry to hear about Nat Spiller. I didn't know him personally but everyone knew him by repute! Your niece must be desolate.'

'Not only desolate, but angry. She still thinks someone killed him.'

'He was so admired,' said Michael. His voice rose, with astonishment. 'Who would want to kill him?'

Lauren felt like saying, 'Well, the prissy Harold Stevens for one,' but she found the idea so incredible she didn't want to put it into Michael's head before the meeting. Instead she said, 'His family to start with, from what Ellie's said. He was so against the developments they were pushing.'

'Come off it,' said Michael, 'Families can have disagreements but blood's still thicker than water.'

'I'm not so sure. Anyway, I said I'd do what Pam kindly calls a bit of snooping–I'm going to see the yachtie who tried to rescue him.'

Michael stretched as he got up and untied the dog's leash from the bench. 'Good luck with it all–just be careful. I've seen you get into trouble before.'

Lauren winced, and opened her mouth to defend herself. But Michael was already on his way. 'I'll see you both at the Climate Protection meeting.'

Lauren was tired after the excitement of the virtual reality experience and a heavy afternoon's work. She might have cried off going to a dull formal meeting if she hadn't been keen to see Harold Stevens in action again. She still thought he was an incredibly unlikely killer, but since Ellie had suggested him, she needed to follow up. Just observing him at the meeting might be useful.

A glass of wine and dinner revived her and by the time she arrived at the Wellington Climate Protection Society's AGM, she was feeling much more cheerful. She was running late and slipped in at the back of the room, to find Pam had kept her a seat. The meeting hadn't quite started, but there seemed to be as many people present–in spite of Harold's ineptitude–as at the first meeting. About twenty, policy wallahs, comms people, retired public servants, useful participants for what Harold had described as a kind of policy think tank, to focus on the Wellington area.

Lauren still fretted that perhaps there shouldn't be yet another climate change organisation, but a policy think tank did seem different, and she wanted to help. That seemed to be the general view. The only problem was Harold as the face of their group. 'He has no charisma,' Michael had said. 'Good on him for managing to get us all together, but we have to do better in terms of leadership.'

Lauren's work that afternoon had been interrupted by two or three discreet phone calls from people who'd joined Climate Protection. She realized that people were happy to go along with the idea of an old-fashioned AGM so that they could vote out Harold from the chair. She couldn't help feeling sorry for him. Seeing him again made it hard to give any credence to Ellie's contention that Harold could have been Nat's killer, he seemed so mild.

As the meeting progressed, it was clear that Harold hadn't expected any opposition to his retaining leadership of the society. He went red, as someone nominated Michael to stand against him, and white when the show of hands gave a resounding victory to Michael. However, he managed to seem gracious and agreed to become the

Treasurer. Scarcely a sop to his pride; it was hard to imagine there'd be much call for funds in this kind of group. Michael too was gracious, insisting that Harold continue as chair for the current meeting.

The only sour note came as the meeting was wrapping up. Pam caused it. 'Before we leave,' she said, 'can I remind you that last week, Nat Spiller died. He was a fearless environmental activist and his death is tragic. So full of promise, so much still to do.' She paused, swallowed, and said, 'Before we leave can we have a minute's silence to honour Nat?'

Harold was already standing, ready to say words of farewell. Now he put his hand on the table as if for support. Then he seemed to shake himself, cleared his throat, and said, 'Thank you for the suggestion, Pam. Let us all stand up.'

They all stood, eyes lowered, for what seemed to Lauren to be rather less than a minute–surprising, those minutes usually felt like five–before Harold said, 'Thank you all, see you next time.' He left the room, walking quickly, and disappeared from view even while little groups were forming and people chatting as they slowly made their way out.

As Michael, Pam and Lauren walked out, Pam hissed, 'That wasn't a minute.'

'I didn't think so either,' Michael agreed.

'Well, you know why, don't you,' Pam continued.

'He did seem very uncomfortable with the mention of Nat,' Lauren agreed. 'I know you might be thinking of what Ellie said, Pam–but it could have been that Harold was still smarting from their quarrel, even though he did go to the funeral.'

Michael asked, 'What's going on?'

Lauren gave him the short version. 'We've been told that Harold had a big falling out with Nat. He thought Nat's methods would tarnish the environmental movement. As if! We've got to have front-line, on the ground activists.'

'Yes,' said Michael, 'That's important, as well as boring respectable people like us.'

They walked on in silence, each wrapped in their own thoughts. Lauren was wondering if Pam had asked for the minute's silence to gauge Harold's reaction. She had just decided Pam didn't have a Machiavellian bone in her body when they reached Courtenay Place. Here their ways parted, Michael and Lauren to catch the bus and Pam on foot to her apartment.

14

At precisely ten o'clock on Wednesday morning Lauren knocked on Steve Painter's door. His house was set above and back from the road. Far enough up the hill for rising sea levels not to affect it, unlike some of his lower-lying neighbours. Across from the houses was the marina car park and beyond that moored yachts rocked gently in the breeze, their steel ropes chiming as they dinged against the masts. Evans Bay was ruffled, the sea slopping around in its confined space, occasional white caps dancing on the water. A plane took off towards the north from the airport runway at the end of the bay. A surefire way of telling which way the wind is blowing, thought Lauren. It's directly into the teeth of Cook Strait southerlies or above Evans Bay into the northerlies. She could see the northerly ascents from her own apartment, but from where she was now there was a good view of the airport as well.

Steve took his time to answer the door. Lauren wondered if he had forgotten, but then she heard footsteps. The man looked like his photo on Stuff, right down to the surly demeanour. His face was weathered, grey hair longish and tousled. He did not sport a nautical beard but the phrase clean shaven was hardly appropriate. His scruffy trousers were dotted with paint spots and his blue jersey, with its leather patches at the elbows, looked much mended. He looked to be in his mid-70s, her assessment confirmed by the liver spots on his hands.

Steve greeted her with a nod and ushered her in only after quizzing her to make sure she was not a journalist. 'You're from the family, aren't you?' Lauren assented, feeling awkward at the deception, but rethinking it, yes, that was the truth, after all she was representing Ellie. 'Can't stand journos, interfering bastards,' Steve grunted. Lauren wondered how much time she'd have with him before she was similarly typecast.

The dim hallway smelt unpleasantly of cigarette smoke and solvents. It was littered with unidentifiable metal objects, curled ends of rope and chain, planks and odd bits of piping leaning against the walls. The living room was more domesticated, though furnished sparsely. Scratches and scuff marks suggested it was a long time since the native timbered floor had been polished. There were a couple of trip hazard rugs, but the three-piece suite arranged to face the television looked comfortable enough, plumped up with cushions. Another armchair, spilling its stuffing, was placed with a view to the bay, an overflowing ashtray on the floor beside it. Books and magazines were arranged haphazardly on the floor beside the chairs. There were paintings around the wall, all marine scenes, some of them quite good, others amateurish.

'You must love living here,' said Lauren, searching for a way to ease into the questions she wanted to ask. 'Across from the bay and the marina.'

'I did.' Steve sighed and sat down creakily in an armchair, gesturing to Lauren to take a place on the sofa. 'It's not the same now. *Lucinda* was moored out there. I still go over to the yacht club and have a beer with my mates, but not having my own boat any more....' He trailed off, the sentence unfinished. 'I'm waiting to hear from the insurance but I haven't the heart to buy another one. Getting on a bit, I suppose. My son's against it after what happened. Mind you,' he glanced out the window, 'half the boats down there are for sale, always are. Well-off buggers shell out the cash and then the boats just sit there.'

Lauren nodded and in her mind she saw his broken boat on the rocks. 'I do feel for you,' she said. 'It looked like it was a beautiful boat. I saw it on the rocks.'

Steve looked at her, surprised by her fervency. As was Lauren. But it broke the ice. 'Yes, she was a real beauty, lovely lines, cut through the water like a knife in a good wind. She and I won lots of races in the old days, although I don't compete anymore.' He paused, sighed, corrected himself, 'Didn't compete anymore.'

He pulled himself together. 'You said you wanted to talk about the young man I found in the water that day? Such a bad business.' He shook his head. 'That poor fellow.' Lauren supposed Nat was young in Steve's eyes, perhaps in her own, too. She nodded as he continued. 'I'm having nightmares about it. I've been over and over what I could have done differently to save him.'

'The police thought you'd done everything you could. That's what I read,' said Lauren gently. 'You shouldn't blame yourself for anything.'

He made a face, shrugged and said, 'But you wanted to talk about it. I can understand the family wanting to know more. I don't know how I can help you, but fire ahead anyway.'

Lauren wanted to talk to him most about his attempted rescue, and what he thought about Nat's condition. But she could ease into that with simpler questions. Timing was important, and so was where Nat went in, because there might have been witnesses. She would have to find out if the police had interviewed any people who may have been in the vicinity.

She cleared her throat 'I did want to ask you if you'd have any idea where he might have gone into the water, given where you found him. You must know lots about the tides and currents around that part of the coast.'

'The cops said he went in opposite the marine lab. I don't know how they knew that, but they seemed pretty sure about it.'

'I'll check that out,' Lauren replied. 'I know his car was left somewhere down there, so maybe that gave them a steer. And his partner Ellie would know where he usually went in.'

'That part of it is probably right, because if it were there, then he hadn't drifted all that far. It was starting to get dark when I came across him. I was really late, shouldn't have been still out on the water but it had been such a marvellous day. I was going to have to navigate with my GPS and my lights on for a couple of hours to get back to the marina, first into the harbour entrance and then right around the point and into Evans Bay. My son would have been furious with me, he didn't like me staying out after dark but I've done lots of coastal sailing with overnights, and I've crossed the Strait every year for I don't know how many years. My son wanted me to stick within the harbour but I was determined to fit in just one more summer.' He shook his head. 'Summer's gone down the plughole now.'

Lauren felt another wave of sympathy. But she must not let the conversation drift. 'So, you think it's plausible that he went in opposite the marine lab. Where is that exactly?'

'Haven't you noticed it before? Between Island Bay and Owhiro?' Lauren shook her head, she vaguely recalled there was some university building along there, she'd once thought of going to an open day but for some reason she hadn't. 'It's by the Dive Shop, you must know that.'

'I think so, is that the one by the Bach café?'

This amused Steve. He seemed to lighten up. 'I can tell you're one of the café crowd. Yes,' he went on. 'There's a little beach opposite the lab. It used to be open but a seawall was built a few years back after one of the storms wrecked the road. If I wanted to go snorkelling along that coast without every driver in the rush hour traffic gawping at me changing into my gear, that's where I'd go.'

He went on, 'There must be a channel in between the rocks. It's an incredibly rocky coast, the Sirens are along from there.' He paused again, 'Poor *Lucinda*.'

Lured to her death by the Sirens, very Homeric, thought Lauren, but pulled herself away from this fancy and back to the subject at hand. The beach opposite the marine lab. She could almost picture it in her mind, but she was annoyed at herself, she'd been along that road countless times. She chided herself on being a poor observer of landscapes, or seascapes in this instance. 'So, do you think he'd been long in the water?'

'Couldn't have been that long, otherwise he wouldn't still have been breathing. A wetsuit gives you flotation and warmth but because he was unconscious and not moving, he would have got cold very quickly. It's early summer but the waters still have a winter chill. I'm not any expert on drowning...thank goodness,' he shuddered, 'but I'd guess it was only a matter of an hour or so at the most.'

'Ellie told the police that he left the house before six pm.' Pam had passed that on to Lauren. 'Apparently she recalled the time fairly accurately because she sat down to watch the news on television on her own and then started preparing dinner. Nat had said he would be back by seven thirty. He would have taken fifteen or twenty minutes to get to the coast.' Lauren was thinking aloud. 'I suppose it would have taken him a while to get his gear on, but he could have been in the water by six thirty.'

'Six thirty sounds about right. I must have spotted him an hour or so later. It's still light, doesn't get dark till around eight, what with daylight saving time. But I was trying to get him onboard for a while, must have been half an hour.' He paused and remained silent.

Lauren had the sense he was reliving it. She plunged straight in. 'Nat's partner Ellie doesn't think his drowning was an accident. She says Nat was always really careful snorkelling and diving, especially if he was out by himself. She thinks someone deliberately went for him, hit him with a rock or something like that. That would make it murder, in my book.'

Steve let out a breath, not quite a whistle, not quite a gasp. 'That's quite something, that puts a different spin on it.' He looked at her. 'But how I can help you? I only found him when he was on his way out. He was near to death. How could I know what happened to him beforehand?'

'You were the person who tried to rescue him, you were the first to see him in the water.' Lauren leant forward, appealing to him. 'Is there anything you noticed, anything that you can recall, that would help us understand what happened? The police seem to have washed their hands of it.'

Steve hunched forward, let his body hang towards the floor, made the whistling sound again, screwed his face up and shut his eyes. 'Let me just think about it for a moment.' He was silent again but it was not an awkward silence. Lauren sat quietly, giving him the time he needed. Finally, he opened his eyes, looked into the distance and began to speak.

'We were making our way towards the harbour entrance. The sea was lumpy so we kept a safe distance from the shore. It's very rocky. But we needed to stay well in sight of land.'

Lauren almost interrupted to clarify. Surely Steve was the only one on the boat. Then she checked herself, realizing that 'we' meant Steve plus *Lucinda* the boat. She smiled to herself, it was just the way men talk about boats, almost as if the boat was his girlfriend. Steve was talking more confidently now.

'I spotted something. A dark shape, might have been a swimmer, but that seemed unlikely. It was getting dark, no one would be swimming this far out. Still, I swung the tiller hard and brought *Lucinda* about.'

He raised his head, spoke to Lauren directly. 'It's awkward, you know, manoeuvring a yacht and trying to keep your eye on something in the water. If you have crew, one of them acts as the spotter but I was on my own. I lost sight of the shape for a moment....I don't mind telling you I swore like a trooper...but as *Lucinda* righted herself I saw it again. It was closer this time, and I could see a bobbing head with wet tousled hair. As we drew near I could see that it was a man and I glimpsed his upper body. He was wearing a wetsuit. I shouted out but got no reaction. *Lucinda* had picked up speed and I had to be careful not to run the fellow down.

'So I risked taking my eyes off him again. We turned into the wind....' Steve checked himself, explained. 'That stops the boat in its tracks, in case you didn't know.' Lauren nodded. 'And I hauled in the mainsail. It was hard to balance as she was rocking furiously, the wind seemed to be getting up. My idea was to start the outboard so I could get slowly alongside the guy.'

Steve broke off and breathed deeply. 'He had black curly hair, pasted down around his pale face. His eyes were closed and it was difficult to tell if he was breathing. His wetsuit must have been keeping him afloat, he certainly wasn't swimming. I whacked the motor into neutral, grabbed a rope and leant as far as I could over the side. Tossed it towards him.' He rubbed his fingers together. 'Actually, it hit him fair square on the head. Didn't mean to, but if he'd been conscious he would have responded. I kept shouting at him, you know, "Hey! We're here! Help is here!"' Steve moved forwards in his chair, making the motion of throwing a rope.

Then he leaned back, looking defeated. 'That's when it really sank in. Christ, I might be dealing with a body. So I said to myself, Steve, you'll be no use to anyone if you go into the drink, too. I repositioned my safety harness, lay flat on the deck and reached under the railing. I managed to grab his collar and I was still shouting, "Wake up, wake up, we've got to get you aboard." It was then that his eyelids fluttered, his lips parted and he made a groan. A soft bubbling sound, a bit hard to distinguish what with the noise of the wind and the sea, but it was definitely him. He was still alive.'

Steve paused. Lauren wasn't sure whether she should prompt him. 'So what happened next?' was on the tip of her tongue, but he gathered his thoughts and went on.

'This was the bad part, it was a nightmare. I tried to get a rope over his head and under his arms, but the boat was pitching and rolling. I kept losing my grip on his collar and then having to manoeuvre back into place to grab him again. Eventually I managed, but then it was, how to get him onboard? Unconscious, a regular size looking guy, I knew he'd be heavier than a sack of sand. I stood up, gave him a heave and sure enough, I didn't have the strength. I only got him up a foot or so before he splashed back down and of course that put him under the water before he surfaced again. You're making matters worse, I told myself.'

Steve gave a convulsive shudder and sat straight up. 'It was when he bobbed up again, half turned around, that I saw the gash on the back of his head. There was fresh blood leaking out through his sodden hair. 'More than just a drowning here,' I thought, 'but this isn't the time to wonder.'

He paused, looking at Lauren as if sizing her up. 'You've probably never been through a man overboard drill.' Lauren shook her head. 'I tried and tried to get him onboard but I just couldn't, he was a dead weight, my strength was deserting me and then, of course...' he hesitated and gulped, 'we hit the rocks, the boat was holed and everything turned to custard. I fell and lost my grip, the fellow slipped out from under the rope and disappeared. I had to try for the cabin to make a mayday call, my own life was in danger and I couldn't do anything for him. And then, well, the boat was moving again, I was just hanging on and then it hit again and I was in the water too. It all became a bit of a blur, I remember landing up on the beach but nothing else. Didn't see the guy again. I can't get it out of my head that I might have pulled him onto the boat when I had the chance.' He shook his head.

Lauren gave a sympathetic nod. Steve looked weary, as if saying as much as he had done had worn him out. He was clearly suffering the after effects of his own brush with death as well as his guilt about not rescuing Nat. But she wanted him to focus on what might have happened to Nat. She wondered if she should offer to make him some tea, but that seemed too much of an impertinence in a stranger's house. She should just press on. 'So have you thought about what might have happened to Nat? How he got to be out there with a gash on his head, drowning?'

'I'll be straight with you. I've been puzzling about it, too. Of course I didn't know the guy so I didn't know whether he was the careful sort. But I don't know how the police can be so sure he lost his footing and got swept against the rocks. Sure, smashed up first, drowned later, that makes sense. When I saw him he probably had hypothermia, would have made it harder for him to revive after being knocked out. But how do they know *how* he was hurt? If you really want to know what I think...' He hesitated again.

Lauren leaned forward. 'Go on.'

'I don't think the wave action was strong enough at the time to concuss anyone, especially not a swimmer with experience. I'd place bets on someone having delivered that blow.'

Lauren took a breath. She felt *she'd* received a blow. She said almost involuntarily, 'Oh no!' He looked at her. She felt embarrassed. 'I'm sure what you're saying will be helpful to Ellie. I promised to look into it. And I was hoping that there wasn't anything to it, that I could reassure her and then she could get on with the business of grieving.'

She had another thought. 'But did you tell the police?'

'They came to see me in the hospital. I was still quite dazed and I can't remember much about what they asked or what I said, but I think they took a statement and got me to sign it. Then later they phoned me and told me it was a courtesy call to let me know they'd decided it was an accidental drowning. I didn't know what to say and I didn't ask them anything else. Still coming to terms with it, I guess.'

Steve looked at her with a half smile, and continued. 'If you're a sailor you get used to surprising events, like storms blowing up from nowhere. You learn to cope with them.'

Lauren responded, 'Not bodies floating past, surely.'

Steve had to agree. 'Well, good luck with your investigating. We sailors have a saying, one hand for the boat, one for yourself. Make sure you take care while you're poking your nose around. There just might be someone who doesn't appreciate that.'

He showed Lauren out the front door. She was momentarily blinded by the sharp sunlight and nearly tripped on a coil of rope blocking the path. She turned around to wave, but Steve had already withdrawn. She walked down the steps, scarcely pausing to look at the view. Her mind was racing. Corroboration of Ellie's story. Well, not exactly, but someone who thought Ellie was right. She must talk to her again, make some notes on Nat's snorkelling habits, get her to confirm what she'd obviously told police about timing. There would have to be irrefutable evidence, she imagined, to get the police to change tack and initiate a murder inquiry. She should also pay a visit to the spot where it happened. Time to get cracking.

15

Lauren was having a bad dream. She was in a choppy sea trying to breathe and swallowing mouthfuls of water. It was a pleasure to wake up, take some deep breaths. What was that all about, she thought, and then remembered. The yachtsman and his belief that Nat didn't drown accidentally. The pleasure of breathing disappeared. She felt grumpy, how on earth did she get herself into this. And what next? She lay in bed for a while, thinking. By the time she'd got up, had breakfast and cleared it away, she'd decided.

Time she talked to the Spiller family. Pam's account of the family lunch suggested there were deep waters there too. She'd already ignored two voice messages from Lloyd Spiller's PA asking to see her urgently. Now, swallowing her pride about being summonsed, she phoned the PA who sounded relieved that she'd finally made contact. 'I know that Mr Spiller is anxious to see you as soon as possible. Would it suit you to come in at 10.30 this morning?'

Lauren looked at her kitchen clock, winced, but said, 'Of course, I'll be there then.' It was ten twenty-five when she presented herself to the receptionist. They were clearly expecting her.

'Mr Spiller will see you at once,' the blonde woman said. She walked Lauren up a flight of stairs, along a corridor, and into an office. 'Here's Mrs Fraser,' she said to the PA and left again.

'Ms Fraser, please,' said Lauren to her retreating back. She hated being taken for her mother.

'Oh, my apologies. I'll make sure it doesn't happen again.' The PA was stiff. She rose, knocked on an inner door and opened it slightly. 'Ms Fraser is here,' she said. Lauren heard a male voice. 'About time. Show her in.'

The PA swung the door right open and Lauren entered the office. She had little time to admire the view before Lloyd stood up behind his desk. 'Good morning, please sit down.' Lauren looked at a pair of tub chairs by a table near the window, but Lloyd had already sat down behind his desk and waved her to the hard-backed chair in front of it. He began speaking. 'I understand, Ms Fraser, that Ellie Petersen has hired you to investigate my son's death. I did ask you to come in, a day or two ago. I'm sorry if you have spent any time between then and now on this absurd business, because I must ask you to stop right now.' He hesitated momentarily, then continued, 'Ellie is not quite in her right mind at present. Her behaviour is upsetting everyone in my family. If you let me know what Ellie owes you to date, I will pay you that and an extra something for your trouble.'

Lauren was stunned. So he thought he could buy her off. Was that how he usually did business?

Lloyd was waiting.

'Mr Spiller,' she said finally. 'I'm afraid you don't understand. I am not a private investigator. Ellie has not hired me. She has asked me if I would do her a favour by looking into the circumstances of Nat's death.'

'Oh.' He was taken aback. He'd been leaning forward over the desk. Now he sat back in his chair. He rallied, leaned forward to talk to her again. 'My son drowned. That's bad enough without all this nonsense as well. The police say that it was an accident, and they should have more expertise than you, Ms Fraser. These are baseless allegations. If you're not a private investigator, I have no idea why my son's partner would have asked you to look at his drowning.'

'I'm sure the police are usually right,' returned Lauren. She had no intention of telling Lloyd why Ellie might have thought she could help. 'But, Mr Spiller, Nat's partner is sure he was too experienced to have an accident out snorkelling.'

Lloyd drew in a sharp breath. It seemed to Lauren he was struggling, grief breaking through the anger. She softened. 'I can understand why you think Ellie was just upset and lashing out, I was inclined to think the same. Now I've talked to the yachtie who discovered Nat in the water. He's not convinced it was an accident.'

Lloyd began to protest. 'You've no right....' Lauren spoke over him. 'Even if the police turn out to be right, I intend to keep investigating. Ellie loved your son. Just because she's upset it's no reason to discount her. I hope your family members will be prepared to talk to me–one of you may know something helpful without realising it.'

Now Lloyd slammed both hands on the desk and stood up. 'None of the Spiller family will be talking to you,' he said. 'No-one had any reason to kill my son, and your so-called investigation is just making life more painful for my wife and my children. I'd like you to leave now.' He came from behind the desk towards her and Lauren scrambled to her feet.

She backed towards the door, feeling she was in danger of being pushed out. She said, trying to preserve her dignity, 'I'm sorry you feel like that. If any of you change your mind and think you have something to tell me, please get in touch. Your secretary has my details.'

With that, she was out the door, breathing heavily. She gathered herself, smiled distractedly at the PA before she took herself down the stairs, head held high.

WAS LLOYD ALWAYS A BULLY? Lauren kept reliving that interview. The force of his personality had rattled her. But it hadn't deterred her. She was determined to carry on. And why was he so keen to stop her? He said it was upsetting the family. Could there have been another reason? The firm's reputation, as Ellie thought? Or something else?

She had an editing deadline the next day and tried not to be distracted by thoughts of the Spillers, be it father or son. But by the end of the day she had decided what she should do next–she would visit the Dive Shop on the South Coast and see if anyone there had seen anything or could tell her more about Nat as a snorkeler.

For years she had been aware of the Dive Shop, but she had never ventured in there. She parked the car in the car park across the road from the shop and near the beach where Nat was thought to have gone into the water. Because it was Saturday, the car park was fairly full–people enjoying the coast one way or another, as well as those sitting with their coffee at the Bach, looking out to sea. She was going to look at the beach where Nat had gone in, but first the Dive Shop. She headed across the road.

She'd assumed the shop would have a masculine environment, even if there were plenty of women divers and snorkelers. Probably like bike shops, which always seemed to have geeky young men on the counter. Lauren remembered that she'd felt as if she were in the wrong place, when she'd been looking for a mountain bike years back.

She was pleasantly surprised. The fit looking young woman behind the counter smiled at Lauren as she approached. 'Hi,' Lauren said. 'I'm a family friend of Nat Spiller, the guy who drowned off the coast a couple of weeks back. I was wanting to find out if anyone here knows anything about what happened.'

The woman said spontaneously, 'Oh, I'm so sorry! But I can't help, I wasn't on duty that day. I think you'd better speak to the manager.'

'Bruce!' she called and a slightly older man emerged from the back.

'It's about Nat Spiller's death. Could I speak to you privately?' Lauren asked. Bruce looked surprised, but ushered Lauren into a small back room which had all sorts of equipment lying around as well as a desk piled with paper and bits and pieces. 'How can I help you?' he asked. Lauren explained that she was acting on behalf of Nat's partner.

'We've already had the cops around. Everyone knew Nat. Helluva shame!' He went on, 'No one saw him that afternoon. The cops thought it was odd that his mask, snorkel and flippers were still sitting on the beach across the road.

'Why do you think he hadn't put them on?'

'No idea, but lots of guys go swimming in their wetsuits. Perhaps he was going to get his gear on later. I don't know.'

'The cops said he seems to have hit his head on the rocks. Have you heard of anyone else hurting themselves on the rocks?'

'I can't say I have, though the sea is very unpredictable around here.' He hesitated, and then said, 'But I wouldn't have thought Nat Spiller would have had an accident like that–he was a very experienced snorkeler.'

Lauren couldn't think of anything else to ask him so she thanked him and walked across the road, paused briefly at her car to grab a rug, and went down to the beach almost opposite.

The little beach was deserted, not surprising, as access was through a barred gate that looked as if it might be locked, and then down some newish concrete steps. It was not like the larger beaches around the south coast that were more inviting. Lauren looked around. The Coastal Ecology Laboratory was just across the road. She guessed the gate was something to do with them. Perhaps they felt they owned this beach but it was part of a marine reserve, after all, and in New Zealand beaches weren't privately owned, not below the high tide mark anyway.

It was a warm day and the beach was sheltered from the northerly. Further out, beyond the rocks, white horses surfed gaily in the turbulent waters of Cook Strait. The edge of the sea was calm, though, with wavelets lapping against the shore. Jagged rocky outcrops sheltered the beach at both ends.

Lauren unfolded the rug and sat down on the sand. She inspected the rocks, uneven, sharp and broken looking, as if the pounding they received from the southerlies had torn shards off them over the years.

It wasn't hard to imagine the lacerations someone might receive if they were flung against them.

She closed her eyes, trying to imagine Nat entering the water. She hadn't known him, but he was a public figure. She'd been to a lecture he gave and seen images of him in the press and a large photograph of him at the funeral. She tried to imagine a tall muscular man with dark curly hair, dressed in a wetsuit.

A loud splash disturbed her reverie. Her eyes flew open and she saw a dark figure emerging from the water. Was she dreaming? Surely it was Nat! He shook out his goggles and bent down to remove his flippers, then walked out of the water ignoring her. The image of Nat shimmered in her mind, and as she focussed, she realised her mistake. 'Justin!' She couldn't help saying his name out loud.

The man turned towards her. 'What?' He seemed disconcerted, not expecting to be addressed by an ageing woman sitting on a rug on the beach.

'Justin–you'll remember me, I'm Lauren, a friend of Ellie's aunt. I was at Ellie's when you called in the day after Nat's wake.'

Justin halted, running his free hand through his damp tousled hair. 'What are you doing here?' he said, an undertone of petulance in his voice.

Lauren thought quickly–get him talking. 'Isn't this where Nat went into the water?'

'What of it?' he replied.

'I'd have thought you mightn't want to go snorkelling here, that's all.'

Justin stared at the ground, shifting his weight from one leg to the other. 'Why wouldn't I? It's where we've always gone.'

Lauren couldn't resist asking. 'Were you with him before he went in that evening?'

'Christ!' Justin exploded. 'You're a nosy old bitch–Dad's already told you to butt out.' He kicked his boot on the sand and didn't apologise when it sprayed up onto her face. He strode up the steps.

Lauren was stunned. Her reverie had been interrupted, she had been horrified to imagine Nat coming out of the water and now she had been sworn at by Justin. It was all too much. She couldn't recall what she had hoped to discover by staring at the scene of Nat's disappearance. A breeze was starting to blow in from the south. She stood up, shaking the sand from her rug. The rug made it worse, she thought, it was a nana touch, so old ladyish. She stumped up the steps, stuffed the rug angrily into the back of her car, slid into the driver's seat. The car's warmth and safety soothed her until the roar of an engine startled her.

The rear vision mirror showed a big black monster of a car–or was it a truck?–behind her–anyhow one of those huge four-wheel drives. It lurched into gear and drove rapidly towards her, before swerving with a squeal of brakes and hiss of gravel. It exited the car park and blasted back along the ocean road. It was Justin, she saw, as she caught a glimpse of the straggly head of hair. He must have been watching her. And now she remembered where she'd seen the car before. It was the one she and Ro had seen speeding, out at Red Rocks. A shiver of apprehension ran through her. What an angry young man he seemed, and so unattractive compared to his older brother.

16

Pam was supposed to be meeting with Lauren on Sunday, to see how the investigation was going. Lauren looked forward to relaying the encounter with Justin, an indication, she thought, of the Spiller clan closing ranks. Lauren was also looking forward to the venue–the Prefab café–where she could rely on the coffee and any food she cared to sample. So she was disappointed when Pam phoned early in the morning to suggest that Lauren came to her place instead. Ellie was coming too. She had more information and she wanted somewhere private to talk.

Pam's house was certainly private–she hardly ever invited friends in, because she was always out. After her yoga class, Lauren regretfully strode past Prefab. Then she stopped in her tracks, went back and bought some date scones for morning tea. Pam was hardly likely to be baking.

She arrived about the same time as Ellie. Pam ushered them along the dark corridor and into her small living room. All the chairs seemed to be in use: piles of books, a plastic bucket with garden gloves, fork and trowel, a cage, or no, not a cage, a rat trap. Pam came to the rescue, plonked the rat trap onto the floor, put the pile of books on top of another pile on top of the coffee table and gestured to them both to sit down.

'I'm sorry I had to bother you at home,' said Ellie, 'but I want to talk to you about something difficult, and I didn't want to be overheard.'

'That's OK,' said Pam. 'I'm sorry, I'm not the world's greatest housekeeper. Anyway, how are you? Would you both like a cup of tea?' The panacea for all human crises. Ellie certainly looked as if she needed a panacea. She had visibly lost weight in the ten days or so since Nat's death, and the dark rings under her eyes told of sleepless nights.

Lauren brightened at the thought of a cup of tea. She was dehydrated after the yoga class and the walk, but Ellie shook her head. 'Pam, Lauren, I need you to help me, I'm really scared.'

'Scared?' They both sat up.

'It's Rodger–oh, I suppose I haven't told you about him, have I? It was all right while Nat was here, we just thought he was silly.' She took a shuddering breath. 'He keeps trying to get me to meet him, have lunch, have coffee, and he's always texting me. I've told him I don't want to, he knows I'm with Nat.' Her voice dropped. 'Was with Nat. Pam, that's the trouble, he's got even worse since Nat, since he–died.'

Lauren could tell Ellie was searching for the word. Died? Drowned? Was murdered? She looked at Pam, who seemed completely nonplussed, and said, 'Ellie, can you tell us who this man is? We don't understand.'

Rodger Brixton. Ellie told the story haltingly. She was embarrassed and upset. He was a middle-ranking council employee whom Ellie had met on a team-building exercise she was running.

Lauren knew about Ellie's small contracting business. It involved facilitating groups, communications and so on and made best use of her people strengths. On this exercise, it seemed that Ellie had excelled herself. The council manager had told her beforehand that the group was dysfunctional, despite its team leader seeming okay–he thought it was the people mix that included more than its fair share of outliers–classic introverts, outsiders who hadn't yet learnt the team ethos, a couple of people under management supervision.

It turned out that Ellie had got rather swept up in the moment at a social get together at the end of the away days. It had become a drinking session. The team building had gone really well. They were staying at the old Waitomo Hotel and they had gone caving, rock climbing and blackwater rafting together. Everyone was cheerful. Apparently, Brixton had cornered Ellie and told her all about his miserable personal life. He had mistaken Ellie's warm listening for an interest in him and so it had begun, his pursuing her. He'd called her repeatedly. She'd seen him sitting in a car at the end of her street.

'And it's still going on,' Ellie wailed. 'Rodger's still phoning me, wants to help me. Help me! Says I have to see him.'

Lauren said, 'Haven't you blocked his calls?'

'Of course I have! I've blocked his personal cell phone, but now he phones me from the city council. And I've got clients there–I can't block that!' She paused on what could have been a sob. Pam stood up and said, 'Now I am going to make us a cup of tea. Ellie, Lauren will talk to you about what we might do next.' She stood up and left the room.

Ellie blew her nose and Lauren sat silent for a moment, taking in what Ellie had said and wondering how Pam had had the nerve to disappear. Then she said, 'You'll feel better, I'm sure, just for telling us about him, but that won't make any difference to his behaviour.' She hesitated. 'Are you sure he's got the message that you don't want to see him at all?'

Ellie sat up, looked affronted. 'Of course I'm sure! When I said not to get in touch, before I blocked his phone, he texted and said he understood, he just wanted to talk to me about Nat.' She gave a shiver. 'As if I'd want to talk to him about Nat.'

Lauren stiffened. 'Do you think he could have had something to do with Nat's death?'

Ellie was startled. 'Rodger didn't even know Nat, he's just pestering me. I've already told you, it's Harold who was angry with Nat.'

'Mmm. So you just want Rodger to stop pestering you. What about a restraining order? I can't remember if it's the police or the courts, but he gets served with one and if he comes near you, you can phone the police to arrest him.'

She'd hardly finished speaking before Ellie started shaking her head vigorously. Then she stood up and came to Lauren, stood in front of her and grabbed both her hands. 'Lauren,' she said, 'I couldn't bear to talk to the police about it. It's been bad enough already, they wouldn't listen when I said I thought Nat's death was suspicious. I just thought you could speak to Rodger for me. Pam says you're good at dealing with people.'

Lauren framed her refusal and opened her mouth to make it, then looked at Ellie directly. She was still standing there, tightly grasping Lauren's hands. She wasn't on her knees, but it felt like that to Lauren. 'Okay,' she said at last. 'I guess I could visit him, find out what it's all about.'

She brushed aside Ellie's thank yous and when Pam came back in with scones and mugs of tea, she ate and sipped in silence. Ellie and Pam were talking about Nat's clothes and what should happen to them, and Lauren only half listened. She was wondering what she might say to Rodger. It was a relief when Ellie said her goodbyes but not before she'd promised Lauren she'd be in touch later in the day to give her Rodger's phone and email contacts.

When she had gone, Lauren caught Pam up with Ellie's request. 'Pam, you really dropped me in it. I'm already investigating on Ellie's behalf and now I'm supposed to sort this out too.' Pam didn't even have the grace to look shame-faced. Instead she looked thoughtful and said, 'But you have to see him, Lauren. Hasn't it occurred to you it could have been him?'

'Of course, he's an obvious suspect, I don't know why Ellie dismissed the idea,' retorted Lauren.

'Ellie's all over the place. She's hardly making any sense and she seems fixated on Harold Stevens.'

'I wish Ellie had mentioned Brixton earlier.' She was thinking on her feet. 'I guess this guy could have thought he'd have more chance with Ellie if Nat were dead, but thinking's a long way from killing someone.' She sighed. 'I'd better see him at his house, I doubt he'd be willing to meet me anywhere.' She gave another sigh. 'It's unlikely, but no more unlikely than Harold Stevens. I'll see how he comes across.'

'Don't keep sighing!' said Pam. 'Look how well you did with that case last year!'

'Suspects didn't keep popping up then,' said Lauren. She picked up her sports bag from the floor and stood up. 'We've had Harold, and that climate guy Derek and now Rodger!'

'What about Derek? Have you found out anything about him?' Pam said, as they walked down her hall.

'Haven't had time yet, but I will. And I'll go and see this guy Rodger as soon as I can.' She gave Pam a hasty hug and set off along the path. As she did so, she called back, 'Just tell Ellie not to come up with any more names.'

Next day, Lauren pulled into an awkward parking space near Brixton's address in Highbury. She'd driven up the tangle of roads from the Aro Valley, that wended their way around hills and gullies– 187 Pigeon Hill Drive. There were steep steps up a pathway through bush and she could not see the house from the road. She'd not phoned ahead, thinking that taking him by surprise after work would be the best tactic.

Pam had got more out of Ellie, who told her that Brixton lived alone. His wife and children had left some years earlier. They had moved to Auckland and the divorce had been bitter. Ellie had only heard Brixton's side of the story and when Pam phoned Lauren to give her the information, Pam said, 'Ellie just couldn't help being a sympathetic listener, more's the pity.'

Lauren made her way up the crumbling path with its white painted stripe across each step, typical of Wellington's hard to access properties. She suddenly felt unsafe. The house was isolated and she didn't fancy running down that path in a hurry if she had to. As the house came into view, she saw it was one of those ugly white stuccoed square houses, its exterior mouldy in places from the damp, bushy location. She walked up the tiled steps into the porch and steeled herself as she knocked assertively on the front door. Footsteps soon sounded inside and the door opened a crack. A man of average height, slim, a neat grey beard, grey trousers, white shirt and a loosened dark tie, grey shoes, a greyish face–a grey man. He looked at Lauren and raised an eyebrow.

'Are you Rodger Brixton?' It seemed like the obvious opening line.

'I am. And who might you be?' He looked apprehensive.

'I'm Lauren Fraser. I'm a friend of Ellie Peterson's aunt Pam. Pam asked me to talk to you. She's concerned about Ellie. Can I come in?'

Brixton seemed to freeze for a moment, then recovered himself. He looked reluctant, if that could be deduced from a slight ripple across his brow, something short of a frown. 'I'm just getting dinner but I can give you a couple of minutes.'

He pushed the door fully open and turned on his heel, leaving Lauren to follow him down the hallway.

The inside of the house was much less scruffy than the exterior. The living room was austere, with very little furniture and no household detritus. Brixton waved Lauren to a low leather sofa, where she perched on the edge. He left the room and she heard him moving about in what she presumed was the kitchen. He returned without any comment and sat on a chair opposite that gave him the advantage of height, and waited for her to begin. She mustered her courage, remembered the speech she'd rehearsed and said in her best managerial tone, 'Ellie has complained to her aunt that you have been contacting her despite her requests for you to stop. Your car has been seen parked at the top of her street. She believes that you think she is interested in you. That's incorrect and she needs you to know that she has no interest in starting a relationship with you or anyone else. She loved her partner deeply. If you persist with this unwanted attention, the police will be called and she will apply for a trespass order.'

Brixton did not reply. He stayed quite still. Lauren became more and more uncomfortable with the silence but was determined not to break it first. Eventually he spoke. 'She's got it all wrong. I've been trying to contact her to tell her something of interest about her partner's death.'

Her partner's death! Lauren was startled. Ellie had said Rodger wanted to talk about Nat, not about his death. She thought quickly. She needed to hold the line for Ellie, but find out what he had to say. 'Ellie doesn't want to talk to you, full stop.' She paused and softened her tone. 'But you can tell me.'

His face flushed. 'It's none of your business.'

He was a nasty piece of work, she decided. She drew herself up, leant forward and looked directly at him. 'If it's important, which I very much doubt, you might as well tell me and I'll pass it on. You're not going to be talking to Ellie, I made myself perfectly clear. Any further attempts to communicate with her will have consequences that you won't like.'

If Brixton was taken aback by her vehemence, he didn't show it visibly. He was again silent and unmoving. The flush that had crept up his neck and on to his face was the only indication that he was having difficulty with the conversation. Creepy.

'It's Ellie who needs to hear what I want to tell her. I don't know who the hell you are. This is between me and Ellie.' His voice was firm and even. Then there was a sudden wobble to it. 'Ellie needs to see me, she needs to hear this.'

'Will you please understand that there is nothing between you and Ellie.'

This time he replied at once. '*You* don't understand what's between us. I know she will want to see me.'

Had she been wasting her breath? She rose, said again that he should not try to approach Ellie, and walked out of the house without a backward glance. She scarcely noticed the steepness of the steps as she walked back down them, she was thinking so hard about Brixton. Did he really have something to tell about Nat's death, or was it a ploy, just an excuse to see Ellie. Or–she paused mid-step–it could even be that he was trying to cover his own tracks with some wild story. She frowned, and drove home still mulling over the conversation.

17

Wednesday dawned clear and bright with hardly any wind. Lauren found it hard to settle to work. She smiled to herself–shouldn't waste windless Wellington days being inside. Nevertheless, she cleared a space at the end of the table for the laptop and opened the file with the story she was editing.

The doorbell rang. Who on earth? Lauren pushed back her chair. Before she could get to the hall she heard the door fly open.

'Lauren? Ro here.' Ro strode into the kitchen and hugged Lauren so enthusiastically that Lauren, who had only half stood up, lost her balance.

Ro righted her and let go, grinning widely. 'Such a beautiful day, I thought I'd persuade you to come for a walk.'

'Goodness, Ro, you're looking so cheerful. Better. What's happened?'

Ro grinned even more widely. 'Come for a walk, I'll tell you all about it. You shouldn't be wasting the day indoors.'

'Ro, tell me what's going on.' Lauren began to feel impatient. Typical of Ro to barge in without even considering that someone else might be trying to work.

'I've scored that fellowship. I'm off to the Antarctic in a couple of weeks. And I'm flying to Christchurch this afternoon to be fitted with my gear!'

'Heavens,' said Lauren. It felt inadequate. Ro was almost bouncing around the room. 'But Ro, you only had the idea the weekend before last! How could it all have happened so quickly?'

Ro opened her mouth to speak but Lauren checked her. 'No, you're right, we need a walk. I'll get my jacket. We can just walk along one of the Mt Vic tracks and you can fill me in.'

Ro waited only until Lauren had shut her laptop, pulled her jacket off its hook by the door and checked she had her keys. She was telling Lauren all about it before they'd even reached the footpath.

'It's a fortnight's trip, writers, artists, journalists and so forth. And it's free!' She did a little twirl by Lauren's letterbox. 'Antarctica New Zealand organises short visits. We're expected to come back and spread the word–how beautiful, how pristine, how the Antarctic must be protected–I don't know! Anyway, after you gave me the idea'–Lauren protested but Ro sailed on–'I checked the application deadline but I was too late for this season. I had a bad twenty-four hours.'

Lauren winced, she could imagine the scene. Ro sitting despondently at home, reading light novels and eating biscuits, her cats around her.

Ro continued as they set off up the Crescent. 'But then I found that Michael Norris had to pull out. He's a colleague of mine in the History Department. Didn't pass the fitness test. So I applied and I'm going instead!'

'Fitness test! He must have been at death's door, Ro, because you can't tell me you've been staying fit this last few months.'

'It's more a fit to travel test, not a test of whether you can pull a dogsled for 10k in a blizzard.'

Lauren laughed. 'Anyhow, that's fabulous, Ro!' They turned off the Crescent and walked down through the park, heading for a track leading into the bush. A glorious view of the harbour, sparkling in the sun, made them pause. Lauren was grateful for the stop. She had accused Ro of becoming unfit but now she was out of breath from keeping up with her friend. 'What will you be doing down there?'

'Just what I told you last Sunday. I put the application together in a hurry but it just fell in place. I'm beginning a history of New Zealand women on the ice. Of course, I can do the main research in Wellington. I bet you didn't know there's a collection of 40,000 photographs of Kiwis on ice in Archives New Zealand. Let alone all the collections of papers in the Turnbull. I bet you never heard of Marie Darby?'

Lauren had to confess that she hadn't. 'The first Kiwi woman to set foot in Antarctica. 1969. Had to make the passage on the first tourist boat. Shocking, isn't it. And they were invited for a cup of tea at Scott Base. Not a heroic tale but it sure highlights sexism. Especially of the Kiwi variety. Especially since the Danes sent women there in the 1930s!'

'Can't wait to read the book.' Lauren was privately amused. Ro was such a creature of enthusiasms.

'The trip will help me get a feel for the material. I'll mainly be at Scott Base, but we'll be able to go out to one of the science stations or whatever they're called, as well as to the heritage sites. A good proportion of the scientists are women now, so I should be able to get a few interviews.'

'Well, you'll definitely have to meet Miriam; she'll be here this coming weekend. And Esther, her postgrad, is going on to the ice too, her first time.' They were now single file on a bush track. 'Tell you what. When Miriam's here, I'll invite some of our friends round to dinner. And when you get down there, look out for Alison too. I think she'll be there already. I can't remember her other name but she was one of the scientists I met in Melbourne. She's at Vic, and she told me she's managing the summer programme. She's involved in core sampling.'

Ro's attention was caught. She stopped still and turned around to Lauren. 'I've been reading about core sampling. One of New Zealand's big contributions to climate science. They're the group that made a big splash by showing that it was warmer millions of years ago and there were life forms in places where now it's just ice.'

Lauren forestalled Ro in lecturing mode. 'Yes, Miriam told me all about it. That's why she got involved, for the biology.'

Ro wrinkled her forehead. 'I think I've heard of Alison. The Vic publicity machine is pretty relentless when it comes to Antarctic work. Anyhow, I need to do my homework. Don't want the scientists down there to dismiss me as just a boring historian, come to gawp at Scott's hut.'

An idea was forming in Lauren's mind as they turned onto a broader track, part of the Southern Walkway. Perhaps Ro could do some digging for her. She said, 'I haven't told you about Nat Spiller's funeral and what his climate activist friends were talking about at the wake, have I?'

'No.' Now Ro was puzzled. 'Why?'

'There's this guy from Vic who's way out of step with his colleagues. Goes on about how they're all being alarmist and sea rise won't be so bad.'

'Could he be right?' said Ro doubtfully. 'Scientists do disagree.'

'I know, but they made him sound like a nasty character, as if he's twisting the facts to be a big-noter, and possibly even for financial gain. Anyhow, he's called Derek Drysdall. He's going to be on the ice this summer. You might run into him.'

'Bound to. Scott Base isn't that big–should I ask him about his views?' Ro was joking, but Lauren replied seriously.

'I wouldn't, but remember you said you'd help investigate Nat's death if you could. Well, Derek turns out to be what police call "a person of interest". Not that our police seem to be the slightest bit interested.'

'Go on,' Ro said.

Lauren explained that Derek was Spiller Construction's tame scientist and that if Nat had put in a counter submission on the Lyall Bay project, Derek would have been really pissed off.

Ro's eyes widened. 'And Ellie thought Derek had reason to kill Nat because of this? Sounds unlikely, surely.'

'Well, we haven't got much to go on and it's just one avenue to follow up.' Lauren was discouraged.

'OK,' Ro sighed. 'I don't want too many distractions, since I've only got two weeks down there. But I'll sniff around, see what the scuttlebutt is.'

'Do be careful, Ro. He may be a really nasty guy.'

'Homicidal, not just another would-be hero, you mean?' Ro laughed. 'Look, I'll find out what I can and I'll report back as soon as I get home.' She gave Lauren a mock salute. The rest of the walk was spent chatting about more mundane topics. They turned down Grass Street, walked back along Oriental Bay and slogged up the track to the top of Maida Vale Road before they parted.

After their walk, Lauren settled back to her work. She reflected that the physical exercise gurus did seem to be right: she felt energised and finished her edits more quickly than she expected. By mid-afternoon, she had sent the corrected script off to the publisher. Well before most people had finished their working day! She did enjoy working from home, and having a manageable workload.

She decided to walk over to Pam's community garden. On a beautiful day, she was bound to be there. She was, bending over a row of carrots, thinning them expertly. She unbent when Lauren greeted her, stretched and rubbed her back. 'Oof!' she said.

Lauren winced in sympathy and said, 'Can I give you a hand, Pam?'

'That'd be great. I'm doing the carrots–can you thin that row of parsnips? Here, take this, it's easier if you kneel.' She handed Lauren a slightly grubby piece of sacking, and they both bent to the task, chatting as they worked.

Pam was still spending a lot of time with Ellie. 'It's not even a month since Nat drowned,' she said, 'so I'm happy to keep her company. Her friends are supportive, but they're all at the age where they're busy with careers and children. Ellie finds evenings especially difficult so I often go over to her place then. I don't mind. As long as I can get over to the garden during the day, I stay sane. Relatively.'

She grinned. 'But have you got news for me, Lauren? Have you seen the stalker?'

Lauren told her about the visit and Rodger's refusal to talk to her.

'Pam, he was weird–he claimed that he had something to tell Ellie about Nat's death. He wouldn't say what it was–it might have just been a ploy. I'm not sure what to make of him, but at some stage I'll have to try and talk to him again. I don't think he'll be annoying Ellie, though–I said we'd be going to the police if he went near her.

'Meanwhile, I'm trying to work out how I can get to see Harold without arousing his suspicions–that is, if he's got something to feel guilty about. Michael and I should visit him to make sure he's not too upset at not being Chair of the Climate Change society. That might be the easiest.'

Pam nodded. 'And Derek Drysdall?' she asked.

'Ah, Derek. I wanted to ask you to do some digging about him, please, Pam.' Lauren stood up and rubbed her knees, thought that asking Pam to do some digging was appropriate, and continued. 'You keep on top of all the latest data on climate change, don't you? We need to know what Derek's standing is in the scientific community–you know, publications, lectures, and so on. It would be good to know how far he's out of sync with his colleagues, given that Nat had been going to put in a submission disagreeing with him.'

Pam said, 'There's been lots of disagreement over the science–I can certainly check him out.'

Lauren moved her sacking, knelt down again and said, 'Ro's going to check him out personally too–she's so much more cheerful, she's got one of those Antarctic New Zealand trips down to the ice, leaves really soon. And Derek will be there; I've asked her to look out for him.'

Pam was delighted to hear Ro's news and said so. She also admitted to some envy–after all, she was the committed environmentalist and would have loved to go down.

'And leave your garden just when it's going to need watering?' Lauren teased. Pam grunted, then laughed. She stood up, wiped her hands on her trousers and said, 'That's done. Should get carrots before Christmas–as long as I keep watering.'

18

It was nearly midnight. Lauren was waiting for Miriam to come through from the Qantas flight. She had promised herself a few days off from thinking about Nat Spiller and how he might have drowned. She was just going to enjoy her new friend's company.

The airport was practically deserted, the only people around were, like Lauren, waiting for passengers from the last flights from Australia. And there Miriam was, looking outdoorsy in a sturdy jacket and tramping boots, pushing a trolley laden with luggage. They hugged. 'You don't travel lightly, enough luggage to stay a month!'

'It's all the Antarctic gear, I had to bring my stuff from Australia. The Kiwis can just get kitted out before the departure from Christchurch.'

Lauren wasn't sure if it would all fit in her small car, but after putting the back seat down and some pushing and pulling, they jammed it in. They made two trips up and down the steps to her apartment block, and half filled her study with the gear. Miriam looked round appreciatively. 'I don't know how many people's computers I've slept with over the last couple of decades.'

'At least it's a laptop and I won't be printing off screeds of stuff at two in the morning. Now, tea?'

'I bet you make a better brew than you get in those pissy little plastic airline cups, sounds great. Let's sit down and have a catch up.'

Lauren realised Miriam was still on Melbourne time, a couple of hours earlier than Wellington. She herself was quite ready for bed, but she suspected Miriam was likely to be lively at any time of the day or night.

They sat in the living room with the curtains wide open, the moon shining a silvery track on the harbour. 'So,' said Lauren, 'what are your plans for the next few days?'

'Well, I haven't arranged anything for the weekend.'

'Just as well, I've invited some friends for dinner tomorrow and I do have some ideas for showing you around. I can't remember if you know Wellington?'

'I've been two or three times over the years, mostly conferences. I know the central city but I haven't spent any leisure time here.'

'Great, we'll put some walks on the agenda.'

'Monday is the first meeting of this Spiller Trust.' Lauren nodded. Miriam had been appointed as the overseas expert on the panel, a coincidence, Lauren thought. Or maybe not such a coincidence, perhaps someone consulted with Alison at the Antarctic Centre about bringing in an independent judge. 'Luckily I was able to persuade them to meet on the date I was to be in Wellington. It didn't take much persuasion, they were saved the airfares.'

She went on, 'Oh, and did I tell you that Derek Drysdall is on the panel, too. Bloody unfortunate pick.'

Lauren said, 'Yes. That doesn't surprise me, he's a friend of the Spiller family apparently.' She held her tongue. She'd decided she wouldn't talk about her investigation just yet.

'Never mind, I daresay he'll be outnumbered,' Miriam replied. She continued, 'On Tuesday, I'm meeting Esther at the Coastal Ecology Lab where I'll be getting together with the Wellington scientists who are off to the ice this summer. Mostly those from our team. Wednesday I fly down to Christchurch.

'I do have a lot of preparation for the trip, so I will be head down with my laptop in any spare moments. What about you? I'm sure you have a life?'

Lauren laughed. 'I've cleared some space, my time is usually fairly flexible.'

'Great, I'm looking forward to spending time with you and meeting some of your friends.'

'Me too–I mean spending time with you and introducing you to my friends.' She yawned. 'But right now, I think I need to get to bed.'

Miriam looked surprised, then, 'Of course, you're on New Zealand time. Can I just have your wifi password before you turn in?'

IT WAS seven on Saturday night and the room was buzzing. Lauren had sent Miriam out for a walk late Saturday, while she prepared the dinner. There were to be eight altogether. When it came to food, Lauren knew most of her friends' likes and dislikes, allergies and moral prejudices. She'd checked again, just to be sure, with Miriam as well. Miriam ate anything, as did Ro, but the other five included a vegan, a vegetarian, a migraine sufferer (no chocolate, cheese or red wine), someone allergic to mushrooms, and a gluten intolerant person. No wonder nobody has dinner parties these days, thought Lauren, as she pulled her pre-prepared chickpea stew out of the fridge. That would be a centrepiece. Then rice, salads, a variety of breads and a few side dishes. For dessert, she threw away the rules. A huge fruit salad, creamy icecream–and a dairy-free icecream substitute that looked awful, but never mind–and Lauren's specialty, a gorgeous figgy steamed pudding that she'd also prepared the day before.

And then the drinks to line up. She expected her friends would bring drinks but she had a couple of best New Zealand chardonnay in the fridge, along with craft beer, sparkling mineral water and apple juice. A wide selection of teas in hand for later and her coffee-maker at the ready.

Now they were all settled in Lauren's living room. Food was piled on their plates on their laps. Her lounge chairs and sofa held five at a pinch, so three kitchen chairs had been brought through. Ro had ignored the chairs and was sprawling on the carpet, gesticulating with her fork and balancing her plate in the other hand. 'I'm so pleased to meet you,' she was saying to Miriam. 'Lauren's told me you've had lots of seasons on the ice, and I've just scored a spot on the summer artists and writers' programme. Another historian had to pull out.'

'Lauren told me you were going,' Miriam replied. 'I guess you'll be at Scott Base. I'm working with the Americans over at McMurdo this summer, but there's plenty of mingling. And you're a historian?'

Ro remembered what Lauren had told her of Miriam. 'Yes,' she said, 'and I had a lot of respect for Jane Standish. She was your partner, wasn't she? I was so sorry when she died–she was far too young.'

Miriam nodded, and said briefly, 'It was a bad time.' She returned to the subject of the Antarctic. 'We scientists enjoy the artists and writers, not so much the celebrities and politicians.'

Lauren was refilling people's drinks. As she leant over to add more wine to Ro's glass, she was tempted to mutter to Ro not to mention that she'd be looking for dirt on Derek Drysdall. Their investigation shouldn't be a subject of gossip among their friends. Then she realised Ro was focussed on her current obsession, and seeing Miriam as a real live example of Antarctic woman.

'Well, I'm not a celebrity,' said Ro, doing her best to charm. 'No doubt we're an interruption but I guess it's good to publicise your work. I'm focusing on women on the ice. Looking to undermine some of those hero narratives.'

Miriam laughed. 'I wouldn't call myself a hero, but there's plenty of women heroes down there, as I'm sure you'll find.'

'Everyone who goes there must be a hero, I reckon. Remember that exhibition at Te Papa,' Megan said. 'It had Shackleton's boat on display, the little one they sailed through the ice floes and then hauled across icy wastes for weeks to get help. My friend Trudy, who's a curator at Te Papa, got on a trip to the Antarctic that summer. She was involved in designing the exhibition.'

'I remember it well,' said Pam. 'Tales of hardy explorers–that one just about tops the lot.'

Miriam said, 'These days we have to be fit, but not hardy!' She turned back to Ro, still sitting on the floor gazing up at her. 'I think this will be the trip of a lifetime for you. And your project sounds great. Are you focusing on a couple of women, or doing a broad sweep?'

Ro said quickly, 'I wonder if you'd come for a meal tomorrow. I think it might help me crystallise a couple of ideas.'

Lauren was surprised. Dinner invitations from Ro were not common. Her house was usually so disorganised and she had no apparent talent for cooking. She looked at Ro who winked at her.

Miriam accepted Ro's invitation and the conversation rolled on enthusiastically. Miriam was so excited about the science she was undertaking that it rubbed off on everyone in the room.

LAUREN HEARD a key in the door. She called out, 'In the dining room, Miriam.' Miriam was there in three quick strides, gave her a hug in greeting. 'That was a long meeting?' said Lauren.

'It was good, the award will be a useful amount for someone to advance their research. Derek Drysdall was being a prick as usual but people ignored him.' Lauren was about to ask more about Derek but Miriam hurried on, 'I'm late because I went to see Esther after it, some stuff she wanted to run past me, before our meeting tomorrow. All a bit of a rush. Esther's kindly brought me home.' She stepped to one side and Lauren realized there was someone behind her.

'Esther! How good to see you again, after that lovely evening in Melbourne. Will you stay and have a drink with us?'

Esther looked diffident, but Miriam said, 'Of course she will, she's going out for dinner but I told her to come in and say hello.'

Lauren settled them both in the dining room while she gathered drinks and nibbles. She walked back in, balancing a tray and heard Miriam replying to a question from Esther. 'This is the first year of the award, it's been put together very quickly. Amazing, really, Nat Spiller died so recently.' She considered for a moment. 'Of course, we were all together at dinner in Lygon Street when Lauren told us about it.' Miriam turned to Lauren. 'When exactly was it, Lauren?'

'It was on a Sunday, the fourth of November–I remember because on the Monday, I saw the wrecked yacht of the guy who tried to rescue him. They didn't know who it was at that time. But on the Tuesday, when I left for Melbourne, I hadn't even got to the hostel where I was staying when my friend Pam phoned to tell me it was Nat who'd drowned. She's the aunt of Nat's partner, Ellie,' she explained.

'That was just after I left for Melbourne,' said Esther. 'I went on one of those ghastly early morning flights on the Monday. I spent most of the weekend before at the lab, trying to finish off work–I was there to all hours!'

Lauren put the tray on the table and handed them both drinks. Now Miriam was talking about Esther's workplace, the Coastal Ecology Laboratory, and how impressed she'd been with it–and with its situation. 'That south coast is magnificent. But it looks as if it could be treacherous.'

'A lot of people use it,' said Lauren, 'and I guess they know to respect it. That was one of the odd things about Nat Spiller's death–he'd been snorkelling there for years. In fact, that evening he went missing, his widow's pretty sure he went in at that beach opposite the laboratory. He often used it, and his car was in the car park nearby.'

'I didn't realise that's where he drowned. A lot of people go in there, because it's near the Dive Shop too,' said Esther. 'I've often seen them....Oh!' She paused, glass halfway to her mouth, with an arrested expression. She looked at Lauren, 'Nat went snorkelling on the Sunday night? That was the night I was working late at the lab.'

The two women looked at her. She put her glass down. She said slowly, 'It's just that I saw something odd on the beach that evening–but there were two men. They looked to be fighting.' She stopped again. 'I wonder if I should tell the police?'

Lauren was so startled, she sat speechless. Then she said, 'I'd rather you told me–I can explain why, it's quite a long story.'

Esther said, 'I'm due out for dinner about now. Could we meet somewhere, say, tomorrow? That's the only time I have before we leave for the ice.'

Miriam chimed in. 'We've got that meeting at the Coastal Ecology Laboratory with you and the others tomorrow–Lauren can drive me there a bit earlier and spend time with you while I do some prep for the meeting.'

19

As they drove along the south coast road, Miriam said 'You're incredibly lucky to have such a wild coast so close to the city–heaven for a marine biologist.'

'Heaven for us ordinary mortals too–I love that on the seaward side, there's just the footpath above the rocky shore and the occasional sea wall. Though those sea walls are going to be smashed within a few decades.'. As she spoke, Lauren was looking along the other side of the road, in the medley of houses old and new, for the Coastal Ecology Laboratory. She almost missed it. It was snuggled in beneath the hill behind, its stone and metal cladding beautifully in tune with its location.

They parked and walked over to the entrance, taking in the thick curved timber ribs that soared up to the second storey, and looked as if they would cope with any weather the south coast threw at them. Miriam and Lauren lingered in the entranceway, looking at the carved kaitiaki, the Maori guardian of the building. Lauren glanced back across the road, uneasily–a great sea view but one of the places you couldn't see the shore from, nor the beach where Nat went in. A seawall screened the sand and rocks beyond.

After Miriam and she had found a space for Miriam to work in,

Lauren climbed the stairs to find Esther in the lab on the first floor, and changed her mind about the view. The room boasted a wide window right across the front wall, looking out to sea. She could see the spectacular exposed rocky reefs of the south coast and right across Cook Strait to the South Island, where the mountain tops of the Kaikouras were silhouetted in the sunlight. In the near view, she could see the gates at either end of the seawall and steps down to the sheltered beach below, and the beach itself, with fingers of rock protecting it on each side.

'What a fabulous spot,' she said to Esther. 'It must be hard to concentrate on your work.'

'Sometimes. But of course the lab's here because of that view.'

'Oh?'

'We do a lot of work on the south coast ecology. And the stretch of sheltered beach,' she gestured, 'is a great place for divers and snorkelers to go in.'

They both stared out the window. The beach was empty, just waves endlessly crashing in over the rocks and running towards the shore. The day was calm but there was still movement in the water. Cook Strait was never a millpond.

There was a pause and Lauren pulled herself back to the reason she'd come. She took some time to explain her involvement in investigating Nat Spiller's death and how the police were insisting that it was accidental. Esther listened wide-eyed, but said nothing. Lauren continued, 'So you remember seeing something the evening Nat Spiller went missing?'

'Yes,' said Esther, 'and I feel badly I didn't know earlier that that was where he went in. The thing is, it was my last day at the lab. Then I flew out to Oz the next morning.'

They were both perched on lab stools, staring out the window. Lauren said, 'So what did you see?'

Esther paused, then collected herself. 'I was tidying away my equipment. It had been a long day. I needed to get some observations finished before I left for Melbourne. Starfish are my passion, but staring down a microscope for several hours is tiring.'

Lauren nodded encouragingly, hoping she was not looking impatient. Esther continued, 'I had brought the microscope over onto this bench and I glanced out the window. That was when I saw them–a couple of guys standing just by the edge of the sea. I knew they weren't from here, and they were behaving quite oddly. I couldn't hear anything of course, just see them.'

Lauren nodded again. 'What was odd about it?'

'I suppose you could say they were facing off. You know, like two blokes raring for a fight. It looked weird. One was in a wetsuit, clutching his snorkel but not going anywhere. Standing facing each other, gesticulating. And I'm sure yelling at each other, though I couldn't hear that. Neither of them was giving an inch. Carrying on the way Italians always talk–using everything, bodies leaning forward, waving their arms, shaking their fists at each other.

'I remember it because it was so weird, I kept staring to see what would happen next. But a timer went off on one of my instruments so I had to attend to that. When I came back there was no one there. I couldn't even see their heads in the water.'

Bugger, thought Lauren, these damned conscientious scientists. 'Do you think it could have been Nat and someone else?'

'I never met him, but just looking at them, I'd have thought they were both guys in their twenties or thirties. They looked kind of similar, same height, tallish, same kind of body shape, neither of them very fat or very thin. Sorry to be so vague, but they were quite a long way away.' She gestured down towards the beach. 'But so rarked up!' She stopped suddenly. 'So do you think it could relate to Nat Spiller drowning?'

'Almost certainly,' Lauren said, 'but it might relate to something worse than drowning.'

LAUREN COULD HARDLY WAIT to contact Pam. Miriam was finding her own way back to Lauren's for her final night there, before she left for Christchurch and the Antarctic. Lauren said a hasty goodbye, before driving back home at speed. She checked herself only when she noticed one of those irritating roadside gizmos that, instead of telling her how fast she was going, was flashing, Slow Down, Slow Down.

Once at her apartment, she poured herself a glass of water, flung herself into a chair with her phone and rang Pam. Thank goodness, Pam was home too. The story tumbled out and when Pam took it in, she was as excited as Lauren. 'That must have been Nat and someone,' she said. 'And they had a fight–Lauren, that's got to be the murderer.'

'I know,' Lauren said. Her excitement was draining away, she felt slightly sick. Ellie was right and this was not a game. She said soberly, 'Esther said they were both about the same size and build. That fits with Harold and Rodger; it could have even been Justin–but Ellie didn't finger him. And I don't know about Derek but we can find out. And what were they fighting about? Who would have known Nat was there? That's what we've got to find out now.'

20

Christchurch International Airport. Ro was standing in an out-of-the-way corner near a departure gate. She was apprehensive as well as excited. Time had flown since this unexpected opportunity to go onto the ice. The preparation had been intense and absorbing. This was her second trip to Christchurch in a week. Now she had all her hi-tech, hi-vis extreme weather gear, all in orange and black, the New Zealand colours. There was no way she could have afforded to pay for it, but Antarctica New Zealand funded all expenses for their invited visitors.

When her neighbour's son Timmy had come over for instructions on feeding Ro's numerous cats, she had shown him her gear and he had persuaded her to demonstrate the whole outfit. The jacket with its huge furry hood made her look as shapeless as a polar bear. Her pants could have taken a direct hit from a fire hose without water getting through. The huge boots with chains on the soles made walking just about impossible inside a building but no doubt would come into their own on the ice.

Ro knew it wasn't hard to impress a twelve-year-old, but she couldn't help a flush of pride when his eyes widened with admiration. She promised to bring him back a souvenir. 'No stupid soft toys,' he said. 'Something real.'

'We're under strict instructions not to leave anything there or take anything away,' Ro had said.

Timmy bottom lip dropped. 'Ohh! You could sneak something out. Just a bit of rock!'

'Careful,' said Ellie, 'or I'll bring you a piece of ice.'

The worst part of the prep had been a trip to her dentist. Ro always was tense and anxious on such occasions, and put off visits as long as possible. But teeth were apparently prone to jangling in a cold environment and her sponsors had insisted on a visit in the lead up. They didn't run to a dental surgery on Scott Base. Ms Lee was fascinated by the reason for her visit and poked for sensitive spots with excessive attention to duty, Ro felt. A couple of fillings later–her responsibility, Ro thought ruefully as her credit card went into overdrive–she left with a free sample of a toothpaste designed to deaden any cold-induced twinges. At least now she would not be running the risk of gruesome attempts at tooth extraction down on the base.

The prospect of this adventure had pulled her out of the ennui of life without a deadline. Ro had relished the race to bring herself up to speed with primary and secondary sources on New Zealand women in Antarctica. The literature was scanty, some of it hard to locate and mostly consisted of personal accounts of time spent in that harsh environment. Valuable and interesting in themselves, but not the same as historical analysis. She could see room for an original take. So even though her hastily put-together proposal to Antarctica New Zealand had been half-baked–and what did they know, they weren't historians–she was confident she could make something of her topic. A change from her usual stamping ground, women in politics, but not totally different. Women seeking entry into a male world, getting a hand up from some of the men and dealing with egos and put-downs from others.

Ro was used to travelling to academic conferences all over the world. She was a meticulous packer, a surprising contrast to her lackadaisical housekeeping. But this time it had been particularly difficult. There would be no shopping for forgotten items in Antarctica. She'd been given a green kit bag for carry-on luggage, and she was now clutching it. And a black canvas bag, known as a boomerang bag. In it, everything she might need for a few days in Christchurch. Apparently planes sometimes returned, even hours after take-off, if weather conditions down south became unfavourable. She fervently hoped that would not happen. If their journey was completed as planned they would be disembarking into the freezing cold, so her outer coat was draped over her arm and she was dangling the heavy boots that she'd need to pull on before arrival.

An announcement blared out and Ro went to security, quite a different process from the usual international departure. No passports required, just a departure card and an ID check. There was no arrival hall on the ice: they'd just walk down steps from the plane.

Ro was weighed along with her hand luggage, which included a bagged meal and a bottle of water–no cabin service. The joint weighing avoided potential embarrassment–it may have been all that heavy gear in her hand luggage pushing up the scales. In the departure lounge the passengers milling around, a mixture of men and women and mainly American or Kiwi accents, were invited to watch a safety briefing about the ice, not just about aircraft safety.

Ro climbed into the bowels of the huge Hercules. Although she had seen images of the internal layout, it was still a shock to see people taking their places on webbing seats around the edges of the cavernous interior. All sorts of boxes and packages were stowed in the middle. Ro found herself a place between a couple of friendly-looking bearded guys, strapped herself in, pushing in the earplugs that had been handed out. The engines roared and they rumbled down the runway, the aircraft shuddering like a beast in pain as they lumbered into the air.

The six-hour trip was hardly exciting and not very comfortable. Around the halfway mark she heard a shout of joy and scrambled to a window. The first icebergs glowed brightly beneath them in the sunshine.

The plane landed softly on the snowy runway near McMurdo Sound. Ro tugged her boots on, wrapped herself into the snow jacket and descended the steps along with everyone else, taking a sharp breath as she was hit by the incredible cold. She stepped gingerly onto the ice and made her way to the transport 'bus', a well-equipped vehicle with snow tracks. She scarcely had time to look around before they were off. They caught sight of McMurdo, the American base where Miriam would be working as part of an international team. At least she would know someone, even if they were on a different base. Apparently the distance was walkable in fine weather, only three kilometres, and the Kiwis were invited over to McMurdo for a movie night every week.

The bus drew up alongside a collection of green buildings. The sun came out from behind a foggy cloud cover and everything sparkled. It was hard to remember that it would be light for twenty-four hours every day. Her new scientist buddy from the plane, Zach, pointed out Mt Erebus rising imposingly in the distance. Ro was struck by a horrid thought. Probably more women reached the Antarctic in that fatal plane crash into the mountain than had ever been on expeditions. How would she fit that extraordinary event into her history?

RO MADE her way through the crowded recreational room. It was her first evening on the base and Alison, who had been assigned as her mentor for the week, had invited her to meet in the bar. Alison was someone she vaguely recognised as they were both on the academic staff at Vic, although she didn't actually know her. But soon they established an acquaintance in common, Miriam, and of course, Alison had met Lauren at the dinner Miriam had arranged on Lygon Street.

Ro edged her way to the bar and caught the bartender's eye. 'Two beers, please.'

'Hi, I'm Tim.' The man grinned behind his bushy beard. 'Speights or Mac?' It was hard to tell all these beards apart, but they seemed to recognise her already.

'Mac, thanks, just halves,' she said, forestalling Tim reaching behind the bar for an enormous glass. 'How much will that be?'

'On me,' a voice interrupted from behind her. A man thrust his way alongside her. 'For my friend here, and whoever she's with,' he said to Tim, who winked at Ro. Ro was flustered by the offer, but put her wallet away. She smiled but not warmly at the man beside her. At least he was clean-shaven, easier to remember. Otherwise average, she thought, fit enough, medium height, dark hair, darkish eyes, thin lips. And a couple of decades younger than her. 'I always treat the new girls,' he said. 'I'm Derek. And you?'

Dammit, this must be the guy from Vic Lauren had asked her to watch out for. She knew she was bound to run into him, with around sixty people on the base. But she hadn't banked on it being this early–or in this way. She scowled but it seemed petty to rebuff him. It had been impressed on her that in this cloistered environment she must not get on the wrong side of anyone. 'Ro, I left girlhood behind a while ago,' she said.

He looked at her knowingly. 'You'll be coming to Arrival Heights, I hear. We're always having to stop work to show the visitors around. So what's your trade? Did you come here to paint pretty pictures?'

'I'm a historian.' Ro was abrupt. 'Thanks for the drinks, I'll take them with me, Alison wants to brief me on tomorrow's programme.'

'Brief you, or chat you up?' Ro turned on her heel. It was best not to reply to such stupid remarks.

Alison seemed a good sort. She'd quite understood when Ro slapped down her beer and muttered about sexist men. She hadn't seen who Ro had been dealing with and told Ro an old chestnut about women expecting to find a man in the Antarctic: 'the odds are good but the goods are odd'. Ro was captivated to hear what Alison had to say about life for women on the ice. They mainly discussed Alison's experiences on the drilling projects, but did venture onto more amusing topics. Ro was secretly pleased that she wasn't off on a camping expedition, that was for visitors on longer trips. She still had to master the Shewee, though, in case it was needed on the day trips. She'd practised at home and had spilt pee on her clothes every time.

21

Michael and Lauren were driving up the highway towards the Hutt Valley. Michael, who gave her the excuse for visiting Harold, had said that Saturday suited Harold so Saturday it was, even though Lauren would have preferred to visit him earlier. Only a few days since Esther had talked to her but it felt longer.

'Twenty-three Arawa Street,' Michael said. Lauren brought up Google maps on her phone and tapped in the destination. A female Australian voice entered their conversation.

'I've got British male,' Michael said. 'Got that authoritative ring to it.'

'Australian female is my buddy. She's terrible at Maori pronunciation but it sounds less "we rule the empire" than when a British voice mispronounces.' They both laughed.

Lauren wondered at herself. She was feeling quite jumpy but it was easy to slip into banter with Michael. 'Are we ready for this?' she asked him, wondering if she should have told Michael about why she really wanted to visit Harold. He'd been her wise counsel during her last investigation

'We deposed him at the meeting and he looked terribly offended. I think we should be building bridges right away.'

'Ever the politician,' Lauren teased, remembering Michael's earlier career. 'The Beehive must be like Hotel California. "You can check out any time you like, but you can never leave."'

'Huh, you've nailed it, but I wish you hadn't.'

Lauren fell silent, then made up her mind. 'Is there time for a coffee before we arrive?'

Michael glanced at the clock on the dashboard. 'Maybe, it's a bit tight. What's on your mind?'

'Quick, take this exit.' Lauren was decisive. Michael swung the wheel and their Australian friend started bleating, 'Make a U-turn when possible.' They both laughed again.

'We could park by the beach here.' They were at Petone. 'There's something I want to run past you.'

Michael swung into a car park busy with people bundling dogs or babies and strollers in and out of their cars. 'We've got ten minutes, let's walk,' he said.

They made their way through the long grasses between the beach and the car park. The beach was firm and crunchy with a fine layer of shells, making walking easy. 'We'll turn back when we get to the pier,' Michael said. 'Now, what's up?'

'I told you that Ellie thinks Nat was murdered.'

'Yes,' said Michael, 'and I've been worried about you getting into another spot of bother.'

Lauren winced. 'Let's put that aside for a moment. What's freaking me out about visiting Harold is that he's one of the suspects, as far as I'm concerned.'

'You're kidding!' Michael raised his eyebrows. 'And I'm the Queen of Sheba.'

Lauren wasn't to be distracted. 'Ellie told Pam and me about a couple of people she thought could have killed Nat–and Harold was one of them.' She hesitated. Should she tell Michael about Derek, and Rodger stalking Ellie? She decided not, at least at the moment, she wanted them both to keep focussed on the meeting with Harold. She continued. 'Ellie talked about a huge spat Harold and Nat had. Harold doesn't approve of direct action and he'd come along to Nat's new group but it was too radical for him. That's why he started our one. And he got Nat banged up in the police cells for a few hours because he dobbed him in. Nat was furious. The police picked him up as he was preparing to scale the Beehive and plant a banner at the top. It was weeks of planning.'

'Sounds like Nat would have more reason to kill Harold than vice versa!'

'Ellie thinks Harold was boiling with resentment. He and Nat were at school together. Harold was unpopular–came from a fundamentalist Christian family. He was very uptight, always hanging about on the outskirts of Nat's circle.'

'God, those fundies. There was a pocket of them when I was at school there. A kid I knew, who was probably gay, killed himself because of his family.'

'Hmm.' Lauren didn't want to speculate. 'I need to get in a few useful questions of Harold, not just about being the treasurer. Like, where was he on the night Nat died.'

'Two agendas. Never a good idea,' said Michael, 'but I'm beginning to know you only too well.

GOOGLE MAPS DIRECTED them through a warren of streets in the flatter part of the Hutt. Arawa Street was in a tree-lined pleasant neighbourhood, nothing flash but the fifties-era houses looked well cared for. Number twenty-three had a small front lawn with a driveway going to the back of the house, and a footpath to the front door.

Michael knocked on the door and then found a doorbell that actually worked. They could hear the chime echoing down the hallway, but no sounds in response. Michael rang again. Silence.

'Perhaps he's in his garden. Let's go round the back,' Lauren suggested.

Michael nodded and they walked down the driveway. A head taller than Lauren, he was able to peer in a window as they passed by. 'No one in the kitchen,' he reported.

There were steps up to a back porch which gave on to a separate laundry and a door into the house. Michael knocked again, to no effect, then tried the door. It wasn't locked. He opened it a crack, calling out 'Harold! It's us–Lauren and Michael. Are you there?'

The only sound from inside was the humming of the fridge and the ticking of a loud kitchen clock. The kitchen, what they could see of it, looked neatly kept and there were signs of recent use. A coffee mug on the draining board, a tea towel slung over the sink bench.

'He must be somewhere out the back. Let's look around.'

'Or he might have popped up to the dairy to get something for his visitors.' Lauren could have done with a cup of tea. 'Does he live on his own?' she asked.

Michael didn't know much about him, but it didn't look like a lively household. No washing strung out on the line, no bikes or toys thrown down by the back door. They walked round the edge of the house. The garage roller door was shut and the back lawn, although neatly mown, showed little sign of any gardening activity that might be occupying Harold. 'Strange,' said Michael.

'Perhaps he's in the garage–look, the side door's open. Cooee,' she shouted. She walked towards the door and peered inside. It was dim, the only light from a small dusty side window. A car was inside, but there was plenty of extra space for the usual things people store in their garage. Something felt not right, though, and Lauren stepped inside. A slight movement caught her eye and she looked towards the back of the garage. 'Christ! Michael!' she called.

Michael came running and they both stared, transfixed. The movement was caused by a figure swaying slightly, a figure dangling from a rope. It was Harold. Lauren recognised his face, even though it was contorted, a strange colour, eyes bulging, tongue poking out of his mouth.

'Is he dead?' Michael's voice shook.

'Certainly looks like it, but we'd better get him down, just in case.'

They looked around. Michael said, 'We'll have to cut him down. I'll find a knife in the kitchen.'

Lauren was left alone with the hanged man. It was all she could do to keep herself together. Her heart was pounding, she felt sick and faint. Michael was back in a moment. He righted the chair that Harold must have pushed off from. 'You climb up, Lauren. Cut the rope and I'll hold him.'

It was very difficult to cut through the rope. It was sturdy woven marine quality. Lauren had to ask Michael to lift the body, to ease the tension slightly. As she was sawing through the last strands, the rope suddenly gave way. Even though Michael was bearing some of the weight, the extra movement shot him off balance. He fell to the floor, with Harold's body landing heavily on top of him. Lauren nearly lost her balance too.

'God, are you all right?' Lauren asked. Michael rolled out from under the body and stood up, looking very pale. Lauren suggested he sit on the chair and he did so without a word. She crouched down to examine Harold. There had been only the faintest hope that there might have been some life left. It was clear there was none. The body had fallen, a deadweight. Nevertheless she placed her ear against his chest and looked carefully at his nose and mouth. There was no rising and falling of breath. The life had gone out of him.

Lauren stood up, felt faint and sat down on the floor with her head between her knees. Michael, recovering, put his hand on her shoulder. 'We need to phone for an ambulance and the police.'

'Will they send an ambulance? He's clearly dead.'

'I don't know, but let's talk to emergency services.' He pulled his phone out of his pocket. Lauren walked outside, desperate for fresh air. She paused, breathing in the warm, scented smells of the lawn and garden. The smell of death lingered in her nostrils. Behind her, she could hear Michael speaking urgently.

Without knowing what she was intending, Lauren made her way to the house again. She opened the back door, calling out. 'Is there anyone there?' Senseless, given what was in the garage, but for all she knew, Harold might have had a flatmate. It was as quiet as a church.

She stepped into the kitchen, looking around. Papers and books were piled neatly on the dining table. Propped up on a pile of mail was a folded sheet of paper with handwriting in it. Lauren peered at it, unwilling to touch anything. It was a note. She poked it open with a nearby pencil, scanning it hastily.

'To whoever finds this: sorry about the shock you'll get when you go into the garage, but I can't carry on. Everything has turned into a mess and I'm so ashamed of myself. No one will miss me. The pile on the table contains my personal documents. Harold.'

Good God. Lauren felt quite sick again. Her eyes fell on a notebook on top of the pile of papers. She used the pencil again, to open it–it was an appointment diary. Harold had written brief notes on most days of the week. She looked closely and read 'gannets, harbour' and 'kaka, Brooklyn'. She heard a siren getting louder as it came towards the house. There was a crunch of gravel as an ambulance turned into the driveway followed by a police car. Without further thought, Lauren picked up the notebook and slipped it into her shoulder bag. The police wouldn't see any significance in it but she might.

THE APPOINTMENT BOOK was not an everyday diary, Lauren realised as she flicked through the pages the following morning. It turned out to be Harold's record of bird sightings. This was the first time she had taken a proper look at it. The discovery of Harold's body had so shaken her that she had felt unable to touch the diary when she arrived home, after she and Michael had given statements to the police. She was fretting about the suicide note. What did Harold mean by saying he was ashamed of himself? The diary might provide a clue, but it had lurked in her handbag until now when she sat down at the dining room table, drew a deep breath and pulled it out.

She turned to the day of Nat's drowning, holding her breath. Yes, there was an entry in telegraphic style. 'O.B. pipit x 2'. Lauren puzzled over the entry. Owhiro Bay, surely? So close to where Nat had gone in. Pipit–they are a coastal bird, she knew, so that would make sense.

Lauren pushed the diary aside. But what kind of evidence was the pipit? She imagined a courtroom scene, TV style, where she was being shredded by a smooth-talking defence lawyer. 'Pipit, at Owhiro Bay, madam? Could it not be Ocean Beach? Or Otaki Beach? Surely pipits are endemic and you can find them anywhere in New Zealand. That's according to nzbirdsonline. Perhaps ornithology is not your strong suit?'

She stood up, told herself to stop crossing unbuilt bridges. The note and the diary were material evidence that pointed to Harold. Perhaps Ellie was right. Her nerves were still jangled, and she slammed the diary into the kitchen drawer, receptacle for keys and bus timetables. Time for a coffee.

22

'Two funerals in a month,' Lauren complained to Michael as they again drove up the motorway to Lower Hutt. 'First Nat's, now Harold. Upsetting, even though I wasn't close to either of them.' She grimaced, recalling a different kind of closeness, clutching Harold's lifeless body as she cut the rope from the garage rafters.

'Who's coming, do you know?' Michael asked. He was attending as chair of the new Climate Protection Society. He could hardly not go, given his role in discovering Harold's body. Lauren and he had already decided that Harold probably meant them to be the people who found him, given that they had an appointment–and neither of them cared to think about that.

'Pam cried off,' Lauren replied, 'and Ellie, who thinks Harold could have been Nat's killer, certainly didn't want to attend. Even though she knew Harold because he hung around Nat.'

'Do you really think he's a suspect?' He corrected himself. 'Was a suspect?'

Lauren realised she hadn't mentioned filching the diary. Best not, even though Michael was someone she trusted. 'Maybe,' she said cautiously, and was relieved that they were nearly there.

'Destination on the left in two hundred metres,' said the phone's navigator.

'There it is, look. At least there's a crowd outside. He seemed such an isolated man, I didn't know what to expect.' Lauren wrinkled her brow.

The chapel was part of the funeral home. Lauren was relieved that it wasn't a church building, she hadn't been looking forward to proselytising. The chapel was modern with seating for about a hundred. As people entered and took their seats, it became half full.

Lauren and Michael perched near the back and Lauren unabashedly stared at people as they came in. From what she could see, the front couple of rows consisted of family groups, no doubt relatives. She didn't know if Harold had brothers and sisters or even if his parents were still alive. Who the other mourners were, she had no idea. Perhaps previous workmates, neighbours, bird watchers.

The service was conventionally Christian, taken by a gaunt man wearing a dog collar. Lauren wondered if that was what Harold would have wanted, remembering what Ellie had said about his fundamentalist family. The pastor's opening remarks were sensitive. After acknowledging that Harold had taken his own life, he said, 'We're here today to honour Harold's life and support one another in our grief.'

The order of service had been printed and distributed. It was tightly structured with hymns and prayers. Lauren felt a lump in her throat when the organist broke into the opening notes of 'The Lord is my Shepherd'. That had been sung at Nat's funeral too, common for funerals, but still moving. She felt comforted by Michael's steady baritone. He clearly knew the words.

Only two speakers were listed for the tributes. The first, a shrunken older man in a dark suit a few sizes too big for him, turned out to be Harold's uncle. He spoke haltingly, remembering Harold as a child, mentioning how much Harold had enjoyed his grandparents' bach at Hukeri and how distressing for the whole family when it had to be abandoned to the sea. It was clear that Harold's becoming a draughtsman and a public servant was seen by the family as doing well. The uncle ended with a long pause, not seeming to know what to say. He shook his head and made his way painfully back to his seat.

Lauren thought it must be terribly difficult to pay tribute when suicide was the cause of death. Perhaps his family thought suicide was a sinful act.

The other speaker, who identified himself as Barry, was much more upbeat. He told the mourners that Harold, despite his reserve, was a good sort, always ready to volunteer for environmental activities. 'Only a couple of weeks ago, I needed help with some work on the scout hut up in the Orongorongos. I called on Harold at the last minute and he put down whatever he was doing and tramped in with me to spend the whole day repainting. When we took a break for lunch we spotted birds poking about in the river shallows. Harold was very excited to see a pipit, reckoned they were quite rare in these parts. It was a long day, near to dark before we made it back to the car park, but that was the kind of man he was, always ready to lend a hand.' He too paused, choked up and left the platform abruptly.

A pipit! Lauren sat up abruptly in her seat and Michael looked at her puzzled. She shook her head, the funeral was coming to an end and they stood for the committal. The coffin was carried out, Barry among the pallbearers and Lauren pushed through the crowd to stand near the coffin as it was put into the hearse.

'Excuse me,' she interrupted Barry who was turning to another woman. 'Can I ask you something?'

'Sure,' he replied politely, but looked puzzled. They extracted themselves from the crush and moved to one side. Lauren said, 'Can you remember exactly what the date was when you were in the Orongorongos?'

Barry was amazed. 'Why do you want to know?'

Lauren grasped for a reason and found herself telling a fib. 'I'm a keen birdwatcher too and I know Harold would have wanted me to record his pipit sighting.'

Barry continued to look amazed, but politely tried to remember. 'It was a Sunday–two weeks ago–that would have been the fourth–the guy I was going to go with had to take his boy to cricket.'

'Thank you so much, I'm sorry for pulling you away.' Lauren was gushing now. Barry nodded, and turned away. Lauren stood still for a moment, her thoughts in a whirl. If it wasn't Harold, who was arguing with Nat on the beach? Ellie had the wrong end of the stick, thinking it was Harold. That left Rodger and Derek in the frame. She sighed and looked for Michael. As she approached, he said, 'What was all that about?'

'Well, Harold's ruled out,' Lauren replied.

Michael raised his eyebrows, but since Lauren hadn't told him about the diary, she certainly wasn't going into long explanations about how OB wasn't Owhiro Bay, but must have been Orongorongos Barry. 'Never mind, let's get back to Wellington.'

As they drove back, Lauren was subdued. She felt obscurely guilty. Taking Ellie's lead she had suspected an innocent man. She had gone to the funeral not out of respect for him or even because she and Michael had discovered his body. Top of her mind had been that she might learn something useful by observing the funeral goers. Now she was left with just the memory of this sad man, Harold. And had his failure to be confirmed as chair of the Climate Protection Society provoked his suicide? In which case, she and Michal were implicated, having plotted his downfall. She found herself wringing her hands, and grasped them firmly together.

Michael had also been silent. Perhaps he was feeling guilty too. 'Do you think he did it because of us?'

'No,' Michael said, almost harshly. 'I think he was gay.'

Lauren was puzzled. 'What's that got to do with it? Did you know that? Was there a relationship gone sour?'

'No, no, no!' Michael banged the steering wheel. 'It's those bloody fundamentalists sitting there brought it all back.'

Lauren knew Michael had left politics because of a blackmail attempt during the Lange years. He had avoided the past by working in Africa for many years. Now he looked pale and angry. He continued. 'Those families in the front row, they reminded me of growing up out here. People were so rigid and conventional, the men mowed the lawns and the women did the domestic stuff. Some families were happy, some weren't, but they all kept up appearances.

'My God, I was buttoned up as a teenager, hiding a shameful secret, but I bet you anything Harold had a shameful secret too. It would have been much worse for him. He wasn't the sort of guy who would find his way into the gay scene–shy, nervous, unprepossessing and with the might of the fundies working against him.'

Lauren considered this. 'I think you've nailed it. He must have been brave to become an activist, even if he did stay on the right side of the law.'

'I'm guessing he had a crush on Nat, but we'll never know. His note wasn't very informative and I don't suppose he kept a diary or anything personal like that.'

Lauren was glad Michael had his eyes on the road and didn't see her blush. Anyhow, the diary was not confessional. Michael seemed to have forgotten that he didn't know why Lauren had ruled out Harold. She turned the conversation to other subjects.

23

The weather had turned foul again. Lauren had hoped for a fine weekend, so that she could go walking. She needed the exercise. And she reckoned a brisk walk really did help her thought processes. But this spring–or now early summer–seemed more changeable than any Lauren could recall. The daily temperatures rose gradually but a fine still day here or there was interspersed with northerly gales, annoying despite the sunshine, or worse, howling southerlies bringing cold and rain. It was a southerly day. Lauren sighed. Harold was no longer a suspect, and her investigation was feeling stuck. She couldn't see how to make progress investigating Rodger, and Derek was down on the ice. Not that she wanted to confront him in person. Of course–she could be checking with Pam how her investigation into his scientific standing was going.

She'd been sitting in a comfy chair in front of the fan heater, a half-drunk coffee and her current novel on the small table by her side. Now she got up and found her phone, before settling back down again. Pam answered her call almost immediately.

'Hi Pam. Are you busy or have you time to talk?'

'Sure do, I was going to spend the morning at the garden, but now look at it. I'd be blown off the hillside.'

'Fortitude, Pam,' she said, 'this is only a bit of weather.' As she spoke, she stretched her slippered feet out towards the heater. 'I rang to ask how your investigation into Derek is going?'

Pam muttered something, sounding guilty.

'What was that?' Lauren felt a wave of impatience. 'We've got to step it up, the trail's going cold.'

'I haven't got as far as I hoped,' Pam confessed. 'It's a tricky business. I've collected all his scientific papers. That wasn't easy because now I'm retired–and even when I was at the Ministry–we didn't have access to all the academic databases.' She lowered her voice. 'Don't tell anyone, Lauren, but before Ro left, she gave me her university user name and password, so now I can get everything I need.'

'Hardly the crime of the century.' Lauren tried not to scoff. But honestly! 'What have you found?' she asked, trying to keep her tone reasonable.

'He's probably outside his area of expertise in making that council submission. He's a meteorologist not a geographer.'

Lauren suppressed a 'so what?'. Pam was no doubt going to tell her anyway.

'His research field is Antarctic weather patterns. He's making a name for himself by claiming that his fellow scientists have exaggerated sea level rising.'

'Is his science shonky?' Lauren asked.

'I'm being as thorough as I can.' Pam sounded defensive. 'There's a lot of stuff to wade through and it's not really my field.'

Lauren tried to remember what Pam's field was before she became a policy wonk. Bugs, she thought. Pam always had something to say about the vast array of insect species that enjoyed their home in the community garden. 'Weather, right?' said Lauren, trying to get Pam to the point. 'Free and frank advice, that's what I expect from a former public servant.' She thought a joke might lighten Pam up.

'There's a big debate going on, it's to do with whether some Pacific Islands like Tuvalu will be totally overwhelmed by sea level rise. Some respectable scientists say there's two processes going on at once, sea levels and land accretion, which may mitigate each other.'

'Yes,' Lauren said, twiddling a pen.

'Meteorological factors may have something to do with mitigation and that's where Derek has made his contribution.'

'Or not?' said Lauren hopefully.

'It looks like his first studies were well received, but his recent Antarctic data has been challenged. Apparently there's a frightful stink brewing up at Vic. When Ro gave me her library password she told me the gossip is that there's some sort of investigation pending. He was very nearly refused permission to go on the ice this summer, and some extra checks have been put in place.'

'But what's all this to do with not having the expertise to do the Wellington City Council submission?'

'That's a bit more difficult,' Pam said.

Lauren sighed. They didn't seem to be getting anywhere.

'I'm trying to find out how specialised geographic mapping is, and whether a scientist from a related discipline could easily do it.'

Lauren rolled her eyes. 'But,' Pam went on, 'apparently Nat was on to something. He'd got one of his climate activist mates who works for GNS to look at Derek's mapping.'

'But how did he get hold of the submission?'

'Don't know, maybe they've been publicly released. But anyhow, this guy reckoned the maps were ridiculous, just coloured drawings he said, not based on any known data.'

'Wow!' Now Lauren was beginning to get excited. 'So was Nat doing more than just putting in a counter-submission?'

'Ellie's been looking through his papers. There was a draft press release accusing Derek of scientific fraud.'

24

Ro rolled out of her bunk. It was her third day at Scott Base and she was beginning to feel comfortable with the routine. Pull on her warm jacket and socks, grab a quick hot shower, towel and dress as fast as possible. Then to the dining room for breakfast and the day's briefing.

She had signed up for today's trip to New Zealand's meteorological research lab at Arrival Heights. It was about six kilometres from the base and the scientists worked regular shifts, coming back to base for the main meal and to sleep. She would be off in the bus with them after breakfast, but she wouldn't be expected to wait out the full shift. The visitors would be transported on to McMurdo for lunch at the American base.

She was beginning to recognize some of the faces behind the beards and had struck up conversations with a number of the women scientists, who mostly were interested in her project, although one or two felt uncomfortable talking about gender and sexism. They wanted to be treated exactly the same as the men, and preferred to avoid noticing if they weren't.

Derek was on the bus, she noticed. She'd assumed that he would be, since she'd learnt that his specialty was atmospheric research, but all the same it was a downer. He raised his eyebrows to acknowledge her and she scrambled to sit as far away as possible. Then she remembered she was meant to be observing him.

The lab was 180 metres above sea level, in a volcanic cone. She noticed how much colder it was as they disembarked. The odd snowflake was falling, but not covering the gravel turning circle. She took in the view, including the large cluster of buildings in the distance that made up McMurdo, much bigger than Scott Base. They were ushered inside, passing through the freezer-type door that she was becoming familiar with. Her first impression of the lab was an overwhelming mass of beeping instruments. The scientists quickly took seats at their workstations while the travellers were still struggling out of their cold weather gear.

A woman was assigned to the four visitors. Ro enjoyed being shown around and the lecture they were given about measuring atmospheric pressure was surprisingly interesting. That finished, there were a couple of hours to fill in before their transport arrived. Rodney, the artist of the group, said he'd like to wander around outside and see if he could find a good sketching spot. Ro, who was feeling rather confined in the small busy space, said she'd come with him.

They donned their gear yet again, signed out of the lab, taking walking poles and a radio, compulsory equipment for anyone walking away from base. They stepped outside onto the gravel area. The sky was blue, with clouds banked up on the horizon, and once again the view struck her as breathtaking.

Since it was such a short distance to McMurdo, only one and a half kilometres, Ro told Rodney that she would walk there instead of going on the bus, and could he let their guide know? By now he was perched on a stool and absorbed with his sketching. He stopped to look at her. 'You'd better take the radio.'

'No, you keep it, it has to go back to the lab. I can see McMurdo from here.'

She set off down the ill-formed rutted road, its edges marked with red flags. Her feet crunched on the ice, but although the slope was steep, her heavy boots and the tyre marks pitting the roadway gave her good traction.

Once she was a couple of hundred metres away from the lab, descending quickly, she became aware of the stillness in the air. There were no noises and no movement discernible, just a very faint occasional rumble, presumably from vehicles moving around at McMurdo. It felt like the end of the world–and it was! This was the experience she was hoping for when she decided to come to the ice–it was what so many of the women wrote about. Alone, all alone.

A breeze picked up quite suddenly and Ro shivered, pulling her scarf and hat more tightly into place. She was at the bottom of the hill now and McMurdo did not look too far away. The cloud bank had gathered, blotting out the sun, and the landscape had changed colour as snow began to fall, at first softly and then more heavily. The world became white, snow covering the dirty tyre tracks, snow in the air reducing visibility and almost obscuring the next marker flag. The sky above her was white as well. She could no longer see the base, but felt confident that the red flags would guide her.

Ro trudged on, conscious of an eerie sensation induced by the blotting out of the world. Her poles grounded her, making a tapping noise as they connected with the ice beneath the snow, which was building up into a thick layer very rapidly. It seemed colder, despite her descent from the hill.

She heard the noise of an engine behind her and suddenly felt afraid. She was walking on the road, after all, and the vehicle would surely not be able to see her until it ran right into her. She picked up her pace and got to the next flag, then stepped to one side. There appeared to be a small hillock on the side of the road, perhaps where the track had been graded. She clambered up and then lost her footing, slithering down the other side. The engine noise came nearer and the ghostly shape of the Humvee, travelling very slowly, loomed up. Ro called out, but of course no one would hear her from the hermetically sealed cabin.

She floundered in the gathering snow. By the time she had regained her footing and begun waving her arms, all she could see was the ghostly shape of the vehicle. In a moment it had vanished completely. 'Shit! They must have expected me to be on the road but they've missed me.'

Ro picked up her poles and made her way onto the road and began trudging in the direction of McMurdo. It was a whiteout, but at least the tyre tracks were fresh. She could not see from one flag to the next, but following the tracks kept her going.

It was very cold now, and snow was falling even more thickly. The tracks were becoming covered. Ro was out of breath. A moment of panic overcame her. She told herself to get a grip. She should count the steps from one flag to the next. She began, 'One...two...three... four....' It was only twenty paces, right, so she should count from every flag and turn back if she failed to reach one. Her fingers and toes felt cold despite the warm gloves and boots. 'Just keep going,' she told herself sternly. 'It isn't far.'

Her self-talk couldn't defeat the panic rising within her. She started to shiver. Suddenly a shape loomed up in front of her. 'Got you,' a rough voice sang out.

Oh no, she thought, surely it wasn't Derek! She felt a momentary relief and stumbled towards him. He grabbed her arm and stared right into her face. 'Bloody tourist. We've been searching and searching. I've got a good mind to leave you out here.' She shrank from his touch, but she had no alternative but to allow him to take hold of her and march her along. A small group soon appeared out of the white landscape.

'Ro! We were worried about you.' Alison's voice was calm but rang with tension. 'Are you OK?'

Ro stumbled, as Derek released her. 'I'm so sorry, I fell over a bank trying to get out of the way and you sailed right past me. I'm OK.' She hesitated and her teeth chattered. 'My fingers and toes felt cold a while ago but I can't feel them now.'

'Let's get you to McMurdo and their doctor can check you out.' Alison spoke firmly as she took Ro's arm. 'Then we'll have a debrief.'

Derek sneered. 'That won't be much fun for you. Alison is famous for her tellings-off.'

'That's enough, Derek, let's get her inside.'

A couple of hours later Ro was tucked up warmly in a visitor's bunk. The doctor had identified the first stages of frostbite in several of her fingers and toes and had treated them by warming them gradually. 'No tots of rum, though,' she joked to Ro. 'We don't do that any more–makes things worse!'

Ro lay in the bunk, brooding over her folly. How humiliating to be rescued by Derek, when she was supposed to be keeping an eye on him. He'd managed to make her feel small, not at all like one of the competent women she was looking forward to writing about.

Then there was a knock followed by the door opening gently. It was Miriam. 'Whatever have you been up to?' The harshness of the words was belied by Miriam's concerned tone.

'Guess I just wandered off,' Ro replied. 'Everything looked clear, I could see McMurdo in the distance, but the weather just closed in.'

'That's why we have all these safety protocols. You're going to get a razzing from Alison, I bet. Leaving the radio behind is serious. At least they found you easily, or so that prick, Derek Drysdall, says. He's in the bar, telling a good story.'

Ro groaned. 'Of all the people.... I was relieved to see him, but hell, I'm never going to live this down.'

'Yes, he really is a swine, and I heard....' She paused, 'But maybe I shouldn't say.'

'I'm all ears,' said Ro.

'Well–he may not be in Antarctica again. He got into a fight with a Texan here at McMurdo, came off worst. Fighting is an absolute no-no on the ice and Alison says they'll recommend barring him, though he can appeal.'

'What was the fight about?'

'The big guy accused him of fabricating data.'

25

More information about Derek came from an unexpected quarter. Lauren was sitting at her table, finishing her breakfast coffee when the doorbell rang. Her first thought was to be pleased that the bell was working. Most of her friends just knocked and called out, and during the day the door was unsnibbed, so that they could walk in.

This was early for anyone else to be calling. When she opened the door, she could hardly believe her eyes. Rodger Brixton. But Rodger Brixton in distress. No longer the unmemorable man she'd visited. Now he looked haunted. His beard no longer neat, his clothes no longer fresh and tidy, and his face. His face! His eyes were red, almost swollen, with big bags beneath them.

Lauren's reaction was involuntary. 'What's wrong?' Then quickly, 'What are you doing here?'

He answered the first question. 'Nothing.' Then, 'Can I come in? I need to talk to you.'

Lauren had recovered from her shock and spoke sharply, 'How did you know where I live?'

'Oh please,' he said, 'you've still got a landline, haven't you? I looked you up in the phone book–same way you found me, I suppose.'

Lauren subsided. She'd been meaning to get rid of her landline. Only an elderly cousin and a friend who lived in Invercargill used it. His visit reminded her to stop putting it off.

'What do you want?' she said, continuing to block the doorway.

He put a hand out, leant against the frame of the doorway. 'Do you think I could come in? I've something important to tell you about Nat Spiller.'

Lauren was incredulous. Now he wanted to talk about Nat? What had changed? There was a pause, she stood in the doorway, he stood leaning against its frame. Then, 'OK, come in,' she said. 'I take it this isn't a confession.'

It was his turn to sound astonished. 'What on earth do you mean?' he said. She shrugged and gestured at him to come inside.

They sat down at the table. Lauren pushed aside her breakfast cup and leant forward. 'So what's changed your mind? Last time we spoke, you said anything you had to tell was none of my business.'

'Look,' he said, then paused. He was clearly nervous. Lauren watched him unconsciously tracing circles on the table with his middle finger. Then he stopped and looked directly at her. 'I thought about it and I did what you asked. I don't want a police record. So I haven't been near Ellie. But I can't stand it any longer, I have to see her, make her understand. She needs me–and once she's sorted out the stuff about Nat's death she'll see that. So if I tell you what I know, you've got to tell Ellie it was me who put you on the right track. In the end, she'll be much happier with me than with that show pony.'

Nat a show pony? Lauren checked herself from interrupting, but he read her face. 'All right, he was genuinely concerned about the environment but he always managed to make sure it was his face in the photographs, his voice on the radio, him pontificating on the TV.'

He stopped. 'Never mind all that, that's not why I'm here. I heard the gossip that Ellie thinks it was murder. So I had something to tell her and you warned me off. OK, I've decided to tell you now, as long as she knows it was me that helped.' His voice cracked, and he brushed a hand across his eyes.

Lauren almost felt sorry for him, but remembered how badly he'd behaved. She'd been leaning forward, her body taut. Now she allowed herself to relax, sat back and said, 'What can you tell me?'

He in turn sat up, leant on the table, swallowed and said, 'You know I'm in the Planning Department at the council. So we had to look at that Spiller Construction project at Lyall Bay. What a lot of nonsense that was,' he continued and seemed about to go off on a tangent about the development.

Lauren interrupted. 'When was this?'

'Not long before Nat was drowned–a week or so I reckon. Justin Spiller came into the office with his mate Derek. They were wanting to see Nat's submission, but it hadn't been lodged. I wasn't dealing with them, but they were hyper, I could hear the fuss right across the office. That guy Derek was really going to town, said he'd get Nat for this.'

'For what?' Lauren interrupted again. 'His submission wasn't even there.'

'They must have known what he was planning to say. He must have told Justin. It was really stupid the way Derek was working himself up. The silliest thing was that it would have made no difference whether or not Nat had put in a submission–Council was never going to agree to them building on that flat land, because they'd had internal Council advice on what's likely to happen.'

'So why are you telling me this?'

'Isn't it obvious? If I were you I'd look at what Derek Drysdall was up to, round the time of Nat's death.'

When Rodger had gone, Lauren thought about the way he'd presented and what he'd said. Surely he wouldn't have come to see her, if it had been he who killed Nat. Unless he was the killer and was trying to put her off the scent. She just couldn't credit that. And what a mess he was! Did he really think Ellie would fall into his arms because he'd come up with some helpful information? She shook her head, he was dreaming. But what he said about Derek. Derek was going to 'get Nat for this'? 'This' had to be more than just a submission against Spiller Construction's proposal. Rodger wouldn't have known Nat was going to accuse Derek of scientific fraud. She smiled briefly at the idea of Derek's 'coloured drawings', then frowned. Derek must have found out Nat was going to expose him–no doubt Justin had warned him. The evidence was piling up, but they still had to put Derek in the frame. Was it he who was arguing with Nat on the beach? What happened then? She hoped Ro might have something to tell her.

26

Lauren paced around her living room. She was expecting Ro to phone. She'd already texted her a couple of times, but there had been no response. Ro had been due back on a flight from Christchurch the previous evening. Lauren had offered to pick her up from the airport but Ro had already made an arrangement with her neighbour.

She decided to drive over to Wadestown. Stopping along Wakefield Street, she picked up bagels from the bakery and, thinking again about the likelihood of anything approaching a decent coffee at Ro's, ordered a couple of flat whites as well. It was an expensive stop-off as she was shamed into buying a reusable mug and then, feeling quite wrong-footed, bought a second one for Ro's coffee. She thought crossly that it was bloody expensive saving the planet.

The city was busy with the lead-up to Christmas, even though it was well past the morning rush hour. The coffee filled the car with a tempting aroma, reminding her as she passed through the government district that the unmistakeable smell of the capital was coffee. It was not like that when she had arrived back in the nineteen-eighties, but by the nineteen-nineties the flat white–Wellington's contribution to world culture–dominated the city's smellscape. If that was what you could call it.

Still musing, Lauren pulled into the small dead-end street leading to Ro's house, miraculously finding a parking spot. Ro answered the door sleepily. 'God, Lauren, what time is it?' She wrinkled her nose. 'Coffee time, I guess.'

'Bagels too.' Lauren rattled the brown paper bag. She stepped into the hall, avoiding the usual jumble, this morning mainly consisting of dumped travel gear. Once seated at the dining table, she began her interrogation.

Ro had just started on a paean of praise for all things Antarctica but Lauren interrupted the flow. 'I'm sure you've had the most amazing experiences, but can you tell me about them later. I want to know if you've got anything on Derek.'

Ro pouted, but obediently changed tack. She caught Lauren up with the whole story of her misadventure, how frightened she had been by Derek's hostility when he found her in the snowstorm and how humiliating it had been to be told by Miriam that he was making a good story of it in the bar at McMurdo.

'That sounds so scary, Ro. Are you all right now?'

Ro waved her fingers at Lauren, wiggling them. 'I'm wiggling my toes too, all functioning now, but it was alarming when I lost the feeling in them.'

'So,' Lauren summed up. 'It shows that Derek is a nasty piece of work, but it doesn't add to the evidence against him. Anything else you can think of?'

Ro picked up her brand new reusable mug and gestured with it. 'Yes, I just remembered. Apparently he got into a punch-up with a Texan who made a crack about him fudging the data. Derek came off worst. Anyhow, news of that got back to Scott Base and it means he won't be on the programme next year. That's what Alison told me. She seemed relieved.'

'Did she say anything about Derek's data?'

Ro looked thoughtful. 'I guess she hinted but down on the ice they have a strict code against gossip and stirring up people. They all have to get along.'

'Mmm,' Lauren replied. 'Sounds like there is something to it–he's got a temper and he's been cooking the books. He must have been furious to hear about Nat's submission, and we have information from another source that he threatened to get Nat.'

'Really?' said Ro, but she was starting to droop, clearly tired from the journey home.

'I'll tell you more later,' Lauren said, standing up. 'You look as if you need a quiet day. Don't forget we've got the meeting to organise the orphans' Christmas outing tomorrow.' She gave Ro a hug and saw herself out.

THE ORPHANS who shared an annual Christmas jaunt were not all technically orphaned. As a group, they were of an age where few had parents still living, unless they had reached alarming ages. Megan's mother was now a hundred and three. And it seemed to the others that it would have been cruel to exclude Megan from their annual Christmas plans.

The group was not fixed from year to year. Many had offspring and some, like Lauren, were grandparents. With the geographical spread of adult children, their presence at the family festivities wasn't always possible. Those without children sometimes spent Christmas with other family, but sometimes it was better to be away with a group of friends, than have your carefully chosen gift for a favourite nephew disappear underfoot in a hail of wrapping paper and tawdry plastic crap.

So the annual orphans' Christmas outing survived and was remarkably free of tension. Last year, they'd walked the Queen Charlotte Track; this year, they planned to be lazier. Keri, who usually took responsibility for the trips, had already emailed the group to suggest renting a couple of baches she knew about at Hukeri, a small coastal settlement north of New Plymouth. The name Hukeri rang a bell with Lauren when the email turned up. She'd heard that name recently. Then she'd remembered. It was where Harold's grandparents had had their house fall into the sea.

The group met in Megan's Oriental Bay apartment to discuss practicalities.

'The baches are pretty basic,' Keri said. 'They belong to two families, friends of my uncle. I was there a few years ago when Dad and his brothers were whitebaiting. They're near the lagoon, lovely situation, but we won't have all the mod cons.'

'Outside dunnies?' asked Karen.

''Afraid so.' Keri was straight-faced. 'Not many spiders, though. Any problems with that?'

'Put toilet paper on the list, then.' Megan wasn't about to confess that she didn't care to go outside in the middle of the night.

A list of all the non-perishables needed for a week's stay was made up. Keri said there was a general store in the village but it would be shut on Christmas Day. They'd have to get milk and so on in New Plymouth on the way. 'There are fridges, Uncle said, but they're beer fridges with a tiny freezer. You know the sort, you can keep a block of icecream frozen in the middle, but not around the edges.'

Lauren thought this was starting to sound a bit grim, and Ro said, 'No turkey then! What are we going to do for Christmas dinner?'

Pam replied, 'Smoked fish is the best keeper and we can get sliced ham.'

Keri said, 'We can do whitebait fritters as well–we'll get frozen whitebait from the general store on Christmas Eve and keep it in a chilly bin.'

Pam tut-tutted disapprovingly and began to talk about disappearing fish populations, but was drowned out in the oohs and aahs of appreciation from everyone else.

27

Lauren woke to the sound of gulls screaming as they wheeled across the sky. It was light but it still felt early. She couldn't consult her phone; it was with her clothes on top of her bag and she was in a top bunk. Lucky she remembered that before rolling out of bed. There were gentle snores from beneath her, where Keri slept on. The odd beep from the bed across the room suggested that Karen was playing a game on her phone.

Lauren clambered down, and tiptoed outside. It had the makings of a glorious day. She walked barefoot through the long dewy grass towards the edge of the estuary. A mother duck swam by with her ducklings. She could see the beach from where she stood, perhaps 400 metres away. The sound of crashing waves and the smell of salt was invigorating.

She decided to go for a walk. Her boots were in the pile at the door, socks still in them, and she decided that the tracksuit bottoms and t-shirt she had on would do for an early morning stroll. She wanted the exercise after sitting in the van for hours the day before. She was also keen to see the cliffs she'd been reading about in *New Zealand Geographic*. Hukeri was one of the most vulnerable seaside communities in the country. With every storm, pockets of land fell into the ocean and some dwellings had already been taken. Coastal erosion was unremarkable in New Zealand but it was getting worse as the climate changed and the sea rose. Lauren remembered that the article had said there were seventeen thousand kilometres of coastline in New Zealand really close to where most people lived.

She cut along a track by the river bank, making for the road bridge that crossed the estuary. Traffic was light, only the occasional car swooshing by. The tiny village was deserted, too. She stopped to read the notices on the window of the Four Square store. Outboards, fishing tackle for sale, bed and breakfast accommodation. Then a notice for a community meeting on Boxing Day. On Boxing Day! That seemed a weird time for a community meeting, Then she realised why. It was addressed to bach owners to give them a chance to discuss the council's proposal of managed retreat for some properties, as well as the proposed subdivision close to the crumbling cliffs.

Lauren walked on, finding a footpath leading towards the sea. The roar of the surf was pervasive, practically the only sound except for the gulls. Her reverie was interrupted by the dinging of a bell. A small girl rode past her, wobbling slightly, on a shiny new bike, obviously a Christmas present.

Within sight of the beach the track veered abruptly to the north. It came close to the cliffs and the damage became apparent. The old track was blocked off and the new one took a more inland route. A dilapidated shed leaned dramatically over the cliff, a landslide of clay and boulders visible underneath. Further on, an abandoned house. It looked as if its back garden had fallen into the sea. Bean-poles leaned at a crazy angle, there were lawn and garden plants still growing on top of the earth that had fallen down, and wreckage, perhaps another shed, on the beach below. Lauren wondered if that could have been the house that was talked about at Harold's funeral–his grandparents', she remembered.

She turned back. She'd lost track of the time, she must get back to the others. They'd be starting to prepare for their Christmas feast.

Christmas Day passed in a joyful haze of eating, drinking and lazing around. No turkey or roast lamb as a centrepiece for the main meal, but the whitebait fritters more than made up for it. The no-present rule was strictly observed but plenty of treats were produced. There were liqueurs and chocolates and a divine Christmas pudding from Karen's great-grandmother's recipe. Pam had brought weird herbal cordials, as well as her own selection of dried fruits and nuts.

Megan had pulled out at the last minute, after her sister had pleaded with her to go down to the farm, since it would be the last Christmas her nearly grown children were at home, and, 'Touch wood,' she'd said, 'you never know how long Mum'll be around.' So to make up for abandoning them, she had slipped into Keri's van two kilos of cherries from Central Otago–the big fat dark red ones bursting with sweetness.

On Boxing Day Lauren was restless. She hadn't yet settled into holiday mode. The investigation was troubling her, in spite of her plan to take a break from thinking about it. She was pleased when Ro suggested that they go for a walk. They retraced her route of Christmas morning. As they walked by the village, they noticed cars pulling up outside a white stucco building. Hukeri War Memorial Hall, 1952, the red letters across the eaves pronounced. 'That must be the meeting I was reading about.'

'What's that?' Ro said.

'It's about the properties at risk from the cliffs crumbling. Let's go in and see what's going on.'

Ro looked doubtful. 'Why? It's not as if you have any special interest in the place.'

'I don't know why, I'm just curious.' Lauren walked across the gravel car park and into the hall's entryway. Ro had little choice but to follow her, looking sceptical.

There was quite a hubbub inside, about thirty people seated on benches. They could hear angry muttering. A guy was standing on the stage operating PowerPoint slides displayed on a large screen. What was showing appeared to be a map of the coastal area, with different colours drawn on it. 'These are just projections,' he was saying, 'and we can't predict where each subsidence will occur. It depends on the tides and wind direction and storm intensity, as well as what plants are holding the cliffs together. But we can be fairly sure that we'll lose a couple of metres a year on the average, and within ten years many of the clifftop houses will be gone.'

'Bullshit!' An older red-faced man stood up. 'These cliffs have been crumbly for years, ever since I've been coming here. I reckon they'll see me out and I don't care what happens afterwards, I'm not going to move.'

The guy on the stage spoke again. 'As I said, we don't know where the cliff will collapse next. You must be aware that some people have already lost their houses'–Lauren remembered Harold's grandparents again–'and any of yours could go at any time. We want a planned withdrawal from the cliff tops.'

There was a mixture of tut-tutting and murmurs of agreement. A woman stood up. 'Some of us would be prepared to move if we got proper compensation, but all you guys are doing with your gloomy talk is lowering property prices. I bet that's so the council won't have to pay so much to buy us out, if they're even going to buy us out.'

'Hear, hear,' said someone, and others clapped.

A Maori guy stood up. 'Kia ora, everyone. This is only a problem because people built houses along the cliff when they shouldn't have. Our settlements have always been on the river. Nobody listened to us back then. You have to have respect for Tangaroa.'

There was a muttering and someone interrupted, 'How does that help with the situation we're in now, and who the hell is Tangaroa?'

The Maori guy carried on, unruffled. 'Tangaroa is the sea god. But what I want to say is that we shouldn't spend our council's money putting right what was wrong in the first place. And it's hard to believe there's a new subdivision giving cheap sections near the cliff top. Kia ora.' He sat down, and a few other people murmured, 'Kia ora.'

Ro nudged Lauren. 'Let's go,' she whispered. Their exit was scarcely noticed and as they left, they could hear someone saying that compensation had already been agreed on, not the amounts, but it wasn't for this meeting to relitigate it.

'That was fascinating, wasn't it?' said Lauren when they were out of earshot.

'I guess so,' Ro looked doubtful, 'but I'd rather be out walking than stuck in a meeting.'

The weather remained sunny and hot. As they walked, Lauren kept thinking how, if climate change went unchecked, there would be communities all over the country torn in strife over this sort of issue, not resolvable. All the more reason to persuade local bodies to reduce their carbon emissions. She decided that her New Year's resolution would be to dedicate herself to climate action. There were not enough activists pushing for change–how someone like Nat would be missed. She reflected that this was one resolution she needed to keep.

Their days were filled with swims and walks. Along the sand, around the estuary, and along trails they found in the regenerated bush that ran down to the estuary near the village.

Halfway through their visit Ro declared herself 'sunned out'. Her fair skin that went with her red hair was pinker than usual. She asked who would like to drive down to New Plymouth to see the Len Lye exhibition, now permanently displayed at the Govett-Brewster gallery. Lauren was keen, and Keri, so the three of them took the van, trying to remember all the last minute suggestions from the others of things they might need that were lacking in the village shop. More pinot gris! More cherries! More chocolate!

Hukeri was out of cellphone range. That made it a real holiday, Lauren thought. But she took her phone with her on the drive to see who might have been texting or emailing. As they drove nearer to New Plymouth she turned her phone on and it pinged, filling with messages and emails.

'Well, that's unexpected. A text from Deirdre.' Lauren tried to sound nonchalant. 'She's driving down the island tomorrow, thought she'd call in and visit–and she's got whanau here. She might stay overnight with them.'

Keri said, 'Whanau here? She's probably some sort of cousin of mine.'

At the same time Ro said, 'I bet it's not them she's coming to see.'

Lauren hoped she wasn't blushing. She hadn't told her friends about her and Deirdre's most recent encounter, except to say that she'd met up with Deirdre at the end of her Melbourne stint.

Back at the beach the next day, Lauren found it hard to settle. They'd worked out that Deirdre couldn't get to Hukeri before three at the earliest, but from lunchtime, every time she heard a vehicle, Lauren looked out to see if it might be Deirdre. Most of the group went swimming in the early afternoon, but Lauren refused and indeed, Deirdre did turn up while the others were down at the beach.

'Hello, so good to see you,' she said and kissed Lauren. On the cheek.

'Merry Christmas. Great you could drop by,' Lauren responded.

There was an awkward pause, then Lauren laughed. 'It was bound to be awkward, wasn't it?' she said. 'Come and have a cup of tea and then let's go for a walk, just the two of us.'

They went into the bach. Lauren introduced Deirdre to two of her holiday mates who were lying about reading, made tea for all of them, and then they set out.

They took what was already Lauren's favourite walk, past the general store, and along to the bridge, before it veered off to one of the bush tracks. By now they were less awkward with each other. Deirdre entertained Lauren with anecdotes about her Christmas with whanau and then explained what she would be doing in Wellington. 'I've been asked to attend a meeting reviewing the work of the Special Tactics group. They're New Zealand's counter-terrorism initiative. I'm not sure why I'm being asked to sit in, it's not my territory. Just before I was sent to Canberra my boss had me sitting in on a traffic policy strategy meeting, too.' She laughed. 'I decided that I must be really offside with him. Traffic policing isn't my favourite part of being in the police.'

'But you must see what's going on, Deirdre. I reckon you're being groomed. They're making sure you've got an overview of the whole organisation so that you're ready to move up the ladder.'

Deirdre had the grace to look embarrassed. 'I suppose that did cross my mind, but counter-terrorism? Traffic policing? Opposite ends of the spectrum, aren't they?'

Lauren agreed, then thought of something else. 'I don't want you to be too important. You wouldn't have time to give me advice.'

Deirdre looked at her. 'But you won't need any advice, that's all behind you.'

She saw Lauren's face. 'Oh no, don't tell me. That environmentalist you phoned me about?'

Lauren's voice rose over hers. 'I told you Ellie was sure it was murder. Now I've done some digging, and I believe her.'

Deirdre had stopped in the middle of the bush track. Now she stepped to the side and leant against a tree. 'You'd better tell me about your digging. I know I explained to you that you wouldn't be able to see the autopsy.'

Lauren tried not to sound pleased with herself. 'Yes, Phyl told me the same thing. But I was able to talk to the police about it, as Ellie's representative. And the bang on Nat's head could have been from hitting it on rocks, but equally could have been something else.'

'So what on earth have you been up to?' Deirdre was abrupt.

Lauren laid out her actions so far: talking to the police about the autopsy and to the sailor who tried to rescue Nat. '*He* thought the head wound looked suspicious,' she said. She explained how Ellie had mentioned a couple of people who had fallen out with Nat, and how the stalker had got on to the suspect list too. She went through what she, with Ro and Pam, had found out before the Christmas holiday, particularly Esther's sighting of two men arguing on the beach around the time that Nat went into the sea.

Deirdre pushed herself away from her tree and looked at the track ahead. 'Let's keep walking. Look, Lauren,' she said, as she stepped carefully over a mounded tree root, 'there doesn't seem to be any substantial evidence that it wasn't an accident. No smoking gun, no real suspects. Esther's evidence might have some traction, but it probably wouldn't be sufficient to open a homicide inquiry. Police look for motive, opportunity, evidence. And they have to have enough evidence to have a good chance of winning a case in court.'

She stopped and thought. 'Of course, it's always worth looking at the family. As you'll know, most homicides are carried out by family or people closely involved with the victim. But as for climate activism, it doesn't seem in itself to be a cause for homicide. You got the wrong end of the stick with Harold. Derek's obviously a nasty piece of work, but it doesn't make him a murderer. And you've already dismissed Rodger as a suspect. I think you're right, he's not likely to have murdered Nat, he's much more likely to harm Ellie.'

'Harm Ellie? No, he hasn't been near her since I warned him off.'

'Oh Lauren.' Deirdre was authoritative. 'The way you described him, he sounds suicidal. It's always a worry when a guy who has been obsessing about a failed relationship–or even a non-relationship, if it's a stalker–becomes suicidal. They have this nasty habit of believing that the object of their twisted affections is better off leaving the world with them. The mildest-seeming men can be very dangerous in that sort of situation. Did you tell anyone else about the state he was in?'

Lauren confessed that she hadn't. Deirdre went on, 'Mind you, it's hard to know who to tell. The police can't usually act unless there's a direct threat, and even then–well, I'm sure you've read about cases where women find it hard to get the police to take them seriously when they know they're in danger.'

Lauren was mortified. She should have thought to take some action. She'd been so intent on trying to figure out who might have killed Nat that she hadn't considered that Ellie might be in danger. She would talk to Pam about it when they got back to the bach. Meanwhile, she stuck to her guns, 'But Deirdre, not all the suspects have been ruled out. There's still Derek.'

Deirdre said, 'Or someone you haven't thought of yet. Look Lauren, I can understand the police letting it lie. They will have washed their hands of it and referred it to the coroner.'

Lauren sighed. Now the track was winding along beside the estuary. She stopped and stared at the water slurping gently at its edge. She said, 'We all know how treacherous the sea can be, so when Pam asked me to investigate for her, I thought Ellie might just be wanting not to blame Nat's carelessness. You have all these weird emotions when someone you love dies. Ellie's main thing was that she knew Nat, knew how careful he was around the sea. He knew the power of the sea–they'd had a friend drowned–so he was methodical, respectful. And the more I've looked into it, the more I feel she's right.'

Deirdre said gently, 'You may be right, Lauren. And I like you for the way you're driven to uncover truths. But if you want the police to change their minds, you'll have to produce more convincing evidence than you've got so far. But please, don't put yourself–or anyone else–in danger.' She paused, and smiled. 'And since I'm not the Police Commissioner yet, you might manage to squeeze some more advice out of me if you need to.'

28

Lauren was in a post-holiday slump. She reflected that the better the holiday, the worse the slump. The friends had been in good form, it was great to see Deirdre, and Hukeri itself was both a lovely holiday spot and an incentive to get stuck into the climate protection work. That is, once the New Zealand shutdown for the summer holidays was over.

One thing she had achieved was alerting Ellie to Rodger Brixton's state of mind. She'd spoken to Pam as soon as she'd got back from seeing Deirdre and Pam had phoned Ellie right away. Together Pam and Ellie had formulated a plan about talking to Rodger's workplace. Ellie had contacts there–after all, she'd been the consultant hired to run the away days where the whole Rodger obsession had begun. Pam had rung Lauren to tell her that Ellie felt she'd made headway with the human resources contact in the Council, who had shown sympathy and understanding and said she'd speak to his manager and make sure Rodger got into an employee assistance programme. Ellie had also beefed up the security around her apartment and was taking special care to look out for Rodger's vehicle when she went out or came home. She swore she would ring the police if she saw any sign of him.

But back to her own situation. No work at present, nothing much going on–and nothing she could do with the information about Derek Drysdall until he got back from the Antarctic. She felt disconsolate, paced about her apartment restlessly in the evenings, wondering if she could pin something on Derek.

One day in early January, Lauren went to Lyall Bay, scouring the cluster of chain shops there for a new travel bag. She'd decided at Christmas that hers really wasn't going to last much longer. She couldn't find exactly what she wanted and decided, as she often did after unsuccessful shopping, that she hated shops. 'Retail therapy? What nonsense.'

To cheer herself up she decided to drive along the beach front at Lyall Bay, enjoying the sight of the breakers rolling in. As she drove she remembered that the Spiller Construction site that Derek Drysdall had been defending was along this road. She could see the big empty section and pulled to the side of the road to have a look. She crossed over to look more closely. The Spiller notice had disappeared from the wire fence. The site was looking forlorn, a heap of rubble in one corner, with weeds growing up through it and all over the rest of the property.

It was in contrast to another building site just beyond it, where the land sloped upwards. It had a smart new mesh fence and a builder's notice announcing Another House. And indeed, there was a house half-built. It looked as if it would have a view right over Lyall Bay, and it was built up and back on the section. Safer then, than the Spiller apartments would have been, but perhaps somewhat lonely and forlorn by mid-century.

The gate in the wire fence was closed but not padlocked. Lauren hesitated, looked around and decided to have a nosey. Didn't everyone like the magic of a half-finished house? All the possibilities, the pleasure of imagining how those rooms would look. She was thinking this as she picked her way over the rough ground up towards the building, and startled as a voice interrupted her thoughts.

'What are you doing here?' Someone was coming around from

the side of the house where the cladding was already up. Justin Spiller!

Lauren was astonished. 'I could say the same to you.' She stumbled over her words. 'I mean, yours was the development next door, wasn't it?'

He scowled. 'That's city council land now. This property belongs to me and a friend.'

'I'm sorry, the gate wasn't locked. I thought I'd have a look. I thought the house would have a lovely view.' As she spoke, Lauren turned towards the gate. But Justin's face cleared. 'Since you're here, do you want to see inside?'

Lauren was already retracing her steps. She paused and turned back, surprised. They didn't sound like the words of someone out to get her. Perhaps pride of ownership had overcome anger at an unwelcome intruder. She hesitated, slightly uneasy at being alone with Justin on a building site. She shook herself mentally. It would be great if the Spiller clan stopped being so hostile.

'That's very kind of you, I'd love to.'

'This way,' he said and led her round the side of the house from where he'd come. A solid door was locked. He pulled the key from his pocket, then turned it and pushed the door open with a flourish. He stepped in and she followed. Inside the flooring was down and the framing for the internal walls was up. He walked her round, instructing.

'This will be the master bedroom. See, it's got an ensuite.' She looked at the joists and tried to imagine the ensuite. 'Another bedroom on this side, one each side of the corridor here, and here's the main bathroom.' They'd reached the end of the corridor and ahead a staircase, mostly completed but with no rail yet, curved round into the top storey. Again Justin led the way. 'It's quite safe,' he said. She emerged into a wide space. The outside walls were built but up here there seemed to be few inside walls. 'This will be one large room,' said Justin. He gestured towards the road. Big window spaces were waiting for their glass.

Lauren walked forward and looked out. The surf was rolling in gently at this end of the beach and children were paddling or swimming, oblivious to the chill of Cook Strait. Families strolled on the beach or sat in groups with toddlers digging happily in the sand. She could see dams, sandcastles and ponds carved up from the water's edge.

Lauren thought whoever bought this house could spend hours staring out the window. The panorama of the beach was spread out in front of her, but far enough away not to be disturbing. The section sloped gently down to the road.

'And a balcony wraps right round the front and on part of both sides, too,' Justin said and he gestured towards a door in a side wall. She went over and tentatively pushed the door open. The decking had begun to be laid, and upright posts were waiting for the balcony railings. She stepped outside and took a few steps towards the front, standing well back from where the decking gave out. She called back in, 'What a great outlook.'

As she spoke, a sharp gust of wind caught the sand on the beach. A fine shower filled the air and the door behind her banged shut. She jumped, recovered and turned to open it. The door handle didn't respond. 'Justin,' she called, 'Can you open the door please?'

On the other side of the door, Justin made a noise somewhere between a snort and a laugh. He opened the door and said, 'I didn't say it was finished yet. You need to be careful around building sites. But you can have a look at the other side if you want.'

Across the room was an identical door. Lauren walked towards it, pushed it open. As she was stepping out, Justin said something and she turned her head to hear. She let out a scream and lost her balance. No decking on the outside, nothing but scaffolding. She grabbed at one of the planks as she fell, scraped her arm. Landed hard on her left foot, which twisted. She lay in a heap on the ground.

Justin was now peering out the door, down at her. 'Are you all right?' Without waiting for an answer, he continued, 'I was trying to tell you, the builders hadn't started the decking on that side.' Lauren was too winded to reply. She managed to sit up, but couldn't stand–the ankle wouldn't hold her weight. Her arm was now bleeding. She sat there for a time, heard the door above her being shut.

Then Justin appeared, picking his way through rubble towards her. The scowl was back, and he was talking at her as he approached. 'Jeez, you're trouble. What on earth did you think you were doing? Just make sure you keep your mouth shut about this–or I'll have WorkSafe on the case. You'd better leave, quickly.' He paused for breath and looked at her. 'God, you're as white as a sheet.'

'I can't stand up. I can't put any weight on my ankle,' said Lauren.

'Fuck it!' He looked at his phone. 'I'm supposed to be somewhere else in five minutes–shouldn't have taken the time to show you around. Now what are we supposed to do!'

Lauren couldn't cope with being berated. 'Look,' she said, 'if you need to leave, just leave. I'll call a friend to help me home.' She felt in her jeans pocket. Yes, she did have the phone with her.

His face cleared. 'Oh well, you'll be OK then. Make sure you use the padlock, when you leave. And don't go nosing around any more building sites–you're trouble.'

With that, he turned and made for the gate. She heard a car start up, and saw his big black monster speeding away. She cursed him and cursed herself for not having noticed his car there. The afternoon was drawing on, the wind was getting up, and it was feeling colder. There were still people on the beach but many were heading away. She could see her own car parked just across the road, tantalizingly close. She noticed she was trembling, and she felt really cold. White as a sheet, was she? In shock, she supposed, and imagined a warm sweet drink, a blanket, a comfy sofa...

She dug her phone out of her pocket, and managed to ring Ro's number. A cheerful voice said, 'Hello, Lauren, where are you? Pam and I are just at The Library, having a drink.'

Lauren tried to answer and failed–to her embarrassment she burst into tears. It was quite some time before both Ro and Pam were helping her up her steps. But not too much longer after that when the sweet warm drink, the sofa and the blanket became a reality. Pam put a cushion under her ankle, and an ice-pack on it and Ro fussed with her arm, tenderly washing off blood and swabbing the scrapes. Lauren was still shivering, and as Ro and Pam were sitting with her, quizzing her about what had happened, she found it hard to be coherent.

'You mean, after you fell out of an upper storey door on to the ground, he just left you there?' said Pam. 'How could he!'

'Well, I said he could go,' Lauren protested feebly.

'Don't be silly. It sounds as if he was just concerned for what an accident on the site could mean for him. You were in a bad way, there were all sorts of things he should have done–given you something warmer to put over you; rung an ambulance; or at the very least, stayed until we arrived. What a self-centred bastard!'

'Do you think he meant you to hurt yourself?' Ro frowned as she asked the question. 'You know, to keep you from any more digging around?'

Lauren frowned too, and then said, 'I don't think so. I think he was genuinely proud of the place and happy to show anyone over, even me. But when I fell, he couldn't get away quick enough. It was odd, though, he reckoned he was calling out to tell me there was no decking where I'd opened the door–but what it did was distract me at the vital moment, because I was looking back at him as I stepped out.' She shrugged. 'I don't know, I felt pretty stupid.'

29

By the following day Lauren's ankle was really painful. It wasn't until a couple of days later that she felt able to walk at all. By then, she had mulled over the incident and was as angry with Justin as Ro and Pam had been. So angry that she determined to bring it to Lloyd Spiller's attention.

It was a mood that would have had her stomping along the Spiller building foyer to the lift if her ankle hadn't twinged every time it hit the ground. So she limped somewhat gingerly, pressed the button for the lift and waited impatiently. She had it in mind to march–limp, she reminded herself–straight to Lloyd's office to confront him. But the lift wouldn't respond when she tried to go to the top floor. She settled for the floor below, marked on the lift controls as Spiller Construction reception.

'Good morning,' said the receptionist, the same young woman as before. 'Can I help you?'

'Yes please, my name is Lauren Fraser. I wish to see Lloyd Spiller.' The receptionist glanced down at her screen, looked back at Lauren and said, 'I'm sorry. He doesn't seem to have a meeting with you scheduled.'

'No,' said Lauren, 'But he will see me.'

'Perhaps he could fit you in tomorrow afternoon? Might I know what it's about?'

'I will see him now,' said Lauren. As the receptionist was explaining why that wasn't possible Lauren turned and walked back towards the lift. She gritted her teeth, caught by the pain, as she passed the lift and took the stairs. Teeth still gritted, she made her way along the corridor to Lloyd's office. She remembered the last time she was there, when he told her to butt out. Justin was taking the family feeling to extremes, she thought. She winced as she came down too heavily on the injured ankle. Now she had reached his door. It was shut.

She knocked and, without waiting, opened it. Spiller was sitting behind his desk, head down, frowning at some papers. He glanced up, then looked again, half rose then subsided. 'What are you doing here, Miss…'–the briefest of pauses–'Fraser?'

'Among other things,' said Lauren, 'to remind you how lucky this country is to have an Accident Compensation Scheme and how lucky that makes you.'

'What?' He looked completely perplexed. 'Miss Fraser, please sit down. I am a busy man.' He glanced at a clock on the wall. 'I have no time for idle chat so be brief. I don't know what my staff were thinking of, letting you in without an appointment.'

Lauren sat down. It was good to get the weight off her ankle. Now they faced each other across the expanse of his desk. Lloyd stared at her and then looked beyond her. Lauren turned to look over her shoulder and saw the receptionist hovering in the doorway. Before the young woman could speak, Lloyd said, 'I'll deal with this, thank you.'

'I trust you will,' said Lauren. 'Your family thinks Ellie's mistaken about Nat's murder.' Lloyd flinched at the word. 'And you may think I'm wasting my time. But that's no reason for your son to put me in harm's way. I could have got much worse than a sprained ankle and bruising.'

There was a pause, then, 'I have no idea what you're talking about.'

'Your son Justin saw me step out of an upper storey door and fall straight to the ground below.'

Now he was engaged. He frowned. 'Where did this happen?'

'Didn't he come by to tell you he was warning me off again? First he played nice and showed me the house he's building. Then he allowed me to fall through that door. He couldn't even bring himself to stay to help me home.'

Lloyd frowned again. 'You shouldn't have been near that house. It's a construction site. How did you come to be there?'

Lauren had calmed down and now she felt slightly sheepish. Still as angry with Justin. But his father seemed genuinely unaware. 'The padlock wasn't done up on the gate and I pushed my way in to have a look. I didn't know it was his house.'

Lloyd raised his eyebrows, looked unbelieving.

Lauren said defensively, 'It just caught my interest. Then Justin came round the side of the house and offered to show me over.'

As she told the story to Lloyd her anger ebbed away and she could feel her voice wobbling. She finished. 'Then he said he had an appointment. Couldn't wait. I had to sit sprawled there all by myself until my friends arrived.'

Now Lloyd looked horrified. He began stiffly, 'Miss Fraser....' Lauren still felt choked up, but this was getting too much. 'Please stop calling me Miss Fraser. I'm a grandmother, for goodness sake. It's *Ms* Fraser.'

He cleared his throat. 'Ms Fraser, you're right. I do think Ellie is mistaken about my son's death and I have asked you to stop poking around in an unhelpful way. But I can assure you, the Spiller family are not in the habit of using heavy-handed tactics to silence opposition.' He looked past her again, but this time at the wall clock. 'My son Justin is due for a meeting with me in just two minutes. By all means stay here while I ask him about this, er, unfortunate incident.'

The words were scarcely out of his mouth when there was a knock on the door and Justin walked in. He came to an abrupt stop when he saw Lauren. 'What are you doing here?'

His father replied, 'Apparently Miss...Ms Fraser' (he took care over his pronunciation) 'is here to ask me to call you to heel.'

'Huh?' Justin looked offended.

'She didn't appreciate you letting her fall out of a door. And she says you threatened her.'

'She shouldn't have been on a building site.' It sounded petulant.

'But you should have asked her to leave immediately, not taken her into a half-finished house. Come to that, why was the gate not padlocked? For God's sake, Justin, you've been told often enough about safety on a building site. You're supposed to set an example to contractors.'

Lauren felt that Lloyd was well off the point. It was Justin's threats that she was concerned about. And, it seemed to her, the way he'd purposely let her fall out of that door.

Now Justin was defending himself to his father. He came up to the desk beside her chair but ignored her and spoke directly to Lloyd. 'Derek was at the site that morning. He left the gate unlocked. I'd gone in just to check that there was nothing lying around before I locked up. Then she came along.' He turned, gesturing at Lauren.

'Derek Drysdall needs some instruction on how to look after a building site, too,' said his father, 'And you should be giving it to him.'

Lauren was startled. She interrupted. 'Derek Drysdall? What's he got to do with it?' Both men stared at her.

As Justin was saying, 'None of your business', his father explained. 'My son is developing that property in partnership with Derek. Do you know him?'

Was it the way he said it? Lauren had the sense that Lloyd didn't care for Derek. She answered, 'I don't know him personally but a friend of mine had rather more to do with him than she wanted when they were in the Antarctic this summer.'

Lloyd grunted. Justin fired up. 'What do you mean?'

Lauren wished she hadn't mentioned Ro. She retorted, 'What I mean is that he endangered my friend when she was caught in a whiteout. He threatened to leave her there.'

Justin leant towards her, too close for comfort. 'That's nonsense. He wouldn't have done that!'

Lauren hadn't intended to talk about their suspicions of Derek. She just wanted the time and space to gather more evidence, without Spillers getting in her way, but it came out anyway. 'Well you might think he's lily-white but you're wrong. It's very likely that Derek Drysdall murdered Nat.'

There was silence in the room. Then Lloyd drew a deep breath. 'Please explain yourself, but don't make stupid allegations.'

Lauren opened her mouth to speak but Justin's voice rose above hers. 'That's completely ridiculous.' He'd gone white. 'He didn't have anything to do with it.'

'You don't know, you can't know,' said Lauren. 'A witness has described someone matching Derek's description, quarrelling with Nat on the beach the evening he drowned.'

'It wasn't him!'

They both looked at him. Justin stared from one to the other. His father, leaning forward, elbows on the desk, Lauren on the edge of her chair. He blurted, 'I was with him. We were...' He hesitated, 'we were snorkelling right down near Red Rocks.'

It sounded absurd, it was a child telling porkies. His father banged his fist on the desk. 'Justin, your mother said you were at our place that evening. And you agreed.' Justin stumbled, 'Well, I....'

'Sit down, Justin.' As he spoke, Lloyd got up and walked to the side door, opened it and said, 'Miss Braithwaite, would you please get my wife on the phone and put her through to me.' He shut the door, came back and sat down heavily. No one said anything. His phone rang. He spoke abruptly into the receiver. 'I want to ask you something. Doesn't matter what you've said to anyone else, but I need to know. Think carefully. The evening that Nat went missing, was Justin at our place?'

There was a long pause as he listened intently. Lauren wished the conversation was on speakerphone. She waited, looked at Lloyd's face, trying to read his expression. He put the phone down.

He spoke quietly. 'Justin. Son. Your mother's been feeling uncomfortable about something ever since Nat drowned.' His voice gathered force. 'She's lost her eldest son. She's grieving. And on top of that, you asked her to lie for you. Why did you do that?' He banged his hand on the desk again. Justin shrank in his chair. 'I don't know, Dad, I can't remember.'

'Don't you lie to me. What's going on?' Justin was trembling. He gave a convulsive sob. 'It wasn't my fault.'

'Justin, what happened?' Lloyd's voice was urgent.

'I told you, I don't know. He went off for a swim. How was I to know his head was bleeding?' He stopped and stared at the floor.

Lloyd spoke again. His voice was still quiet, gentle even. 'Son, were you with Nat when he planned to go out snorkelling that night?'

'No, no, I wasn't. Well, I wasn't snorkelling. It's no fun snorkelling there now, with that stupid Marine Reserve. Derek and I go out past Lyall Bay where we can still go spearfishing and get shellfish. I just go swimming at that beach sometimes. She knows.' He jerked his head at Lauren, who in her mind's eye saw herself sitting there on her picnic rug.

'Justin.' It was all Lloyd said. Justin visibly startled. 'Oh yeah, anyway, I was driving past and saw the bro's car in the car park, had a couple of things I wanted to clear up with him.'

He said he'd pulled into the car park himself and walked down to the gated beach where he knew Nat would be. 'I was right, he was there, had the beach to himself, what was left of it.'

'What do you mean?' his father sounded sharper.

Justin winced. 'I just mean it was high tide, not much left. Nat must have just arrived, had got into his wetsuit and was laying out his snorkelling gear.'

Lauren could imagine it–the tiny area of shingly sand still exposed and the man, sorting his gear. Would he have been pleased to see his brother?

Justin was into his story now. 'I wanted to talk to him about the submission he was putting in about our Lyall Bay development.'

Justin didn't observe his father flinching. Lloyd bit his lip and stayed silent. Justin continued. 'He was hopping about pulling on his booties, wouldn't listen properly–though he stopped when I told him you knew he was going to oppose it.'

For the first time, he looked directly at Lloyd. 'I told him you always know what's going on.' Lloyd was impassive. Justin's eyes dropped again. 'Anyway, Nat was bloody rude. Said Derek was a creep and his submission was bullshit. Said climate change was more important than the development.' He stole another look at Lloyd. 'Didn't care that this was my first go being in charge of a development.'

'So what then, Justin?' said his father.

'So he wouldn't see sense. I could have killed him!'

The words hung in the air. A moment's silence. Lauren recalled the image of two men facing off on the beach. Justin realised what he'd said. 'But I didn't, of course I didn't!' he stammered. 'Silly bastard tried to jolly me along. He said he wouldn't snorkel, the wind was starting to blow from the south and clouding up the water, he'd just swim, wanted me to come with him. Called me chicken when I refused. Just walked off into the water without resolving anything.' Another pause. 'Okay, I was pissed off.'

The pause lengthened. Lloyd prompted again.

'I,' he hesitated, 'I picked up his diving belt. Threw his knife on to the beach. Pulled out the diving weight and threw it towards Nat. God, I've never pretended to be an ace shot–how did I know it would hit him on the head? It was awful when he stumbled and fell on his knees.' There was another pause, as Justin screwed up his face and shut his eyes. He opened them again and continued. 'But he got up again, seemed all right–all right enough to call out that I was a prick.

'He gave a bit of a lurch, steadied himself with his arms out, rubbed the back of his head–but then plunged in and he was all right. He was dog paddling towards the swimthrough.

If I'd gone out to make sure, Nat would probably have just given me grief. Silly bastard. He *was* all right. Shouldn't have been swimming when the weather was turning. I don't know what happened to him.'

His recital petered out. He sat, shoulders hunched, still looking at the floor. An errant tear ran down his cheek.

A profound silence filled the room. No one spoke, no one moved. Lloyd rested his elbows on the desk, held his head in his hands. Lauren was upright in her chair, frozen with horror.

Then Lloyd spoke. He cleared his throat, put his arms down on the desk and looked at Lauren. 'Ms Fraser,'–afterwards she recalled that he'd used the honorific she preferred–'Ms Fraser, I would like you to leave. We have family business. Please go.'

Lauren gasped. 'But....' She said again, 'But....' Then looked at Lloyd. Of course she had to go. He needed to deal with it. She rose, felt unsteady, clutched the back of the chair momentarily. She made her way to the door without another word and left the office.

30

Lauren walked down the steps to Ellie's apartment. She felt unaccountably nervous. Ellie had been right all the time. Nat's drowning was the result of foul play. The investigation had hardly been straightforward. They had looked in all the wrong places.

She took a deep breath, recalling the discovery of Harold's body. She reassured herself that the suicide had nothing to do with the investigation, even though it may have had everything to do with Harold's feelings towards Nat. That was one puzzle they would never solve. If only she had followed Deirdre's dictum–suspect families first–she would have looked harder at Justin to begin with. She sighed, Ellie had been so convincing.

She knocked on the door and Pam answered. She gave Lauren a brief hug and said, 'Come in, we're waiting for you.' They went down to the living room where Ellie rose to greet Lauren. 'Thank you for all you've done.' She seemed quite composed. Lauren had been dreading more tears. Ellie went on, 'Lloyd phoned me last night. I was so pleased that you'd called first, so I knew what to expect. Well, not entirely.'

Lauren raised her eyebrows. Ellie said, 'Of course, Lloyd always has his own way of dealing with things. I half expected him to go for some sort of cover-up, but no. He called the police while Justin was still in his office. Justin was taken into custody. Best lawyers of course, and he was out on bail right away. Lloyd said there will be a charge of manslaughter and a prison sentence.'

'That's a relief,' Lauren replied. 'I did wonder if he'd do the right thing.'

Pam muttered something that Lauren didn't quite catch. 'What was that?' she said.

'I was saying that he's still a bastard.'

'Who do you mean, Lloyd Spiller?'

'Yes, he was the one responsible really. If he hadn't put all those expectations on Nat and on Justin too, we'd never have had this ghastly business.'

Ellie looked thoughtful. 'Maybe. I just can't process what I think about Justin and Lloyd at the moment. Pam, did you tell Lauren that he even offered to buy me a house? I turned him down flat.'

'Blood money,' said Pam. She sounded as if she could have gone on at length about the Spillers, but Ellie interrupted her. 'Lauren, I need to say thank you for warning me about Rodger, too.'

'I know he got into the employee assistance programme–has it helped then?'

'It's been brilliant for me,' said Ellie. 'My contact at the Council let me know that he's gone to Taupo. I don't know what the story was, but I don't care either. I don't have to worry about him any more.'

'So what will you do now, Ellie?' Lauren asked.

Surprisingly, Ellie blushed. 'Nat did leave a legacy. I'm sorry, Aunt Pam, I should have told you first, but I've only just found out.'

Lauren thought she could guess what was coming, but Pam looked mystified.

'I'm pregnant.'

Pam gasped. 'But Ellie, I thought you and Nat had agreed....'

Ellie interrupted. 'That was what Nat wanted, but in the circumstances....' Then she was at a loss for words.

Lauren jumped in. 'That's wonderful news, Ellie. He would have changed his mind once presented with the fact. It happens all the time. I'm sure you'll be a wonderful mother.'

31

There was a tide of shuffling, murmuring around the crowded lecture theatre, interspersed by shouts of recognition and the slapping of footsteps up and down the aisles. Lauren spotted Pam on the opposite side, in a row near the back. With the thrust of excited people behind her, she had to march right down the stairs and, feeling conspicuous, walk across the front of the theatre. At least she got a good look at the guest speaker, a distinguished-looking woman standing alone to one side while technicians fiddled with the equipment and the hosts of the event chatted to one another.

Pam saw her and waved. At the same time Ro, entering from above, caught sight of them. Lauren and Ro both squeezed past people who swivelled in their chairs to let them through. 'We'll need binoculars from here,' Ro grumbled. Lauren was amused. Pam may have been a back seat person but not Ro.

The crowd settled as an older man in a well-cut suit walked to the podium. 'That's the new dean,' whispered Ro loudly, 'Smarmy.'

'Shh,' said Pam as the dean began his introductions with a surprisingly competent greeting in Maori. Lauren mused that it was de rigueur these days. She was pleased that she no longer had to officiate at public events. Despite at least three short courses and numerous staff meetings where the woeful lack of te reo was raised, Lauren could not get her tongue around it. But she got the gist of what the dean was saying–a standardised welcome. He soon handed over to a rather dishevelled bearded man, clearly another Antarctic scientist. His job was to extol the achievements of the distinguished visitor. 'Great that it's a woman,' Ro muttered. 'Miriam says she's one of the best.'

The event had been advertised as a public lecture on rising sea levels, the annual venture into the limelight from the Robert Falcon Scott centre.

'Shit!' Ro nudged Lauren. 'There he is.' She pointed to a latecomer who was making his way slowly down the steps looking for a seat. 'That's him.'

'Who?' said Pam.

'Derek Drysdall, of course.'

At that moment he glanced towards the group of women. There was a spare seat on the other side of Pam, but he hastily averted his eyes and clambered past some people to take a seat in the middle row.

The theatre stilled as the speaker moved into position and rustled her notes. Lauren shifted awkwardly in her seat which rolled as she moved. Lecture theatres! This one was brand new, but they hadn't got any more comfortable since her young days when she was squeezed into rows at Cambridge. Not that lectures were the main events then, it was the tutorials. Her mind took her back to those awkward silences when she was a green young girl facing a bespectacled older woman, who seemed to regard her–or perhaps all young women–with contempt. There was the memorable occasion when Lauren had spent the weekend at pubs and parties and had hastily dashed off an essay on *Lysistrata.* No Wikipedia in those days, she'd just skimmed the old Loeb classic text she'd hastily borrowed from the girl on the stairs below. 'You express yourself nicely,' her tutor had said. Lauren had sighed with relief, taking it as a compliment. But then the withering remark. 'A pity you had nothing to say.'

There was a nudge from her left side and Ro whispered, 'Concentrate, you're off in a dream.' Lauren returned to the present and picked up her pen. Taking notes was the only way she'd ever been able to pay attention right through a lecture. In fact, the scientist was wildly interesting. The four screens across the breadth of the theatre were magically illustrated with shots of tropical islands and scenes from Antarctica. The beauty of the natural world, Lauren thought to herself, and we're destroying it.

The science being presented was complex, but the lecturer had a way of making it seem simple. Sea levels were rising alarmingly, the evidence showed. But the impact of rising seas was sometimes unexpected, not always devouring the land in front of it, sometimes even building up the shore line. The message was clear, though. The world was heading for a disaster unless rapid action were taken.

The lecture held Lauren's attention to the end, then it was question time. Beside her, Ro was getting restless, shuffling her feet and muttering. Lauren looked at her quizzically and was rewarded only with a shake of the head. There was the usual gamut of questions, technical or self-aggrandising from the scientists and the public's ranging from intelligent to daft.

Suddenly Ro was on her feet, waving her arms. It wasn't her turn, but the chair allowed her, probably to stop her from being a distraction. 'Are you certain your data is accurate,' Ro almost shouted. 'There's been an enquiry into the Antarctic meteorological data from last season.' She turned sideways and gave a hard stare in the direction of the centre of the theatre where a commotion erupted. All the eyes that had been turned on Ro turned towards the figure of Derek Drysdall who had stood up. 'Can I reply to that?' he shouted.

'Not now, Dr Drysdall,' said the chair looking awkward. Drysdall stayed on his feet and pushed his way out into the aisle. As he thumped up the steps towards the top exit, his face red with anger, he scowled at Ro and muttered, 'Pack of interfering lesbians'. Ro sat down again and waited for the lecturer to reply. The woman said, 'These conclusions are based on many years of data. I'm not aware that there's been an enquiry into the data from last season, though I do recall a blip in the weather data.' She looked towards the Centre director for clarification.

He looked embarrassed and shook his head. A murmur spread across the audience. The dean intervened, answering smoothly, 'I understand that there were some technical difficulties in the previous season and if the enquiry finds any fault in the data, we will publish a retraction. Thank you.' He looked at his watch. 'No time for more questions, I'm afraid. Let us thank the speaker in the usual manner.'

People clapped and began to disperse. Ro beamed at Lauren and Pam as they rose to leave. 'Serves the bastard right,' she whispered loudly.

MIRIAM HAD CHANGED her plans and flown on to Wellington from Christchurch where her flight back from the Antarctic had landed. Now she sat at Lauren's kitchen table with a drink in her hand watching Lauren wobbling around as she prepared dinner for the small group invited for the evening. 'It was so kind of you to invite me back,' said Miriam with a warm smile. 'I'm looking forward to our trip to the Wairarapa'–she stumbled over pronunciation of the unfamiliar place name. 'Never been there, and I hear there's some interesting fossils out there. Pity about your ankle, though, no walks.'

'And I'm sure you don't like shopping?' Lauren gave her a mischievous grin. 'But you could do with a rest after–what–six weeks on the ice?'

'That's true–I am run down. Being at McMurdo was arduous. But of course it was exciting, too, and I do want to get back to the lab and work on our samples.'

'All work and no play...' Lauren trotted out the tired proverb but she did understand perfectly. Her own investigation had become all-absorbing and had given her life a fillip. But she could do with a break, too.

Miriam continued. 'And another thing is, I don't want to go straight back into the heat of Melbourne. It's shaping up to being the hottest summer on record–thanks, climate change!' She nodded, perhaps to the universe. 'The city will feel like an inferno after the ice.'

'Well, we're doing our best to copy you Aussies, sadly. Have you heard about the Nelson bushfires?' The fires were currently raging. A state of emergency had been declared a few days back and thousands of people were being evacuated, as well as pets and livestock. It was being described as the largest fire in New Zealand's history and was certainly the largest aerial firefight, with dozens of helicopters at work on the blaze.

'Yes, indeed,' Miriam replied. My next door neighbour on the plane pointed out the pall of smoke that could be seen as we got near the top of the South Island.'

They looked at each other. What was there to say? Lauren turned the subject back to their trip. 'You'll have to drive,' she warned Miriam, 'but it's only a couple of hours and we can get to see the fossils.'

Miriam sniffed. 'I suppose I can manage that little tin can you keep in your car park.'

'Huh,' began Lauren. Her comeback was interrupted by a knock on the door. It was Ro, who pecked Lauren on the cheek, strode into the kitchen and enveloped Miriam in a great bear hug.

Lauren began to feel left out as Antarctic talk poured out from both her guests: McMurdo, Humvees, Arrival Heights, sea ice, core sampling drilling .... Before she could get really miffed the doorbell rang again. This time it was Pam and Megan who had met on the footpath.

A round of drinks in their hands, Miriam led off by saying, 'What on earth have you all been up to? I turn up after being at the end of the earth to find Lauren limping around with some cock and bull story about being pushed out of a window.'

'Defenestration, it's called in the trade,' offered Ro.

Pam was indignant on Lauren's behalf. 'It's not a joke. Lauren could have come off much worse. It was Justin who killed his brother, after all. It might have been partly an accident as they are claiming, but I think Lauren's was one accident too many to be a coincidence.'

Megan looked puzzled. She hadn't heard the whole story but no one was going to fill in all the details, it seemed. 'How's your niece?' she asked Pam.

'She's doing OK. She'll be grieving for Nat for a long time, but it's helped her to know what really happened to him.' She looked solemn but then smiled. 'She's terribly grateful to Lauren for working it out, though Lauren would be the first to tell you that she was gob-smacked when she found it was Justin.'

'Anyway, Ellie has sworn off the whole Spiller clan with relief, turned down the father's offer to buy her a house. It seemed too much like a pay-off. And she's back working. I think Justin is out on bail, but he's been ordered to steer clear of her. And the stalker's gone off to Taupo.'

'Wow, sounds as if she's managing to move on. But surely once she's had the baby, the grandparents will be all over it.'

Pam looked doubtful, but Lauren said, 'I think you're right, babies have a way of sorting people out.'

She changed the subject. 'It was a pity we wasted so much time on Derek Drysdall,' Lauren said. 'I still think he's a real bastard.'

Pam was saying something about at least having learnt a lot about climate science, when Ro butted in. 'It's all over Vic–he's off to Queensland. Apparently he's got a funded chair from some climate change denier up there who makes his fortune from coal-mining. Hard to believe though–that enquiry's still going on, how would he dare show his face at any university!"

Miriam was appalled. She hadn't heard the news. 'That's one Kiwi we'd rather you kept.'

'But we're happy to send him to Oz.'

Lauren went back to the kitchen to start serving up. A wave of warmth swept through her. Friendship, she thought, how lucky she was.

32

Deirdre was late. It was nearly ten past eight in the morning and she still hadn't arrived. Lauren wondered if she should set off on her own. Deirdre had finished her Canberra secondment at the end of January, and was now back in the city, settling into a new apartment near Te Papa. Lauren hadn't yet been invited to visit and certainly not to help Deirdre set up in her new place. She took this to mean 'keep your distance' which she found surprising. She'd even talked to Michael and Kiano about it when they visited. Michael was his usual sensible self, pointing out that Deirdre needed time to draw breath and settle in. Kiano quoted an African proverb: 'If love is a sickness, patience is the remedy.' That made Lauren laugh.

Only a week or so later, Deirdre had met her for coffee and when Lauren mentioned she was doing the waterfront walk each morning, finding that her ankle could manage flat surfaces more easily than hills, Deirdre had invited her to join her on her walk to work in the morning occasionally. Now Lauren was sitting on one of the wooden seats outside Te Papa, looking at harbour activities and starting to feel chilled. Autumn was definitely on its way.

The ping of an incoming text message had her scrabbling in her bag for the phone. 'Sorry I was delayed and I'm getting a cab. Lunch instead? One pm at the National Library caff, only if it suits.'

Lauren swore. That was going to put her whole morning out. She didn't have to go of course, but she knew she would.

She walked back along Oriental Bay to her car, parked at the other end. Her thoughts drifted back to the events of the summer. At least it wasn't climate change in-fighting that had led to Nat's death, just the old Cain and Abel story, brotherly conflict as old as time. Mind you, she thought, warring politics are as old as time too. She reminded herself that this was the year she was going to throw herself into climate change activism–and she would not be put off by any internal dissension if it should arise. She and her friends had been following the young activist Greta Thunberg, full of admiration at the impact she had made with her school strike. A school strike was planned for Wellington today, as part of coordinated international protest. Some people in her circles seemed to think that it was for young people to fix the climate problem because they were the ones who would be most affected, but Lauren vehemently disagreed. The older generation could not just walk away from the crisis they had created.

Late morning saw Lauren driving across town. It was always surprisingly easy to find a park in the parliamentary precinct. She scrabbled for change for the meter, cursing the fact that she'd forgotten to top up her parking app. The library's Home café was busy as usual, librarians on their lunch hour, researchers taking time off their serious pursuits and a scattering of public servants from nearby government buildings. Police HQ was just up the road. She caught herself hoping that Deirdre would not be in uniform–she didn't want to draw attention to herself.

She caught sight of Deirdre entering from the side door. She was looking very professional in a grey tailored suit which emphasised her lithe figure. She hadn't yet noticed Lauren, who stood up from the table she had bagged and waved her over. They exchanged smiles and a brief kiss on the cheek. 'Sorry about this morning,' Deirdre said. 'Police business. Anyhow, how are you? You're looking good.'

Lauren was feeling her way into the conversation, unsure as to where it was heading–nowhere, probably. She accepted the compliment with a nod and suggested they hang their jackets on the back of their chairs to mark the table as taken. They lined up at the counter where the queue was slow-moving as usual. Lauren felt uncharacteristically awkward, as they went through the usual back and forth, deciding whether to choose from the over-stuffed glass cabinet or from the blackboard menu. 'I suppose you're in a rush?' she ventured.

Deirdre glanced at her phone and winced. 'The pressure's on but that's no reason for me not to eat properly. Skipped breakfast so I'm starving.' She ordered the pasta special and a long black while Lauren more modestly chose a pita bread stuffed with something Turkish as well as a coffee.

'Well, what's the latest–or daren't I ask?' Deirdre looked across the table with a glint of amusement in her sharp brown eyes.

'I'm just back to the usual. I told you Justin was arrested for his brother's death. I'm not sure what the charge was–there've been lawyers crawling all over it. Pam tells me he's out on bail but under strict instructions not to hassle any of us.' She paused. 'I guess I'm feeling at a loose end.' She pulled herself together, nothing attractive about someone down in the dumps. 'But there's an Extinction Rebellion protest on Friday night. I'm thinking of going to that. I want to do more than write submissions.'

Deirdre rolled her eyes. 'Just don't go scaling tall buildings.' She said it almost fondly.

'And you?' Lauren asked.

'You were right, I do seem to be being groomed. It seems a long time since I was on the front line, there's so much desk work now.' She looked around and lowered her voice. 'It's all very hush-hush, but you would realise that we're worried about terrorism.'

'I can imagine. But you know, Deirdre, a lot of policy work is about scenarios. Some things might not happen, but we need to be prepared.'

Deirdre sighed. 'It's all very interesting, but I'm a practical person really. It's not that I want to go back to sirens and car chases–not that there's much of that in an average cop's shift–but I did like working with people, making a difference.'

Deirdre's phone buzzed. 'I'll have to look at that, sorry.' Her phone was on the table and she glanced down at it, frowning as she picked it up. Her face took on a greyish pallor. 'Jesus Christ! Unbelievable.' She stood and looked at Lauren. 'Sorry,' she said again and grabbed her jacket.

'But Deirdre, your pasta hasn't even arrived yet–if you missed breakfast you at least need to have some lunch.'

But Deirdre was on her way, almost colliding with the young man who was bringing their meals. Lauren flushed as he looked enquiringly, placing the two plates on the table. 'It's okay, my friend had to leave suddenly. Just take the pasta back to the kitchen.'

He smiled at her sympathetically, and did as he was told. Lauren ate her own food without enthusiasm. As she was on the last sip of her coffee, she became aware of an unusual buzz around the café, different from the usual comings and goings.

A woman about her age, at the next table, stood up suddenly, muttering, 'My God!'

'Are you all right?' Lauren enquired. 'What's going on?'

The woman waved her phone. 'Someone's been shooting into a crowd of people in a mosque in Christchurch. Lots of fatalities, apparently.'

'Unbelievable,' said Lauren. 'Sounds like a terrorist attack.'

The woman paused. She was fiddling nervously with her scarf. 'We never thought it would happen here, did we?'

Lauren thought that Deirdre would be in the thick of it. Her terrorism work had suddenly become real. Her heart lurched. The world she knew was fast receding.

AFTERWORD

The background for this work of fiction is our concern with the threat of climate change and our interest in climate activism. While we were writing we read widely, watched documentaries, attended lectures, took part in protests, contributed to environmental organisations and kept up with daily news reports of climate science and climate change related events and disasters.

There are far too many sources of information to be acknowledged, but the following resources were particularly helpful to us in understanding how climate change will impact on New Zealand and how Antarctic science can contribute to waking up the world.

Neville Peat, *The Invading Sea: Coastal Hazards and Climate Change in Aotearoa New Zealand*, Cuba Press, 2018.

Rebecca Priestley, *Fifteen Million Years in Antarctica*, Victoria University Press, 2019.

Thin Ice: The Inside Story of Climate Science. Film directed by Simon Lamb & David Sington, 2013.

As well, Kennedy Warne, 'Three feet high and rising', *New Zealand Geographic* Nov-Dec 2015, is an evocative portrait of how climate change is threatening a small beachside community, similar to our fictional Hukeri.

And Phillipa Werry, *Antarctic Journeys*, New Holland, 2019, has nice detail on Antarctica.

ACKNOWLEDGMENTS

We want to express our gratitude to all those who helped us during the writing of this book. Fleur Beale assessed the manuscript for us and gave us wise advice, based on her long career as a published author. Judith Mason read a draft attentively with a sharp eye for accuracy and consistency. Jim Welch copy-edited and proofread, and was meticulous in hunting down errors and infelicities.

Judi Lapsley Miller's photo artistry (www.artbyjlm.com) gave us the wonderful image of Wellington's wild south coast, which was used by James McDonald, our brilliant cover designer (JAMESMCDONALDBOOKS.COM) to produce the cover for *Rising Tide*. We really appreciate their painstaking efforts.

Thank you, Ingrid Horrocks and Bridget Williams Books, for allowing us to use the poetic quote that is our epigraph. It comes from the essay, 'It's just there: clicking on the crisis' in Tony Doig, ed., *Living with the Climate Crisis: Voices from Aotearoa,* BWB texts, 2020.

Our thanks also to Sean Audain from Wellington City Council, who gave us the virtual reality experience of rising seas he designed, which is fictionalised in the book. Afterwards, he spoke to us about us how cities around the world are preparing for the rising tide. The virtual reality experience is the subject of a newspaper article, accessible at: http://www.stuff.co.nz/technology/gadgets/103246531/virtual-reality-game-shows-wellington-after-sea-level-rise.

Christine Borra of *Your Books* guided us expertly, as usual, through the book production process,.

Finally, we want to thank independent booksellers who make our books available to readers. In particular, Carole Beu of *The Women's Bookshop*, Lorna Bingham of *Another Chapter* and Tilly Lloyd of *Unity Books Wellington*, gave us helpful advice on sales and marketing.

ABOUT THE AUTHORS

Jennifer Palgrave is the pen name of writing partnership Lois Cox and Hilary Lapsley. Lois and Hilary are based in Wellington, which provides a rich setting for their books. This is their second Lauren Fraser novel.

For more information, visit their website at:
www.jenniferpalgrave.wordpress.com

Jennifer Palgrave's books are available in print from independent booksellers in New Zealand and from mightyape.co.nz and fishpond.co.nz. As an e-book, *The One That Got Away* is available for Kindle from amazon.com. *Rising Tide* will also be available in a Kindle edition.

ALSO BY JENNIFER PALGRAVE

The One That Got Away

Lauren Fraser is easing into a comfortable retirement when her historian friend Ro reveals a shocking secret. Ro's research has uncovered the attempted poisoning of a New Zealand prime minister.

Despite herself, Lauren is drawn into the mystery. Who was the would-be murderer and can they be brought to justice after thirty years? Who has been involved in covering up the plot and why? As they get closer to the truth, Lauren and Ro find themselves in danger. One death follows another, and it is no longer a cold case they have on their hands.

This gripping novel is set in Wellington, New Zealand's capital city, where Lauren and her circle of lesbian friends are celebrating Jacinda Ardern's fresh new coalition government. Will Lauren and Ro succeed in exposing malign global forces that destroyed a former government, and still operate today?

'A rollicking good read.' *Waiheke Weekender*

'... a good yarn, very well plotted, and interesting characters.' *John Lapsley, columnist, Otago Daily Times*

'A fun enjoyable story. There's a failed assassination attempt and a secret coverup ...the investigation goes beyond the cold case ...and takes on the people who are still around and willing to murder to cover their tracks. A ripping yarn, definitely worth a read.' *Lisa Finucane, Nine to Noon, Radio NZ*

'I very much enjoyed entering Lauren's world. It was a good, fast paced read and I loved the political intrigue!' *Hon Grant Robertson, MP*

www.ingramcontent.com/pod-product-compliance
Ingram Content Group UK Ltd.
Pitfield, Milton Keynes, MK11 3LW, UK
UKHW041637190726
13854UKWH00006B/2546